Brothers
by
Blood

D.L. Rogers

D.L. Rogers – Author
June 2008 Release
All Rights Reserved;
Any similarity to any living person is strictly coincidental.
This is a work of fiction; based on historical fact.

THE WHITE OAKS SERIES: by D.L. Rogers

Tomorrow's Promise: Survival on the Plains – Book 1 in the original trilogy, released 2008
Brothers by Blood – Book 2 in the original trilogy, released 2008
Ghost Dancers – Book 3 in the original trilogy, released 2007
Caleb – Book 4 in the continuation of the series, released 2010
Amy – Book 5 in the continuation of the series, released 2011
Maggie – Book 6 in the continuation of the series, released 2012
Beginnings: Into the Unknown – Book 7 (and prequel) in the continuation of the series, released 2013

Other Books by D.L. Rogers

Elizabeth's War: Missouri 1863 – Released 2014
The Journey – Released 2009
Echoes in the Dark – Released 2009

Cover design by: Jackie Polsgrove-Roberts and Glen Dixon

DLRogersbooks
www.dlrogersbooks.com

-Dedication-

This book is dedicated to God for giving me the ability to put these stories into words and giving me the strength not to give up the fight. And to my family. To my children and friends who have believed in me from day one, encouraged me and helped me to "stay the course" to see my words in print so others can better understand these tumultuous years through the eyes of Blue Fox with Two Hearts and George, his *BROTHER BY BLOOD*.

"We want no white men here. The Black Hills belong to me. If the whites try to take them, I will fight."

Tatanka Yotanka (Sitting Bull)

Prologue

Death hovered outside the window of the ranch's main house. In time, the glass would no longer hold back the darkness of eternity and Morning Flower Woman would be swept away into the world beyond.

Thirteen-year-old Blue Fox understood this all too well, but still refused to accept his mother would die. Even as she gazed at him now, her eyes like black coals peering from hollowed sockets, he refused to believe she would leave him.

Staring at her visage, Blue Fox shivered. The thin, frail form clinging to life was but a shell of the strong woman she'd once been. He lifted a cool, wet cloth and gently wiped her brow.

"Come close to me, Blue Fox," she whispered in her native Lakota.

Blue Fox tingled with dread, but moved closer at her urging. Sour breath made bile rise in his throat. He touched her arm, the skin loose and sweaty, then jerked away as though burned.

Her fingers beckoned him closer. With every ounce of will he possessed, Blue Fox slid onto the bed facing his mother. Her skeletal arm curled around his small frame.

"I will leave you soon, Blue Fox," she rasped.

"No." His voice echoed against the emptiness of the unfamiliar room. "You'll get better. You just need more rest. And more broth. I'll get you some." He tried to get up, but she held him tight in her death grip.

"You will hear what I must say."

"You need your strength." He tried to pull away again, but she kept him where he was.

"I am beyond help, my son. The Great Spirit has chosen to take me, and I am ready. My only regret is that I must leave you." Her voice wavered. Blue Fox's throat tightened and he tried hard not to cry.

He closed his eyes and forced a happier vision of his mother into his mind. A smile lit her face and large, almond-shaped eyes sparkled in the sunlight that warmed their village. She laughed, a sound that made Blue Fox feel safe, loved. He ran into warm arms that surrounded him like a blanket, her soft whispers like a gentle breeze against his skin.

A tear slipped down his cheek and splashed to the bed linen. He opened his eyes and watched the wetness spread across the stark whiteness of the sheet like the disease ravaging his mother's body.

"You are strong, Blue Fox. I have faith you will find your place in life. You are here with Ben and Sarah because the time of our people will soon end. It may not be tomorrow or the next day, but the Lakota will not survive much longer as they have always lived. Free. Unhindered by borders or white man's laws. Of this I am certain." She paused, struggling for breath. "But you, Blue Fox, must learn to live among those who remain. The whites."

"But, *ina*, Mother, I don't want to live among them. I want to return to our village." Blue Fox ached with despair. He only wanted to be with his mother and her people, sharing her love and guidance.

"You do not listen, Blue Fox. Like me, the Lakota are dying. I will not allow you to die with them. That is why you are here, at White Oaks, with Ben and Sarah..."

"But I don't want to be here!" Blue Fox interrupted. "You'll get better. I know you will. You just need rest and lots of food. Then we can return to our village. Together."

"This is not to be, Blue Fox. You must accept that I will die. You will be alone, except for Ben and Sarah." She took a shuddering breath and tears slipped from her eyes.

"You must believe I know what is best for you. These are good people and I trust them with your life."

"But they're white!" he shouted, making the bed shake.

"As was your father," she reminded him.

Her words silenced him. He didn't remember his father; he was too young when he'd died. And now she, too, would leave him. All he remembered of his young life was Morning Flower Woman and the Lakota.

"But I have never been white," he whispered. "The only reason I speak their words is because you force me to."

"With good reason, as you will learn." Seconds passed before she spoke again, her voice barely a whisper. "If I could change what is to happen, Blue Fox, I would. But I cannot. Therefore, I must do what is best for you. These people will give you what the Lakota cannot. A future."

Blue Fox knew his mother had made up her mind and there'd be no changing it. They'd had this discussion many times in the last two months since their arrival at White Oaks.

Silence enveloped the room. His mother's arm protectively around him, Blue Fox wanted nothing more than to stay surrounded by her wisdom and love forever.

Her arm tightened and she sucked in a deep breath. Blue Fox closed his eyes and held his breath as he waited for her to exhale. Her body quivered and air slowly leaked from her mouth.

Blue Fox was unable to move. Unable to accept that his mother was truly dying. That she would leave him.

Breathe, he commanded in his head again and again. Seconds passed. He opened his eyes; hers were wide and brimming with tears.

"I love you, Mother," he whispered. Hot tears spilled over his cheeks.

She raised her hand high enough to caress his wet face then took another shuddering breath. Slowly, the air issued from her lungs one last time and her hand fell limp to the bed.

"Mother," Blue Fox cried. "Mother. Answer me!" He shook her, but she just stared.

Deep in his heart Blue Fox knew she'd never again say his name, never again smile or laugh. Shaking, he stared at what remained of Morning Flower Woman of the Lakota Sioux.

He slid from her grasp and off the bed. Unable to look at her unseeing eyes, he ran past Ben and Sarah who had entered the room, down the stairs and out of the house to the barn. He threw himself into a wall—pounded, kicked and yelled, his face soaked with tears.

"Why? Why? Why?" he cried over and over. He pounded whatever he came into contact with—screamed and yelled, kicked and punched until he had no energy or voice left.

Exhausted, he curled up in a pile of hay like an abandoned kitten.

"I'll never be white," he whispered. "I am Lakota."

Chapter One

"You will go back." Ben Walters' voice was controlled.

"I won't." Blue Fox crossed his arms over his chest. "I'm never going back."

"You have to. It's what your mother wanted. And we promised her we'd see that you were schooled."

"But I don't want to!" Blue Fox shouted across the front room, his voice echoing off the walls and strange furnishings. "They hate me. And I hate them right back!"

Ben's wife, Sarah, stepped forward. Her hands were twisted together and her eyes were filled with concern. "Calm down, Blue Fox. We don't want you to do something against your will, but it's what your mother wanted."

"I don't care. I won't go back. I can't!" He stomped across the room, sending up little puffs of dust from the threadbare rug covering the floorboards.

"Blue Fox." Ben took a deep breath, "You don't have a choice. As long as you live here, you will do as you're told. We promised your mother and we intend to keep that promise. No matter how much you fight or scream you will go to school. And you will learn."

Blue Fox glared at Ben—tall, lean and commanding with only a few streaks of gray in his ebony hair.

"And what if I don't?" he asked.

Ben pursed his lips, and Blue Fox saw his anger rising.

Sarah stepped closer and put her hand on his shoulder. "Blue Fox," she whispered. Blue Fox's breath caught and he jerked away, unfamiliar with her touch.

"We only want what's best for you. I understand the other children were cruel today, but eventually they'll learn to accept you."

"Eventually?" Blue Fox snorted. "And how long am I supposed to listen to them call me half-breed and Injun?"

Sarah's hands shook as she plopped down in an overstuffed chair beside the fireplace. He hadn't even told them about the threats, only the children's hurtful teasing.

8

"I'm sorry," she whispered. And Blue Fox saw real sorrow in her face.

"But if we stick together, we can solve this problem, Blue Fox," she continued. "You must go to school. You must learn, or what will there be for you when you're grown?"

He shook his head. "I'll return to the Lakota."

"No you won't," came Ben's stern voice. "You were left in our care, and we intend to see this through. You'll go to school and that's the end of it. I'll talk with the teacher if it's necessary, but you will go back."

Blue Fox tried to speak again, but Ben cut him off. "Don't, Blue Fox. I'm through talking. You're going back. There will be no more discussion."

Ben stalked up the stairs. Sarah turned to Blue Fox as she stood. "We only want what's best for you, Blue Fox."

"You don't know what's best for me," he shouted, then turned and raced to his room.

Blue Fox slammed the door behind him, then flopped on his belly onto the bed. He pounded his fists into the soft mattress.

"I don't want to be here," he cried. "Why can't I be among my own people? I want to go home." He rolled onto his back and threw his arm across his face. As though suddenly in the room with him, he heard his mother's voice.

"These people can give you what the Lakota cannot, my son. A future."

He jerked upright, looked around the room and took in its sparse and unusual furnishings. A single window, lacy curtains, a small pitcher and basin on a bureau, and a picture of a man hanging on a cross on the wall.

"Mother?" Only silence. He felt like a dagger was being driven into his heart, the world closing in around him. He hated this place, hated these people, and hated most of all the children at the school.

But his mother had always taken care of him. Always known what was best for him. *Could he do anything less for her now than what she asked of him as she'd died? Had asked these people to do for him?*

He sighed in defeat. "Only because it was your wish, Mother, will I go back. Not because they say so." He lay back

9

down, closed his eyes, and drifted to sleep. He dreamed of gently rolling hills, gently flowing rivers and of a happier life with Morning Flower Woman and the Lakota.

Blue Fox stepped inside the chalky-smelling, book-lined room and stopped. He took a deep breath to calm his pounding heart. Slowly, two and three at a time, they turned, until twenty-one white faces stared at him. Some had eyes as wide as milk saucers, others' lips curled with disgust. But all questioned. All wondered why he'd come back.

"Half-breed." The word was whispered through the students like a soft breeze. His skin pricked, his insides constricted, and he recoiled as though rocks were hitting him, the word so bitter in his head.

The teacher pounded her stick.

"Enough!" she shouted. "There'll be no more of those names used here. It is 1869 and that kind of nonsense will not be tolerated. Do you understand?" Her dark, hard eyes swept the students, who quickly regained their composure.

"The next time I hear such language, the offending student will be paddled and their parents notified." She stared out over the sea of wide eyes and nodding heads.

"Good. Now open your spelling books to page 25."

Blue Fox took a deep breath. *I don't belong here. They know it. I know it. I hate it here.*

His thoughts splintered when he realized the teacher was speaking to him.

"Mr. Devlin, are you paying attention?" She called his white name, annoyance in her voice.

"He don't know how to," a boy on the other side of the room shouted.

The room erupted with laughter. Blue Fox stiffened in his seat. Even the little boy beside him had a grin on his face. He flushed with embarrassment.

The teacher rapped the stick again. Silence descended. "Mr. Devlin?"

"Yes, ma'am," he whispered. "I'm listening."

"Very well, we shall continue."

10

The teacher droned on for hours until, finally, she snapped her book shut and rang the lunch bell.

"Remember, Mr. Devlin, lunch is only one half hour."

He looked away and nodded, feeling even her dislike of him.

He ran outside the white schoolhouse into the warm September sunlight. Other children raced to benches, huddled together, pointed and snickered. He turned his back and walked toward a huge oak tree behind the dusty building. He sat down in its shade and ate the lunch Sarah had packed for him alone and in silence. When he finished, he watched the other children laugh and play and felt an odd stirring in his heart, but he didn't understand why.

Minutes later, the teacher rang the bell, recalling the children to their seats. Blue Fox forced himself to his feet and started back. At the door four boys waited, glaring with open hostility. One, with wide shoulders, stood a head taller than Blue Fox. The other three seemed to hover around the bigger one like flies swarmed around buffalo.

"Half-breed," they whispered as he walked past. Their laughter exploded behind him.

He whirled, his hands clenched into fists.

"Come on, Injun. What's you gonna do? You gonna fight us all?" one of the boys goaded.

They clamored up to him, then shoved their way into the classroom. Blue Fox's chest heaved when he sat down, their taunts floating like a heavy cloud in his head: Half-breed. Injun.

The scuffing of shoes and chairs quieted and voices stilled when the teacher stepped to the front of the room again.

Blue Fox took a deep breath, willing himself to pay attention. But when he looked down at the slate board in front of him, he couldn't tell what was on it. Nothing but curved, squiggly lines that meant nothing. The teacher drew more of the same pictures on the board at the front of the room. He watched in silence, but understood nothing.

He willed himself through the remainder of the day. But when the dismissal bell rang, the teacher stopped him before he made it out the door.

"Mr. Devlin."

He turned and walked back the short aisle to her desk. He looked at the deep wrinkles in her white face, the gray knot of hair tied tightly at the nape of her neck. He stared at her hands, long and spindly, wrinkled and gnarled with age.

"I have reason to believe you cannot read," she said, snapping him from his perusal of her.

He nodded.

"Then you shall stay after school each and every day until you can at least read at the level of the younger students."

He kept staring at her hands, hands that reminded him of the birch trees by the river—white, with mottled spots all over them.

"Is that agreeable, Mr. Devlin?" He wished he didn't have to come here. He wished he were back among the Lakota. Wished his mother were still alive. But she wasn't, and no amount of wishing would change that. He nodded.

"Yes, ma'am."

"Good. We'll start tomorrow after the final bell."

She gathered her belongings and swept past Blue Fox as she left the building. He turned to leave and stopped cold. There in the classroom still in her seat sat Karen, the prettiest girl in school. Golden hair curled below her shoulders and deep, blue eyes sparkled like a cloudless sky at sunrise. Eyes that watched him.

Her stare didn't waver.

Blue Fox studied her eyes, wide in their assessment of him. Her cheeks flared red, but she didn't look away.

She picked up her books, her long golden hair falling over her face to hide the small nose and full lips. But instead of walking out of the building, she walked straight toward him.

"I noticed you've been watching me." She stood so close Blue Fox could touch her. He smelled the floral scent wafting around her. Saw the swell of her small breasts beneath her blouse when she breathed. He felt as though a magnet drew his eyes to hers.

Blue Fox could feel his face burn. He looked away, knew his cheeks showed his embarrassment. Silence hung in the room for several moments, heavy like the air after a long,

12

drenching rain. Finally, he forced himself to look up again. Her head was cocked to the side and her brows were drawn together.

"I'm sorry if I've embarrassed you." Her voice was gentle. "Would you like to walk me home?" Her eyes sparkled and her lips curled into a smile that lit her entire face.

Heat raced through Blue Fox's body. No girl had ever spoken to him, let alone the prettiest one in the class. He didn't know what to say. Didn't know what to do.

Time stretched in front of him. Karen stared at him. Her eyes sparkled in the sunlight that streamed through the open window to her right.

"Would you like to walk with me?" she asked again.

Blue Fox was still unable to speak. He could only nod.

She hooked her arm through his elbow. A rush of excitement raced through him as they turned toward the door. She chattered words Blue Fox didn't hear as they walked to the exit. All he saw was her face.

She stopped and stepped away from him. "You haven't heard a word I've said," she pouted, her hands on her hips, her books tucked inside her elbow.

Blue Fox looked away, his face heating again.

She stared at him a few seconds, which made him even more nervous. He shuffled his feet back and forth, looked everywhere but at Karen. He looked at the empty chairs, at the pictures on the walls, even at the rows of tables where the children sat. Then he remembered they were alone in the room.

She sighed and leaned forward. She touched his arm and drew his eyes back to hers.

"Would you like to kiss me?" His heart nearly stopped. "It's all right. I'll let you."

Blue Fox felt like he'd turned to clay. He couldn't move. Just stared. She moved closer. Her books clattered to the floor. Her face grew fuzzy the closer she came until wet, soft lips brushed his. He felt her hands on his shoulders, heard her soft breath through her nose as her lips lingered.

His body grew hot and blood raced through him. He grew stiff and was horrified at his reaction to her touch. *What was happening to him?*

Her hands slid to his back and drew him closer. Without thinking he put his arms around her shoulders and he touched the softness of her hair that lay on her back. He closed his eyes and was overcome with desire. He pulled her closer. She whimpered, sending a rush through Blue Fox's already hot body.

She tried to pull away, tried to work her way out of his embrace, as though suddenly aware of what she was doing.

"Don't," she whispered.

But his senses had gone wild. He pulled her back to him, crushed her lips against his. She pushed at his chest, but he held tight, savoring the taste and feel of her sweet, soft lips.

Suddenly Blue Fox was spun out of her embrace like a child's top. Harvey, the big boy who'd brushed past him earlier in the day, was standing in front of him, his white face twisted with rage. Behind him were the three other boys.

"You got some nerve, Injun', puttin' your dirty lips on a white girl," Harvey drawled. His voice dripped with contempt and his finger stabbed Blue Fox in the chest with each word.

Harvey grabbed the front of Blue Fox's shirt and jerked him so his nose was only inches away from the white boy's face.

"Now, half-breed, I'm gonna put you in your place."

He shoved Blue Fox away like garbage. Blue Fox gained his balance and stepped back, his eyes darting around the room for a way to escape. To his left was the open window. *If only he could reach it and dive through...*

"Don't even try it," Harvey growled, jutting his chin toward the window.

Blue looked at the four boys and Karen behind them. Anger boiled in his belly.

"Go to hell." He curled his hands into fists.

He ran for the open window.

But Harvey was quick for his size. He jerked Blue to a halt halfway through the frame, holding Blue's feet as he dangled helplessly on the sill. Harvey yelled instructions to the other boys while Blue struggled to escape the clutching hands. Blue kicked and jerked his feet and legs until he managed to pull loose and fall outside.

He landed on his back, the wind knocked out of him. Gulping for breath, he rolled over and forced himself to his

14

knees, then to his feet. He regained his balance and turned to run, but Harvey's boys already blocked his escape. Slowly, he straightened his back.

"Come on then, if this is what you want. Let's get it over with!" He raised both fists over his head.

The boys remained still. They waited until Harvey walked out from around the building like a strutting rooster and stopped in front of Blue.

"We don't want your kind here, Injun. This is our school and not for dirty half-breeds like you. Since you don't appear to be hearin' what we're sayin', we're gonna have to teach you a lesson, so you won't even think about comin' back. Ain't that right boys?" Harvey turned and looked at each boy individually.

The others nodded vigorously. "We don't want your kind here," one shouted.

"Go back where you belong," added another.

"Seems we're all agreed," Harvey said. "'Cept you, that is."

Blue's eyes darted from one boy to the other. Which one to take on first?

Harvey started to talk again, but Blue wasn't going to give him a chance to strike first. He rammed his shoulder into the stomach of the boy closest and knocked him to the ground, gasping for air. He whirled in time to dodge a punch by another. When the punch missed, Blue thrust out his fist and hit that boy in the face. Blood spurted from his attacker's nose. The boy scuffled away, howling in pain, clutching his bloodied face. "He broke my nose! He broke my nose!" the boy shouted over and over again.

"Damn Injun'," Blue heard behind him, a split-second before he felt a crushing blow on his back. He staggered, but managed to stay on his feet. He turned and barely ducked another punch at his head. Jerking left, he stuck out his right foot and tripped the approaching boy, who teetered sideways then fell to his knees. Not giving him a second to regain his balance, Blue kicked him in the back and sent him sprawling to the ground.

But two of the boys were up and moving again and now Harvey joined the fray. Grabbed from behind, Blue's arms were pinned behind his back. Breathing through clenched teeth, he

15

fought with wild desperation to get free. He swung his head back and forth and kicked his feet at anyone who came near him.

"So you think you're tough, Injun'?" Harvey paced in front of Blue. "I'll show you tough."

The words had no sooner left Harvey's mouth when Blue felt as though a log was crushing his stomach. He gasped for air, gagged as he tried to fill his lungs. The boys laughed and, through the blur in his eyes, he saw Harvey square off in front of him again.

"I'll teach you a lesson you won't forget, half-breed. We don't want you here. Now you've touched a white girl. And for that you'll pay." The instant Harvey finished speaking, the next blow came. Blue's cheek exploded with pain. He felt blood surge down his face from a gash under his left eye.

Blue tried desperately to tear himself out of the boys' grip, but the pounding continued.

Finally, his arms were released and he staggered to his knees. A blow to his back sent him sprawling forward. Dust choked him. They continued to kick him on both sides and he was sure his ribs would shatter. He curled into a ball to ward off the attack, so they kicked his head. He closed his eyes. Lights flashed bright and sharp.

He heard a voice. Karen's voice. *Was she trying to help him? It was too late. Darkness was coming.*

"I told you I could get him alone," she said, her voice haughty with victory.

Blue managed to lift his head enough to see Karen standing in front of Harvey, her fingers caressing his face the way they had his only minutes ago.

"Yes, you did," Harvey said. "But I only asked you to get him alone. I never told you to kiss him. Why'd you kiss him? You're *my* girl, remember?" He grabbed her chin between his fingers.

Her lips pursed in petulance. "I only wanted to see what an Indian tasted like."

Her words pierced Blue with more shame and blinding pain than the beating he'd just received.

16

Through the buzzing and lights in his head, he watched her jerk back from Harvey and walk away, her skirt swinging with the sway of her hips.

Seconds later, darkness consumed him.

When Blue woke, his head was pounding and the sun sat low in the sky.

He touched his face and groaned at the pain that surged through his jaw. Blood and dirt caked his cheeks and hair. His eyes were swollen and hurt like the devil, his lower lip still bleeding and tender.

Blue leaned back against the white clapboards of the school and surveyed the schoolyard. He had no idea how long he'd been there. Looking down at his torn clothing, he grunted at the thorough job the boys had done. His trousers were ripped; raw, bloodied knees showed through. Tattered sleeves barely clung to the shirt hanging on his body and both his elbows were cut and oozed blood.

He hiked himself up against the building. Blinding pain hit him like a knife between his ribs. He moaned and hugged his chest. Steadying himself, he started forward, forcing one foot in front of the other trying to stay upright.

The world reeled and he put a hand back against the schoolhouse to keep from falling. Minutes later, one step at a time, sweat pouring in his eyes and using the wall as his support, he managed to reach the street.

He saw none of the boys. He saw only townspeople going about their business, hustling from one shop to another. Propped against the schoolhouse and in obvious need of help, he noted their uncaring expressions as they passed. Women moved from one side of the street to the other to avoid him, and children pointed, their eyes wide.

The world started to spin again. Blue leaned up against the hitching rail, tried to steady himself, but it didn't help. He couldn't breathe. Was dizzy. He grabbed at the post, tried to hold on, but neither his hands nor fingers worked.

Seconds later, he was spiraling down a long, narrow tunnel into cold blackness, unable to stop himself from falling.

17

Blue tried to sit up, the memory of his assault bringing him back to consciousness. Pain exploded in his brain. He grabbed his head, laid back down and tried not to cry out at the bright lights that burst like cannon fire in his head.

"Don't move so fast, Blue. You're pretty busted up," someone said.

The voice was familiar, but Blue couldn't place it. A vague form hovered over him, but he couldn't distinguish the face through his blurry eyes.

"You just be still, you hear?" the voice commanded.

"Who is it?" Blue asked.

"George. George Hawkins."

Now the voice matched the face: Hawkins, the smartest kid in school. Blue remembered how George's thick-lensed spectacles always slid down his nose and a stray lock of limp, brown hair always fell across his forehead, causing him to constantly push something up or off his face. George was quiet. He never spoke to anyone, not even the teacher unless she called on him.

"Thanks for the help," Blue said. He felt the words scratch his parched throat.

George nodded. "I know what it's like to be bullied by Harvey and his boys. Till you came, I was their favorite target."

Blue studied George. The thick glasses, his awkward appearance, and the gentle way he administered to his wounds. Blue felt a sudden kinship. George was an outsider, too. Blue tried to sit up, but pain shot like hot embers through his chest and he groaned.

"Take it easy. You could have a busted rib or two. You need to move really slow."

"Ouch! That's the truth." Blue moaned. He slowly repositioned so George could wrap his chest.

"This your room?" Blue swept the room with his hand and looked around while he tried not to grimace each time George wrapped another strip of cloth around his ribs.

Bare, whitewashed walls loomed in silence around him. George's bed, a lopsided chest-of-drawers, and a washstand were all that filled the room, adding to its bleakness. Blue felt a pang of pity for George. Even *he* had more than this boy did, living with people he didn't want to be with.

Blue looked up at the boy. George's face flushed red, but he threw back his shoulders and raised his chin.

"Yeah, it's mine," he answered in a strong voice. "It's not much, but it's all I got. Pa does the best he can for us, him being crippled up and all." George shoved the hair off his face, pushed up his glasses and gave Blue a crooked smile.

"Where's your ma?" Blue asked.

The boy's face clouded, but he held his back straight.

"Took off when I was a babe," he answered. "Don't you know, she just up and left when I was a tiny thing. The way Pa tells it," the boy sat down beside Blue, a mischievous smile on his face, "she took off one night with one of them cure-all elixir salesmen whose belly spilled out over the drawers of his too-tight red and black checkered suit. Pa says Ma wasn't much to look at, but she sure hitched herself up with one of the sorriest-lookin' excuses for a man he'd ever seen."

George hooted with laughter and Blue couldn't help but join him, stabbing pain and all. In that moment Blue knew, if he wanted, he could have a real friend. Someone he could trust. All he had to do was take that first step.

"I was real little when the war broke out," George continued. "While my pa was away, I played soldier every day. I slashed my sword in the air and killed all the Yanks to help him out. I won the war for him," he added wistfully.

Blue thought about George's words and how little he really knew about this society. He'd been a small boy when the war was fought, shielded from its horror by a mother who wanted him only to be safe and happy, while this boy had been at its center, wanting to kill Yanks to make his father proud. He was drawn from his musing when George spoke again.

"After Pa came back from the war, he took a fall off a horse that crippled him bad. Now we're making it the best we can."

Blue suddenly saw a reflection of himself. But in George's reflection, he saw no self-pity. The boy stood proud against what he was—the son of a cripple and a woman who'd run away from her husband and baby.

19

"Got any other family, besides your pa?" Blue asked to dispel the sudden silence in the room.

"Nah. Just me and Pa. It's always been just us." George shoved his hands deep into the pockets of his threadbare pants, showing a hint of his loneliness.

He turned serious eyes to Blue. "That's what I'm gonna be, don't you know? A soldier, like my pa." George's voice was solemn. "He was an officer, just like I'll be. I'm even gonna go to West Point, like he did." George pushed his glasses back up his nose then swiped at the stray lock of hair across his forehead.

Blue stared at the gangly, awkward boy in front of him. *George, a soldier?*

"They make a man out of you at the academy," George added, as though he'd read Blue's thoughts, his voice so full of hope Blue knew he was completely serious. "And see if I don't get there." George laughed again and Blue smiled, unable to join his laughter because of the pain in his ribs.

With his sudden good spirits Blue forgot some of his pain, both physical and emotional. He knew it was still there, but it was somehow—different. Less.

"What about you, Blue? How come you're with the Walters?"

Sudden visions of a calm, happy life raced through Blue's mind. Times he'd shared with his mother, Hihannahci Wanahca Win, Morning Flower Woman, in the Lakota Village with her people. Every day, they walked hand in hand. She taught him the ways of The People, while he chased rabbits and bugs through the lush, green countryside. He drifted among the memories.

"Blue?"

"What? Oh, sorry," Blue stammered. "What did you say?"

"I asked how come you're with the Walters?"

Blue shifted, causing a stabbing pain in his chest. He'd never confided his innermost thoughts to anyone before. But he sensed he could tell George anything.

"My ma was a Lakota Indian, but my pa was a white trapper. He found my ma after soldiers had attacked her village and destroyed it. He nursed her back to health then married her."

He looked down at the gold band circling the middle finger of his left hand. He twirled it as he spoke. "This ring was my ma's wedding band. It's made from a gold nugget my pa found in the Dakota Territory."

He tried to remember his father. But no memory came.

"What happened to them?" George asked?

"My pa died when I was just a baby. Then my ma got sick. So she brought me to the Walters."

"Why them?" George asked, shoving his glasses up again.

"I guess Sarah lived with my mother's people for a while and my mother trusted her. And she had nobody else."

They lapsed into a heavy silence.

"So here we are," George said to break the stillness.

"Here we are," Blue agreed, trying to cheer up. "Guess I'd better be getting back to White Oaks or Sarah's going to send a posse out after me. I usually head straight for the ranch as soon as school's over. She'll be worried." He put his hand on his ribs. "And when she gets a good look at me, she's going to be hellfire mad." Blue shook his head and smiled, thinking about the look he was sure to see on Sarah's face.

"At least she cares about you," George said.

Blue stared into the boy's eyes and sensed deep sadness.

George helped Blue to his feet. Staggering like two drunks, his arm draped over George's shoulders, Blue felt almost giddy. They stepped through the doorway and entered the paling sunlight of early evening.

Midnight, Blue's horse, stood tethered in front of the ramshackle building George called home. The black horse snorted and swished his tail in greeting.

"Thanks." Blue jerked his head toward the animal.

"No big deal. It was the only way I could get you home." George gazed at the animal and Blue saw admiration in the other boy's eyes.

"Anyway," George continued, snapping back to what he was saying, "it was like that horse knew you needed him. He stood stock still while I hoisted you up on his back, then he followed me home like a puppy."

Blue stepped forward and stroked Midnight's nose. "He's a good friend. Ben and Sarah gave him to me when I first came to them. Up till now he's been my only friend." Blue turned to George, a questioning look on his face.

He clapped George on the shoulder. The boy's face lit up, his smile so contagious Blue found himself grinning, too.

"Thanks again for helping me out."

George's smile was almost blinding.

Blue untethered Midnight and lifted his foot into the stirrup. He groaned like an old man as he pulled into the saddle. "I'll see you in school."

"You're going back?" George shouted in disbelief.

"You bet I'm going back. And I'll keep going back, George. I won't let them beat me. All this time I've been fighting Ben and Sarah, when I should have been listening to them. Now I realize the only way I'm going to show the others is by learning." He paused and looked up at the sky. "I want to do the best I can for my mother," he added softly.

George nodded.

Blue gathered the horse's reins in his hand. Settled as comfortably as possible in the saddle, he waved good-bye to his new friend and headed Midnight toward White Oaks.

Chapter Two

Every step Midnight took jarred Blue with pain, but he found himself enjoying the smells of White Oaks as he drew closer to the ranch. Freshly plowed fields. Cattle and hay. Sarah's cooking.

He recalled George's words as he entered the yard. *"At least she cares about you."*

Yes, Sarah did care about him, even though he'd fought her caring since the day he'd arrived at White Oaks with his mother. But George was right. Blue now understood Ben and Sarah did care for him. He knew because he saw it in Sarah's eyes every time he turned away from her, not allowing her to give him the love she so desperately wanted him to have. When he wouldn't let Ben teach him how to ranch and instead gave him hard words and his absence. Now Blue knew. If he had let himself, he would have seen their love sooner.

Blue nodded his head. His mother was right. Sarah cared. And when she got a look at him she was gonna show him just how much. The thought warmed his blood. Sarah Walters, the woman who, to the entire town, was his aunt. But in reality she was no blood relative—only a woman who knew his mother because she'd spent a year in captivity with her people.

Now, because of George's simple words, the wall he'd built around his heart seemed to melt away. It was almost as if the beating by Harvey and his boys had been a good thing—in a cleansing sort of way.

He urged Midnight forward. He needed to get home. Now.

Blue turned Midnight into the oak-lined lane, which lead to the big white house sitting proud against the orange sky. To his right was the barn, behind it the bunkhouse, although deserted because Ben and Sarah had no ranch hands. He scanned the courtyard, noticing the well to the rear where it was handy to draw water from the back of the main house. And just up the trail was the small house recently vacated by Caleb and Prudy, the

23

free black couple who'd moved into their own tiny farm a few miles from here.

The hinges on the front door to the main house squeaked and drew his attention. Sarah stepped out onto the porch. Even from where he was, he could tell by her wide eyes she was worried, by the way she bit her lower lip and twisted her apron. But today he allowed her concern to warm him, instead of anger him, as it had in the past.

Gathering her skirt she descended the steps. She walked slowly at first, but as Blue's battered features came into her view, she ran.

"What happened!" She grabbed Midnight's bridle and stood beside the animal, looking up at Blue.

"Nothing much." Blue tried to hold back the groan of pain as he lifted his leg over Midnight's back and dismounted.

"Nothing much! Who did this to you? Who was it?" she demanded. Her voice rose and Blue watched her blue eyes cloud with anger.

"Blue, who did this to you?"

"Some of the boys finally got to kick up their heels," he joked as he led Sarah and Midnight toward the barn. "Mostly, they kicked 'em up on me."

Sarah gasped and Blue watched her jaw move back and forth before she exploded.

"Those heathens! Bastards!"

Shocked by her outburst, Blue couldn't help but smile and allow himself to enjoy her tirade and anger on his behalf.

"By God, we're going to do something about this," she yelled.

"You can't do that!" he shouted.

"And why not?" she asked, her hands on her hips.

"Because it'll only make things worse. I have to handle this myself." He looked away, drew a deep breath and turned back. "I'm not a baby."

"Oh, Blue. Of course you're not, but I can't bear to see them taunt you like this."

Blue studied her face and saw the love and caring there plain for him to see. *Why hadn't he seen it before?*

24

"Besides," he added. "Something good came out of this. I made a friend."

Joy leapt into her face and his heart swelled.

"Tell me," she pulled him toward the well, "while I clean some of this blood and dirt off you."

He told her about George while she dabbed his dirty face with the hem of her skirt. He watched her face pucker and twist as his tale unfolded, as though she, too, felt his pain.

"You may not believe it, Blue, but I do understand what you've been through. How you feel alone and how you desperately want someone to be your friend."

Blue grunted. *Yeah, sure she knew. Safe here in her big house with Ben. She knows, all right.*

She covered his hand with hers and her warmth flowed to his heart.

"Haven't you ever wondered why your mother brought you here when she realized she was dying?"

Blue nodded. "She told me it was because you lived with the Lakota. She trusted you and Ben. She said The People trusted you, that you had even earned a name of respect from them."

Sarah snorted most unladylike. "It was a name of respect all right, but I had to live through hell to earn it." Her eyes grew glossy with her memories. Blue watched her as she spoke, her voice now quiet.

"I was brought to The People by Man-Who-Runs, your uncle, after the Lakota attacked our wagon train. When I entered the village with him, The People laughed and ridiculed me. I struggled every day just to keep my sanity. I tried to escape. Even tried to kill myself." Her voice cracked with emotion and her gaze drifted downward to where she rolled her wrists upside down to expose two thin-white scars. She raised sad eyes to Blue. "I hated your uncle and everyone in his village because I thought they'd killed Ben and kept me from going home."

Her eyes brimmed with tears, but then her face grew hard.

"It was a long time before I was accepted by The People. I had to fight for that acceptance." She paused and withdrew an oval locket from around her neck, touched it tenderly.

"It was your uncle who gave me my name of respect, after I fought three women to get back this locket that Ben had given me that I'd lost in the attack." With a faraway look she stroked the locket resting at her neck. A moment later she continued. "I became Wi Tapeta Yuha Win, Woman with Fire Like the Sun, and after that, The People accepted me."

Blue watched her expressions and realized she really did understand his feelings.

"When I finally allowed myself to feel again, I began to study and learn their ways. I came to care for your uncle. Very much. And when the army came that day at Bluewater Creek, I wanted to stay with him. He tried to send me away, but I wouldn't go. I watched, helpless, as he was gunned down by the cavalry."

A tear slipped down her cheek before she swiped it away with the back of her hand and her back straightened.

"When I returned home I was treated like I had the plague. People called me names like Indian Lover and Squaw, a vile name given to Indian women by white men." She paused again, checked Blue's arms for more cuts and bruises. "For years I struggled to be accepted among my own people. And by my own husband." Her words were as soft as the breeze that floated around them. Blue gasped, surprised by her words.

She stopped speaking and took a deep breath, her eyes sparkling with unshed tears. She took Blue's hands into hers.

"Do you understand what I'm saying? Sometimes acceptance must be won over a long period of time and after a great deal of pain. But when that acceptance comes, its nectar is sweeter than that of any fruit and can be savored for the rest of your life."

Blue nodded. He did understand. Now.

A smile lit Sarah's face. The stillness of the early evening enveloped them for several moments. Then Sarah jumped up and slapped her thighs.

"Come on now, let's get you inside and into some clean clothes." She grabbed Blue's hand and led him into the house.

Later that night alone in bed Blue thought about all Sarah had said and he believed he did understand what she'd told

26

him. And when he fell asleep, amidst all his pain, a smile curled his lips.

He woke the next morning stiff and sore, but again vowed Harvey and his kind wouldn't keep him from returning to school. Although he hated the musky-smelling room filled with white children of all ages, he suddenly wanted to fulfill Morning Flower Woman's dream for him. He would learn to live in the white world. And to do that, he had to attend the white man's school.

He dressed that morning with great care, each movement causing some part of his body to ache. Dressed, he went to the kitchen and greeted his new parents. Ben had still been out on the range the previous evening when Blue rode in and hadn't seen his battered face or body.

Ben's chair scraped across the floor when he came to his feet.

"Those bastards," he said through clenched teeth.

Blue was pleased by Ben's outburst, as he had been by Sarah's, and wondered how, for so long, he'd been able to push these people from his heart. Just by looking at Ben he could see the man cared. A great deal.

Sarah touched Ben's hand. He set his chair up and eased back into it, obviously working to control his rage.

"Have some breakfast," Sarah offered.

"I'll be late," Blue answered. He grabbed his lunch bucket then turned warm eyes toward Sarah.

Sarah's eyes filled with pride. Ben stood up and stepped toward him.

"I'm proud of you, son." Ben laid his hand on Blue's shoulder. "Even though you took a beating, you're still determined to prove you have just as much right to be in that school as those other boys. You go and learn, and show them you're as good as they are. Better," he added.

Blue's chest swelled. "And I'm gonna keep going back," he said. "Again and again. I'm gonna learn as much as I can. For my mother," he added softly.

Blue left the house with new purpose in his step. He gingerly saddled Midnight and rode slowly toward school.

As he drew closer, his heart began to race and he started to sweat. He took a deep breath and reassured himself he had to go back, to prove to himself he was as good as they were. And for Morning Flower Woman, to fulfill her wish for him to learn was suddenly all consuming. He wanted to learn everything he could. Why the sun rose in the east and set in the west. Why birds flew and dogs ran on all four legs. Why it rained and why it stormed. He would learn how to add, subtract and read, so no man could take advantage of him because he was unschooled.

Blue entered the schoolroom as the teacher rang the final bell. Students were headed to their seats, but the room suddenly fell silent. Blue looked around and noticed the surprised stares of Karen, Harvey and his pack, stopped in mid-stride in the middle of the room.

Blue looked at each of them and swore silently he wouldn't let them see him squirm. Searching the room, he spotted George, a grin the size of the Missouri River on his face. Blue nodded and smiled in return before he turned back to Harvey and his group. One by one they went to their seats, surprise still evident on their faces. But maybe there was something more than just surprise in their faces. Something he had never seen before.

Perhaps he would never gain their acceptance, he mused, but at least, today, he had earned their grudging respect.

Chapter Three

Every day after school Blue rode Midnight around the perimeter of the ranch, alone with his thoughts.

Six months had passed since his brush with Harvey and the boys. He'd recovered, but there were parts of him that still hurt when he moved a certain way. Sometimes lights flashed bright and quick in his head, gone as fast as they'd come, but leaving behind a painful reminder.

He repositioned in the saddle and stared out over White Oaks. He sucked in the warm March air. This was home. Here he had nothing to prove. Here he was loved.

Stopping at the crest of the north hill, he gazed out over the land. Spring was beginning to bloom. Buds appeared all around him. New leaves on the oaks swayed in the gentle wind and the sun was warm on his face. Birds, squirrels and rabbits darted in and out of the underbrush. To the east, he heard the lowing of cattle in the pastures. And to the south was the small pond surrounded by bushes and trees he and George would swim in when the weather warmed up.

A spiral of smoke from the kitchen chimney of the main house was visible in the distance where the barn, corrals and other outbuildings clustered around it. Blue felt safe here. Accepted, as Sarah had suggested.

Must be suppertime, he mused, his stomach and the smoke reminding him he was hungry. His mouth watered at the thought of chicken and dumplings swimming in thick gravy.

He thought about Ben.

"This will all be yours one day," Ben had told him one night, watching the sun set over the valley. He'd been stunned, but Ben had gone on to explain.

"When Sarah and I arrived here years ago, this ranch was owned by a fine elderly lady named Emma. We came to love her like a mother and she loved us like her children. Her last gift to us was this ranch."

He gazed deep into Blue's eyes. "That's why it's only fitting it should go to you, for we love you as our son."

29

Blue saw tears in Ben's eyes and a sense of belonging enveloped him. A belonging he hadn't felt since his mother died.

He thought of Morning Flower Woman and sighed wistfully. In her wisdom, she'd brought him to the only people she knew would care for him as their own. He knew this ranch and these people had become his heart. Here was where he belonged. White Oaks was home.

A horse snorted behind him and he turned to watch George ride up. His friend waved a hand in greeting.

Blue waved back and George reined his horse up beside him. Since their first meeting, Blue had noticed remarkable changes in his friend. He'd gone from being shy and self-conscious to confident and sure. Blue didn't want to take credit for the change, but he knew it had happened ever since they'd begun spending time together.

During school, they shared each other's company, and after school, they rode to each other's homes to spend more time together. They wrestled, rode, and played games.

They worked cattle and horses at White Oaks with Ben and helped each other with their lessons. Blue felt a bond as strong as brothers.

Today when he looked at George, he saw sadness on his friend's face.

"What's wrong?" He shifted uneasily on Midnight's back.

"Everything," George answered. "Pa's gone on a drunken binge, shouting he can't find work, that nobody will hire a washed-up, has-been, crippled soldier like him." George scanned the valley. "I told him to use some of the money he's got put away for me. But he started screaming how he wasn't going to ruin my life like his is. Seeing me go to the Point is all he lives for."

Blue remained silent. He knew George hurt, but the only thing he could do for his friend right now was listen.

"I finally got him settled down and put to bed," George continued. "But I couldn't stand the quiet. It was like the walls were laughing at me with their silence."

Blue gazed at his friend, felt his pain. Suddenly, an idea flashed into his head. He turned to George and shouted.

"Come on. You're having dinner with us!" He turned Midnight around and sent the animal racing toward the main house.

Unable to argue, George followed. They reached the courtyard several minutes later, the horses lathered and winded.

Blue jumped to the ground, threw the rein around the hitching post and raced inside, the door slamming in his wake. George dismounted and was right behind him.

"What in blazes is all the racket?" Sarah yelled from in front of the big iron stove. A smile lit her face, as it always did, when she saw them.

"Well, look who came dragging in?" she teased. "George. Blue. What's all the commotion?"

"Sarah, sit down. Please," Blue said, his heart pounding. The idea had come to him full-blown and he was too excited to wait for Ben.

"I will, I will, just give me a second." She pulled out a chair and sat down. "What's so all-fired important?"

Blue took a deep breath and plunged in. "I've asked George to stay for dinner."

"Well, that's fine, Blue. You know George is always welcome."

"But that's not all I want to ask," he continued in a rush. "I want Ben to give George's pa a job."

"What?"

"What?" George echoed. Shock registered on both Sarah's and George's faces.

"I want you to ask Ben to give Mr. Hawkins a job. He's in a bad state, Sarah. He can't find work in town and it's making it real hard on George. They could stay in the bunkhouse. Then George and I could ride to school together. We could see each other all the time."

His words flowed like a flood from his mouth, and he watched George and Sarah's expressions change from one of shock to consideration.

"Well," Sarah began, but was cut off.

"Where in the world did you come up with such a hair-brained idea as that?" George asked Blue. "You know my pa

31

can't do heavy work. Can't hardly even sit a horse anymore. What could he do around here?"

Blue pondered the question. "Help with the garden. Sarah has so much to do in the big house, every year I see the garden get worse and worse. " He looked over at Sarah. He knew Sarah always kept the garden well-tended and in good condition, but she nodded knowingly.

"You're right, Blue. Every year I have less and less time to spend in the garden. It's a lot of work. And the barn always needs cleaning and new hay. Why, I bet if we really put our minds to it, we could come up with a dozen things your pa could do."

Blue smiled, his heart bursting with love. She understood what he was trying to do and was going along whole-heartedly.

"There you go," he said to George. "A dozen things your pa could do."

One thing Blue knew, George's father wouldn't take charity. Even though he was a broken man, he still had his pride.

"Well..." George sounded skeptical.

"Come on, George. What would it hurt to ask Ben? Your pa could work and earn wages to boot. Maybe not a lot, but something for his labor. And it's better than not having anything. Right Sarah?" he asked, hopeful.

Cautiously, she nodded her head.

"There, it's settled." Blue slapped George on the back.

"Wait just a second," Sarah reminded him. "We've still got to check with Ben first. But," she leaned forward, her voice conspiratorial, "I have an in with the boss. I think he'll listen to my request."

A week later, George and his father moved into the empty bunkhouse.

Soon a regular routine took over. George and Blue rode to school together every day. They spent afternoons lazing under the shade of one of the huge oaks in the fields, their noses pressed to books, studying, each helping the other with words or equations they didn't understand.

One warm day after studying for hours, George stood up and screamed, "Enough!"

They raced to the swimming hole, pulling their clothes off as they ran, and dove into the cool water splashing and dunking each other.

Blue broke the surface and spit water out of his mouth. Slowly, he started toward his friend across the pond.

"Oh no you don't!" George laughed, paddling for the bank. "You're not going to dunk me again. And it's time for me to get even for past transgressions!" He pulled himself out of the water, turned and raised his arm above his head, his finger pointing into the air like a preacher.

"You shall not defeat me," he cried dramatically, then rushed to the bushes where they'd left their clothes.

"Now, George," Blue called, knowing what was going to happen next. "Come on, George. I'm sorry. I won't ever make you run home naked again. I swear," Blue pleaded. He knew George would never let his revenge rest with mere begging. He'd get even first. Blue paddled faster, but George had already grabbed their clothes, wadded them up in his arms, and grabbed the reins of both horses.

"Fair is fair, Blue, my boy. Farewell, dear friend. I'll see you at dinner, if you make it home before the fireflies come out!" George hooted with laughter, threw himself into the saddle and fled far enough away to dress then head for home.

Blue stood on the muddy bank. *What could he expect? Fair is fair.*

He sprinted home, hiding behind bushes and trees and made it to the back door before he was spotted.

Sarah screamed when she caught sight of him and ran out of the kitchen. Blue tried to hide as he raced upstairs to his room. The door slammed behind him, but not before he heard George's howl of laughter from the front porch.

Chapter Four

"I'm gonna get a job." George clucked his horse toward White Oaks, the day's schooling done.

"What?" A shock of alarm ran through Blue. "What do you need a job for? We've got plenty of work to do around the ranch. Paid work, remember?"

"I know and I thank Ben and Sarah for letting me do it. But I know they haven't got a lot of money to pay me with. Least not me and pa. Besides, I don't want to strap them, having them think they have to pay me and all."

Blue stared at his friend.

"What makes you think they can't pay us what they give us?"

George turned the shade of a ripe tomato. "I heard them. I didn't mean to," he rushed on. "I was just passing by the front room when I heard Ben say how bad the accounts were, and that he was afraid there wouldn't be enough to put up what was needed for winter. Sarah asked about you, me and my pa, but Ben said he wouldn't discuss it—as long as we worked, we got paid."

George frowned. "I can't keep taking money when I know it's making it tough on them."

Blue thought about his parents and pride ran through him. Only they would keep paying someone for a job they didn't really need done when they didn't have enough.

He leaned over and slapped George on the back. "You're right, my friend. And starting tomorrow, we're both going to hit the planks to find jobs!"

The following day Blue fidgeted, waiting anxiously for the clanging of the bell that ended the day's lessons. And when it did, he was out the door in a flash, George right behind him.

He stood at the top of the main road that led into town, and his heart quickened. People lined the boardwalk streets, went in and out of the general store, bakery, hotel, and at the far end, the livery. Somewhere within the framework of that town, someone would give them a job.

Their first stop was the hotel. Blue and George stepped through the front door and stopped. Wealth surrounded them like a soft, shimmering blanket. A huge chandelier hung from the ceiling, its gas lamps sputtering with light, although it was full daylight. Fancy carpet covered the floorboards, and all around, ornate chairs and paintings adorned the room.

Blue's heart quickened, overwhelmed by a place of such grandeur.

"Come on. Let's talk to the man behind the desk." George headed toward the clerk. Blue followed, but stayed quiet, happy to let George do all the talking.

"Sir," George said.

The man looked up from his paperwork, adjusted his glasses and eyed both boys. "Yes. May I help you?" he drawled after a long perusal.

"We're looking for work," George said. "We can do anything needs to be done to keep a place like this looking fancy."

The man took a deep breath. "Just a moment. I'll get the owner." He ambled away as though the boys were nothing more than a nuisance he was forced to deal with.

A few minutes later a tall man with a round belly strode into the room.

"May I help you?"

George stepped forward. "Sir, my name is George Hawkins and this is Blue Devlin. We're looking for work. We can sweep or dust or wash dishes," George said in a rush.

Blue stood mute behind his friend and tried not to look the man square in eye, although the man looked both of them over like slabs of prime beef. When the inspection was over, the man stepped toward George.

"You can work in the restaurant. You can gather the dirty dishes, scrape plates, wash dishes, and sweep the floor," he said to George. "You," he said to Blue, "I have nothing for." Without another word he turned and walked away. "If you want that job, follow me," he said over his shoulder, waving for George to follow.

George ran after him. "Don't worry, Blue. You'll find something," George called back to him. "Don't give up."

35

Blue watched his friend disappear through the door. It had been so easy for George. Would it be easy for him? But he knew the answer to his own question. He'd seen how the owner looked at him, tried to make him feel lowly and worthless.

Still determined, Blue pushed the thought aside and walked through the door to the planked sidewalk outside. He took a deep breath and forced himself to keep looking.

He started with Winstead's Bakery. Stepping through the door, he headed toward an older woman who waited behind the counter.

"Yes?" she asked with an arched eyebrow.

"My name is Blue Devlin and I'm looking for work. I could help with the baking or cleaning up. Anything you'd need me to do," he added.

"Devlin, you say?" She eyed him. "Hmm. Just a minute." She disappeared through a curtain. Blue was looking around, imagining what the pastries in the case would taste like, when a rotund, balding man stepped through the curtain.

"My wife says you're looking for work," he said, his tone clipped. "Got no need, boy. This is my place and my wife and me take care of everything." He stopped, stared at Blue a second, then added, "Even if I did need help, I wouldn't hire no 'breed."

Blue tamped down his temper then turned and stalked out the door without a word.

He tried the bathhouse next, but was greeted by the same scathing looks. "Got no need for a pretty boy like you in a place like this," the owner hooted. "Let alone a pretty boy Injun!" The man howled with laughter as Blue raced out the door and back into the street.

Depressed and unable to look any longer, Blue returned to White Oaks with nothing but a head full of "no's" to show for his efforts.

Blue slammed through the kitchen door and stalked toward his room. He was stopped in the front room by George, who'd been waiting for him to get home.

"How'd it go?" he asked, anxious.

"You don't want to hear about it."

"Bad?"

"Bad." Blue didn't want to talk about his humiliation. All they could see when they looked at him was a 'breed or an Indian. He was more than that, damn it. And he was going to prove it.

Sarah called them to dinner and George let the issue drop. But gathered around the table, Blue was forced to listen as his friend prattled on like an old woman about his new job.

"I'll be in charge of keeping everything clean," he said proudly. "In the kitchen I'll take care of gathering the dirty dishes, washing them, and stacking them, you know. And in the lobby, I'll make sure the floor is swept and see no dust gathers on the furniture or pictures."

Blue listened to George ramble and felt more and more dejected with each passing minute.

He looked up and noticed Sarah staring at him, her eyes soft with understanding. She knew what he was going through. She felt it and he loved her more for it. She stood up and offered dessert to stop George's rambling. Blue was more than grateful as he dug into the white cake, hoping to ease his hurt insides.

By Saturday Blue was ready to give his search for work another try. He dressed carefully, combed his hair and set out.

He started with Anson's General Store. The bell over the door tinkled when Blue pushed through. A smile came to Anson's face when he saw Blue and his hopes soared.

"Hi, Mr. Anson."

"Blue. What can I get for you today?"

"Well, sir, I'm looking for a job." The man's expression changed.

"I could stack boxes and goods and sweep the floor," Blue said in a rush.

Anson shook his head. "I'm sorry, Blue. I don't have a job for you."

Blue stood frozen, hating those words. Did he not have a job because he was a 'breed he wanted to ask, but held his tongue.

"Nothing?" Blue managed.

"Nothing," Anson replied.

Blue couldn't keep the words from spilling out of his mouth. "Is that because of what I am?" he asked, his tone bitter.

Anson appeared taken aback, but Blue saw hostility jump into his eyes. "Of course not. You're welcome in here anytime."

"Anytime I have my uncle's money to spend," Blue shouted.

"Go on, get out of here, Blue. I don't need to listen to your talk. Git!"

Blue hurried outside, his heart pounding, his anger boiling to rage. Couldn't people even give him a chance? He took a deep breath. He wouldn't let them beat him. He shoved his hands into his pants pockets and headed down the street.

He tried one of the drinking saloons. The man slammed the door in his face. He even went to the ladies dress shop, but there too, he was told she wouldn't hire anyone like him. His self-esteem was being crushed like a pebble under a giant rock.

Every refusal built more resentment in the pit of his belly. But he was determined to succeed in finding someone in town who'd hire him.

There was only one place left. The livery. He loved horses and thought it would be a fitting place to work, even if it was only shoveling manure. Hopeful, he stepped into the livery's dark interior.

It smelled of dung and dust, sweat, horses and hay. To the rear of the building he heard melodious whistling.

"Hello?" Blue called.

The whistling stopped and a man shuffled toward him.

"Hello, young man," the hunched-over old man said through teeth stained dark from tobacco juice.

"I...sir, I'm looking for a job," Blue stuttered. "Would you have something for me to do around here? I'll work for small wages and do whatever you want. I'll clean stalls, feed and water the animals—even groom them if you want." he added in a rush.

The man studied Blue for a moment. Placing his hand on his gray, whiskered chin he moved his head back and forth eyeing Blue.

"You that half-breed kid, ain't you?"

Blue drew a heavy breath. "Yes, sir. I'm Blue. The half-breed," he answered, deflated. He didn't want to hear it again, so he turned to leave.

"Just a minute, sonny. Just 'cause you're a 'breed, don't mean I won't hire you."

Blue stopped in his tracks, turned slowly, afraid he might be imagining the words. The man, with gnarled lines running from his gray eyes to his mouth, was smiling.

"Sir?"

"Said, just 'cause you're a 'breed don't mean I can't, or won't, give you a job. Known plenty of 'breeds in my day, which has been too many to remember," he said, a twinkle in his eyes. "But wasn't a one wasn't a good worker or even a good friend."

Blue straightened. "I'd be an excellent worker. I know horses. I work them out at my aunt and uncle's place all the time. I'm a good rider, too. Like I said, I'll do anything, just name it."

"Sounds to me like you'll do just fine." The man grinned. "Got yourself a job. You can start after the school bell rings. My name's Jackson and I own this here place."

He held out his hand and Blue took it, a new sense of purpose enveloping him.

"Thank you, sir. Thank you. You won't be sorry," he managed, pumping Jackson's hand before he ran from the building jumping and shouting with joy.

He untethered Midnight, swung into the saddle and they raced for home.

Every day Blue left school and rode the stretch of road to the livery, new purpose in the straightness of his back. He was happy. He had good parents who cared about him, a best friend who was closer than a brother, and now he had work. Work that made his back hurt, his senses rebel and his pride swell. He was no longer a burden on Ben and Sarah. He'd even insisted on giving them a portion of his weekly pay, regardless of how small it was. And even old man Jackson was kind and caring and prattled on endlessly about 'the old days' as Blue worked.

Life was good, Blue thought, tossing another bale of hay onto the loft. Oh, he still ached whenever he thought about his mother, but finally now, he'd found his place.

Sitting on the porch late one night at White Oaks, apple pie heavy on their stomachs, George leaned back and gave Blue an intense stare. Blue knew a question was coming, a serious one. Sometimes when they sat alone on the porch of an evening, George got melancholy when he talked about life and death. Blue hoped it wouldn't be a discussion like that tonight. He was too full and too happy.

"How'd you get your name, Blue?"

Blue smiled, thankful this conversation wasn't going to turn deep. He grabbed a piece of wood and his knife and started to whittle. He chuckled at the memory of the story his mother had told him of his birth.

"According to my mother, I was named Blue because of my blue eyes, so strange to her people." He paused. "But Blue Devlin isn't my full name," he added with a smirk. "Blue Devlin is just my white name."

"What? I've known you all this time and I don't even know your real name?" George prodded. "Well then. What is it?"

"Blue Fox with Two Hearts."

"Blue Fox with Two Hearts?" George nearly shouted.

Blue grinned and nodded. "The way the story goes, the day I was born there was a ruckus in the yard outside our cabin. My father grabbed his rifle and went to find out what the commotion was. When he came back, he told my mother a fox was trying to catch one of the few chickens we had in the yard. My mother, certain the animal's presence was a sign, added Fox to my name in the Lakota tradition.

"The days I spent with the Sioux were the happiest of my life." Blue sighed and thought back on his time with the Lakota. "I remember watching the other boys hunt make-believe buffalo and play the hoop game."

"Hoop game?" George interrupted, his face screwed up with curiosity. "What's that?"

"It's a game where the children tossed arrows into a round hoop on the ground." Blue answered quickly, anxious to explain. "Whoever put the most arrows inside the hoop, won," he finished, warm with the memory. "I watched them, anxious for the day I could play the games with them."

"You just watched? You never played with them?"

Blue's happy thoughts fled. *Why hadn't he ever played with them? Why had he always watched, but never joined in?* His thoughts twisted at the unsettling questions.

"Didn't you ever play?" George asked again.

Blue avoided the question with more memories. "When the weather was warm, I swam with some of the other children. And once in a while, they'd let me play the hoop game with them." He thought back over the scenes of his childhood. "But most of the time, they told me I was too little and to go away, so I spent most of my time with my mother." He felt sudden anger rise inside him.

But he didn't understand what he felt. *Had he known even then he was different from the other children? Was he allowed to play only when they needed another body to complete their team or they felt sorry enough to let him join their game?*

He sat silent for a few minutes before George pulled him from his thoughts. "But where'd Two Hearts come from?"

"I got that from the Lakota, too. It shows I have a heart in the red world and one in the white world." Blue snorted. "I guess even then without my knowing it, I was set apart as a half-breed." He threw down the piece of wood and flung the knife into the floorboard.

"But that's all in the past," Blue said, trying to dispel his sour mood. "Now I'm here. I've got you and Ben and Sarah. What else could I ask for?"

He looked at his friend and tried to push away the sadness gnawing at his insides. But it was too heavy. He was happy right now, tonight, but he knew someday soon that happiness would flee when George left for West Point.

He'd go into the world and become the soldier his father always dreamed he'd be.

But Blue didn't want to think about that now.

"Race you to the corral post," he shouted, clamoring down the porch stairs, George fast behind him.

41

Chapter Five

Blue's eyes wandered the confines of the schoolroom, but stopped at the teacher's desk, empty of the usual clutter of books and papers for the first time he could remember. Today was the last time he'd come here. The last time he'd listen to the teacher drone her lessons. The last time he'd see Harvey and his bunch.

It was the last day of school. A twinge of regret passed through him.

Although he'd hated coming here for so long, he knew he'd fulfilled Morning Flower's dream to learn. And that was mostly due to the woman standing in front of him. She still wore her hair in a severe knot at the back of her head. She still droned on like an injured cat all day. But her attitude toward Blue had softened, even changed to a possible liking, as she'd worked with him to teach him to read and write what he could already speak.

A small smile of satisfaction curled his lips when he thought back over the past three years. How hard it had been. How difficult the studies. But he'd learned so much, despite everyone's belief that he was just a dumb 'breed'. And he'd shown them he was as good as any of them. Better than many.

He recalled the day Harvey and his boys beat him up, the only time, and the lasting friendship he'd gained from it.

He looked at George who fidgeted in his seat, anxious for the day to end, too. A pang of dread rushed through Blue. When summer was over George would leave for West Point to become a soldier, to complete his father's dream for his future.

And when George left, what would become of him? He watched his friend shove his glasses up his nose and swipe at the stray lock of hair that still defiantly fell across his forehead.

What would he do? Blue knew he had a place at the ranch as long as he wanted it. And he felt safe and happy there. *But what kind of future would he make for himself, the way George would when he became a soldier?*

Time grew fuzzy and the teacher's voice blended into the walls around him. Before he realized it, the final bell sounded and the students rushed from the building, screaming and jumping in delight.

He got up to leave, then spotted Miss Fletcher at her desk arranging the last of her books. He walked to the front of the room and stood before her.

She looked up, the lines around her face deep in question. "Yes?"

"I, Miss Fletcher, I want to thank you. To say you were right, about learning and all."

She took a deep breath and smiled, deepening the cracks in her face, but lighting her face with joy.

"Thank you, Blue." She scanned the room, now empty except for George and Blue, and the smile faded. "So many don't understand. And even less take the time to thank me." She looked back. "You're very welcome, Blue. Now use what you've learned," she whispered.

"Yes, ma'am."

He gathered his belongings and strolled to the door where George waited for him.

"It's finally over, Blue," George said. "All those years of listening to Miss Fletcher's lessons are finally over."

Blue nodded in agreement, a somber mood settling on him like dust on a statue. The long-awaited end of school wasn't as joyful as he thought it would be. In the end, it meant the eventual departure of his only friend.

Blue straightened and looked over at George, still trying to fit the split-rail fence together. The summer was passing too fast. It was only a few weeks until George would leave for the Point.

One more rail needed to be anchored before they were done, but Blue decided he couldn't wait.

"I'll give you a head start to the pond," Blue challenged. He dropped the fencepost.

"We're not done yet," George protested.

"We'll finish later. Come on, I'll give you to the count of five. Don't waste any time. You know you'll need every second to beat me." Blue began to count.

George dropped his end of the rail and tore through the trees ahead of Blue.

"Three, four, five!" Blue shouted before he sprinted off. He could overtake his friend within minutes if he wanted, instead he lagged behind, allowing George to beat him to the pond. He threw off his clothes and dove into the cool, refreshing water seconds after George.

"I beat you!" George shouted when he broke the surface, his face awash with happiness. Staring at his friend, Blue marveled at how much George had grown and changed. But now, with a mere smile, he easily transformed back to the young, awkward boy Blue had first met.

They splashed and dunked each other in the water for nearly an hour before deciding they'd better finish the fence. The sun was dropping low over the ridge and Sarah would have dinner ready soon. One thing they both agreed they didn't want to miss...was dinner.

They dragged themselves from the pond laughing and wrestling. Putting on his shirt, the thought of how much George meant to Blue pierced him to his soul. He felt like he'd been gut-punched and he had to take a deep breath to keep his control.

Pain raced through Blue like a bullet. He gathered his clothes, pushed through the bushes hiding the pool, and walked back toward the fence.

George ran up beside him, panting from his swim. "What's the matter?"

Blue stopped and turned to face his only friend. *How could he tell him all he felt? Tell him how much it would hurt when he left, without making George feel guilty about having a plan for his life?*

"I was just thinking about how things are gonna change when you leave," Blue said.

He didn't have to say anymore. George swung his arm around Blue's shoulder and the two walked in silence back to finish their fence work.

44

Blue pushed thoughts of George's departure from his mind. He'd enjoy every remaining moment with his friend. No matter how short.

Summer ended too soon. George was to leave for West Point the next day. Sitting on the wooden swing on the front porch, Blue spoke little, his thoughts too painful to put to voice. He looked at George, across from him in a rocker, and forced a smile.

"You practicing for old age, George?" he teased, trying to ward off his somber feelings. "Looks like you've got a pretty good idea about how it works."

George rocked harder, his face screwed up in thought. He suddenly stopped and looked into Blue's eyes, his own now misty.

"You're closer to me than any brother ever could've been, don't you know, Blue? I hate like the devil to leave you and White Oaks. Since I've been here, I've felt like I had a real home with a real family." He looked away, but not before Blue saw a tear roll down his cheek.

"I know," Blue said gently. "Ben and Sarah have that way with people. If you let them, they'll become whatever you need." He paused.

The boys remained quiet a few minutes, Blue working hard to keep his eyes dry. Finally, he was able to speak.

"George, I want you to know you're the first and only real friend I've ever had. You're more like a brother than a friend, like you said. It scares me to death you're leaving, but I know you have to do this to live your dream, and your pa's." He paused to gather his thoughts, careful how to word them.

"The years can change people, George. I hope they won't change you."

George leaped up out of the rocker and crossed the distance to Blue. He grabbed Blue's shoulder in a firm grip. "Something that'll never change is the way I feel about our friendship, Blue. No matter what, we'll always be friends. Always."

Blue grabbed George's hand and squeezed. "Always," he whispered, barely containing his tears.

"And to prove I mean what I say, we'll make a pact, here and now," George said. "We'll make a promise that no matter what, you and me are friends above anything else."

George reached into his pants pocket. "And to seal the vow, I say we become brothers. You and me, forever."

Blue's heart raced. He watched George open his pocket-knife and, without hesitation, slice an inch-long gash in his palm. Then, taking Blue's hand, George did the same to his. They grabbed each other in a firm handshake, their blood mingling.

They were more now than just friends. They were brothers. Brothers by blood.

The next morning broke bright and warm, a contrast to Blue's inner turmoil. Today he would say goodbye to George. And even though he still had Ben and Sarah, he felt as though a part of him would ride away with George.

Blue entered the kitchen where Ben, Sarah, George, and Mr. Hawkins sat at the table eating eggs and bacon. Mr. Hawkins, Ben and Sarah talked softly. But George sat quiet. He stared at his plate, his fork moving eggs from one side of the dish to the other.

"There you are," Sarah said cheerfully, trying to dispel the pall hanging in the room. "I've got a plate already made for you. Sit down." She placed the food in front of Blue. George looked up and in his eyes Blue saw a reflection of his own agony.

Breakfast progressed, but only the parents spoke. Although they tried to bring George and Blue into the conversations, Blue couldn't manage more than a few words. His throat hurt with his effort to stay strong and he could see George struggling the same way.

By the time breakfast was over, the boys had managed to rearrange their food, but had eaten nothing.

"You all packed?" Mr. Hawkins asked George.

"Yes, sir," George responded, his voice flat.

"Then it's about time we head out. The train leaves this afternoon and it'll take us a while by buggy to get to the station. You don't want to be late."

46

George turned pained eyes to Blue before he headed out the door to gather his belongings, Blue right behind him.

They reached the bunkhouse and Blue helped George gather his bags. Blue tried desperately not to embarrass himself, to act like a child and cry all over himself. After all, they were men now and needed to act like such. But it was hard, so hard. The agony tearing at Blue's insides made him want to be five years old again so he could run into his mother's arms and weep at the pain he felt.

"Sarah packed some food for you." Blue handed George a bulging sack he'd grabbed on his way out the door.

George took the sack, tucked it inside his bag then turned back to Blue. "I don't know what to say, except I wish you were coming with me." He paused and looked down at his shoes. "I know this is what I've wanted my whole life, but now that it's here, I'm not ready for it."

Blue swallowed the lump in his throat and nodded. As much as he wanted George to stay, he knew his friend needed to go. To find his own destiny.

"Just think of it as a great adventure," Blue said. "You'll be fulfilling the dream you and your pa have had for you your whole life."

They left the bunkhouse in silence and walked back to the front porch where Ben and Sarah waited.

"It's time to say goodbye," Blue said.

George stepped up in front of Ben. "I'd like to thank you, sir, for all you've done for me and my pa over the last years. We've felt like part of a family here. It means a lot to us." He offered his hand, but Ben hauled him into his chest.

"You just take care of yourself, and come see us whenever you can. You'll always have a place here with us, George, whenever you come back. Don't forget that."

"No sir." He sniffed and stepped in front of the woman who had replaced his long-forgotten mother.

"Ma'am, you're a wonderful lady and it's been more than a pleasure to be among your household." Again he offered his hand, but Sarah scoffed and pulled him into an embrace and held him tight.

Sarah whispered something in George's ear and when he pulled away, his eyes shimmered with tears.

George drew his back up, turned and strode down the steps toward Blue. "I guess it's time to go," he said, his voice husky. "You sure you won't change your mind and ride into town with us?" he asked, hopeful.

Blue shook his head, fighting to keep control. "I'd rather say good-bye in front of family, not strangers." He sucked in a deep breath.

George pursed his lips and nodded. "Yeah. Me, too."

Blue lifted his palm and traced the cut, now crusted by a thin layer of brownish scab. "Brothers," he said. "Always."

"Brothers," George replied. "Always."

They drew each other into an embrace and held on. Blue knew their lives would change forever after today. They pulled apart and Blue walked George to the wagon and threw his bags in the bed. Blue tried to stall the inevitable, searched for something to say, anything to make George stay. If even for a few more minutes.

"What did Sarah say to you that got you so flushed?" Blue finally asked as George was just about to pull himself up onto the wagon seat.

George lifted loving eyes to Sarah. "She wished me luck and told me she felt blessed with not only one son, but two."

Blue grinned and nodded. He reached out his hand one last time. "Always," he mumbled, his voice trembling.

"Always," George managed.

"Give 'em hell, George." Blue saluted then swiped at his tears. He watched George roll down the tree-lined drive out of White Oaks—and out of his life.

Chapter Six

Blue stretched his back, trying to work out the kinks. His mornings were spent at the livery with Mr. Jackson, the afternoons with Ben, running fence and checking the stock. Even though Ben tried time and again to get Blue to give up his part-time work at the livery, Blue felt a certain loyalty to the only man in town who'd given him a job.

Blue leaned on the shovel and thought of George. He missed him something awful. In the weeks since he'd been gone, only one letter had come from his friend, written in haste. George wrote he was so busy he didn't have a spare minute to himself. He worked from daybreak to sunset, drilling and doing schoolwork. By the time he finished, he was so exhausted he fell into bed, asleep before his eyes closed.

A spasm of loneliness cut through Blue. He finished mucking the stall, hoping it would ease the sadness in his soul.

The day passed and the ache lessened, replaced by an unanswered question. *What was to become of his life? Would he spend the rest of his life working for someone else, mucking stalls, feeding someone else's stock? Or would he step into Ben's shoes as owner of White Oaks? Or was there something else out there for him to discover, just as George was doing?*

He dropped the shovel and sighed, wishing his life could be different somehow. He decided he needed to get some air and started toward the front of the livery when someone shoved in through the doors.

"What the hell do you mean, they got a treaty?"

Blue stopped and listened to the deep voice.

"I don't give a good God damn if they got a treaty says they own the whole damn territory. I heard there's gold up there and if that's true, I'm goin' up there to git it."

Blue didn't move.

"They was given all that land up there around the Black Hills where they say the gold was found," a second, more shrill voice replied. "Talk is, them Injun's are making it tough on anyone who goes looking for that gold in them hills. They're getting restless about us coming on their land."

"I told you I don't give a damn about any treaty. All I care about is getting my ass up there and finding gold, if it's really there."

"Oh, it's there, all right," the shrill voice said. "I seen it with my own eyes. Nuggets as big as silver dollars. So much gold up there a man could get rich overnight."

"Well then, I damn well intend to git my share of it while I still can, Injuns or no," the deep voice said. "Let me tell you something, Rosen, ain't no damn Injuns gonna stop me from finding my fortune. Especially if it's just settin' there waitin' for me to take it."

The men stopped talking and Blue's heart flipped in his chest. He looked down at the ring he wore on the pinky finger of his right hand—the ring made of gold from the Black Hills. The same hills these men were talking about invading to grab that gold.

"Hey! What does a man have to do get service around here?" the deep-voiced man shouted.

Blue stepped out from the stall in front of two men with long, greasy hair dressed in dirty, trail-worn dusters. Dark eyes that grew wider when they saw him hid none of their loathing.

"Well, well, well, Rosen. Looky what we got here," the first man said. He shoved a piece of straw into his mouth, exposing several rotted teeth.

"Not sure, Hollister," Rosen replied. He looked around the stable. "Where's the old man?"

Blue tensed. "He's feeling poorly today so I'm watching the barn." The men scrutinized him even more closely, their looks scathing.

"Sure you didn't kill him?" Hollister laughed.

Blue ignored the question. "What can I do for you?"

"The roan, fetch it for me." Hollister pointed. "Fetch the paint beside it too, boy, and be quick about it."

Blue led the paint out first. He stepped toward the adjoining stall to get the roan, but Hollister stopped him with an arm across his chest.

"On second thought, don't touch my horse. I'll get him myself."

The skin pricked on Blue's neck. "That'll be two bits for board and feed." He tried to keep his voice even.

"I ain't paying no damned Injun. You might take the money and run off." Hollister led his horse from the stall.

Blue said nothing and held his temper.

"I don't care where you say the old man is. He'll just have to take it out of your pay." He hooted with laughter then jammed his knee into the horse's belly and jerked up the cinch.

"Come on, Hollister. Let's just get outta here," Rosen almost whined.

The two men turned and stepped toward the door, but Blue rushed to block their way. "You don't leave till I get your two bits. Each."

"Petty uppity for a 'breed, ain't he, Hollister?"

"He damn sure is."

Hollister grabbed Blue by the shirt. "You step out of my way you little injun bastard and let me pass. Else wise, I'll beat you like the runt you are and take great pleasure in doing it."

Blue shoved the man away from him and stood his ground. "You owe Jackson two bits for boarding those horses. You won't be leaving until you pay what you owe."

Blue thought his heart would jump right out of his chest it raced so fast. He was taller than Hollister, although Hollister carried more bulk. He drew himself up as straight as a pole, hoping to intimidate the man with his height and youth.

"Damned Injun. I got other notions, boy." Without warning Hollister backhanded Blue across the face. Blue was staggering to stay upright when he hit him again from the other direction.

Blue yelled and charged at Hollister's waist and the two fell onto the hay and manure-covered floor. They rolled, jumped to their feet and faced each other like two charging bulls.

Hollister threw a punch, but Blue stepped aside.

"You want me?" Blue shouted. "Come on, here I am." He rolled his fist, swung and connected with Hollister's nose. The man cursed and charged. He lifted Blue like a sack of oats and threw him at one of the stalls.

Blue slammed into the slatted stall, but managed to stay upright. He shook his head and steadied himself. He whirled, clenched his fists, and got ready for the man's next attack.

Instead, it came from behind. He'd forgotten all about Rosen! Pain shot through Blue's neck and his knees buckled. He dropped to the ground and shook his head, trying to clear the lights that exploded in his brain and drained him of his strength. He scrambled to his feet, but his legs felt like water.

A boot slammed into Blue's shoulder and he stumbled into a stall and hit his head against the wall.

When the lights in his head stopped flashing and the buzzing in his ears faded, Blue pulled himself off the ground and staggered to the water trough. The men were gone. He took deep breaths and waited for his legs to stop shaking before he dunked his head into the water. Hollister's words echoed in his head. *"Damned Injun."*

"What the hell is so wrong with being an Indian?" Blue shouted to the empty walls. "What have I ever done to make them hate me so much?" He closed his eyes and shook his head, causing the lights to flash again. "They don't even know me."

Anger boiled deep in his belly. He straightened his back. "Those sons-of-bitches still owe Mr. Jackson two bits each. And I'm going to make sure they pay what they owe."

His legs still wobbly, he strode through the livery doors, finding Hollister and Rosen his only thought.

In the middle of the main street he noticed a newly arrived stage across the way, but he didn't spot the men. He looked up and down the dusty street, toward the ladies clothing shop and past the hotel. A few people mingled on the planked sidewalks and in the road, but neither of the men he sought was among them. *Maybe they've already ridden off.*

Or had they gone down the alley between the hotel and the saloon? Or were they behind the general store? He stumbled up the rutted street looking for their horses. He checked between each of the buildings, but saw nothing. A feeling of bitter defeat coursed through him as he headed back to the livery. But he stopped cold when he heard a familiar voice.

Blue peered around the dust-laden stagecoach and saw Hollister standing next to a young woman with Rosen a few feet away. Nobody else was around the coach, only Hollister, Rosen and the frightened girl.

"Come on, honey, give me a little kiss." Hollister had hold of the woman's shoulder. Her bonnet sat askew on her head and Hollister boldly stroked her arm.

Rosen stepped forward. "Come on, Hollister. We don't need to draw no more attention to ourselves. Let's get outta here."

Hollister ignored Rosen and stepped back from the woman. He pulled a silver whisky flask from the waist of his pants. The metal container flashed in the sunlight when he lifted it to his lips before he swiped the back of his ham-sized hand across his mouth.

"Come on. Leave her alone, Hollister," Rosen said, annoyance now in his voice. "You know I don't cotton to abusing women. A breed, maybe, but not no woman."

Hollister shoved Rosen away from him. "If that's how you feel, then get the hell outta here. I got business with this little lady. Don't I?" He turned back to the frightened woman, took another swallow from the flask, then shoved it back into his duster.

"Come on, darlin'," Hollister drawled. "Let me show you what a real man can do." He grabbed her neck and planted a kiss on her mouth.

She tore herself away and wiped her mouth with her gloved hand. "Please. Leave me alone."

Blue heard the terror in her voice.

Rosen backed away, disgusted, and started down the sidewalk.

Blue's body clenched with rage as Hollister ran his meaty fingers along the woman's cheek. She whimpered and struggled to get free of his grip.

"I'll scream," she threatened.

Hollister laughed. "No you won't." He leaned forward and whispered in her ear. Her eyes nearly popped out of her head and she started to shake.

"Come on, Hollister," Rosen shouted from down the walk. "We got better things to do. Let's go!"

"You go!" Hollister shouted back without taking his eyes off the woman. "Leave me alone. I'm busy."

Blue looked around for help, but no one else was close enough to see what was happening.

"No!" she cried.

Without thinking Blue bolted from behind the coach toward Hollister. He slammed into the man's side, shoving him away from the woman. She screamed and staggered from the blow and he and Hollister tumbled to the ground. Blue jumped to his feet and kicked a stunned Hollister in the chin, sending him back to the ground.

Blue whirled, ready for Rosen, but the man stood on the walk, his hands raised in front of him, shaking his head.

"This one ain't my fight!"

Behind him, Hollister sat up with a roar. Blue whirled. The furious man spit blood, but when he focused on Blue, he chuckled.

"Didn't get enough at the livery, eh, boy?" He pulled himself to his feet. "We can remedy that right quick..."

Hollister's right fist cut through the air, but Blue was ready. He ducked, dropped to the ground and swept the man's ankles with his foot. Hollister crashed into the stage, bounced, then fell to his knees.

He gaped at Blue, his face twisted in fury. Using the back of his hand, he swiped blood and spittle off his chin. "You dirty little shit. I'm gonna teach you a lesson you won't soon forget."

Blue glanced around at the gathering crowd. He didn't expect any help and wasn't offered any.

Hollister jerked to his feet and staggered toward Blue. Blue shoved him. Hollister stumbled backward toward his and Rosen's horses tethered outside the stage depot. Blue shoved him again. And again. Hollister collided with the back end of the roan, already skittish from the two brawling men. The animal jumped sideways and Hollister slipped and fell in the middle of a warm, fresh pile of dung. He sat up and stared down at his hands and arms, covered to the elbows in horseshit.

Blue glared down at the seething, dung-covered man.

"Now who's dirty?" he couldn't help ask.

The crowd erupted into wild hoots of laughter and the sheriff elbowed his way toward Blue and Hollister.

"That's enough. Break it up!" the sheriff shouted. "Blue, you get on back to work. And you," the sheriff motioned for Hollister to get up, "you come with me."

The man stood up, reeking of horse manure. The sheriff curled up his nose and looked at Hollister with unveiled disgust.

"Then again, you're not going to my jail smelling like that." He screwed up his face. "A bath sounds more like the way to end this spectacle. Come on folks, clear out. The show's over." He pushed the man forward. "You. Let's go."

The sheriff shoved the stinking man toward the bathhouse. But Hollister stopped, turned and glared at Blue. In a voice so chilling it sent tingles up Blue's spine, he called, "It ain't over yet, Injun."

Blue rode into White Oaks later that day, a feeling of triumph riding with him. He'd proven to the people in town, to Hollister in particular, he wasn't just some damn half-breed. He was proud and deserving of their respect just like anyone else there.

But a feeling of foreboding shadowed that triumph.

Even though the woman had thanked Blue numerous times for his assistance, only a few of those in the crowd had told Blue he'd done a good thing in helping her. He could still see Hollister's eyes flashing with such hatred it made Blue shiver. And the last words he'd muttered before Sheriff Randall dragged him off for a bath echoed over and over in his head. *"It ain't over yet, Injun."*

Blue cringed remembering the words. He'd embarrassed the drifter in front of the whole town. Him, a half-breed kid. That wasn't something a man like Hollister would forget soon. If ever.

"You're just in time for supper," Sarah shouted from the kitchen when the front door slammed behind him.

"Yes, ma'am." He dropped onto the divan in the front room.

Ben wandered in and Blue caught the questioning look in his eyes when he noticed his dirtier than normal clothes.

"Problem today?"

55

Blue shrugged. He didn't want to come running to them like a kid every time he had a problem. "Little one."

"How little?"

"A couple of drifters wouldn't pay for boarding their horses at the livery because old man Jackson wasn't there. Wouldn't pay a half-breed."

Ben stiffened but didn't move other than that telling motion. "And?"

"I told them they had to pay me. They didn't like that much. They knocked me around a little then left."

"How little?" Ben crossed his arms over his chest.

Blue heaved a sigh. "More than just a little, I guess." He paused, looked deep into Ben's eyes. "It made me mad, Ben. Real mad. I wanted to beat them to a pulp." His words started to come out fast now as he told Ben about the incident. "They beat me up and left without paying. So I went to get paid."

"Did you?"

Blue sighed and made a face. "Not exactly. Not unless you call humiliating one of them in front of the whole town getting paid." Blue couldn't help but smile as he remembered the surprise on Hollister's face when he found himself flat on the ground in a pile of horseshit.

"They were picking on some young, frightened woman just off the stage," he continued in a rush. "I just couldn't help myself when I saw that. I didn't think, just charged. We wrestled and fought a few minutes until..."

He laughed out loud. He couldn't help it, the vision of the dung-encrusted Hollister fresh in his mind.

"Until what?" Ben asked, impatient.

"Until I pushed him into a warm fresh pile of horse crap."

Ben tried to keep a straight face, but in seconds the two were laughing uncontrollably.

Blue regained himself enough to finish the story.

"The last I saw was Sheriff Randall leading him toward Baker's Bathhouse." Blue laughed again, until Hollister's chilling eyes flashed into his mind's eye. He stopped cold.

"What's wrong?" Ben laid his hand on Blue's shoulder.

56

"Hollister was mad. Real mad, Ben." He shook his head. "He said it wasn't over yet."

Ben's face went rigid. He took a deep breath, but quickly relaxed. "Don't worry about it, son. Like you said, he's a drifter. Nothing will come of it. Come on, let's get supper." He put his arm around Blue's shoulder when he stood up. "We'll keep this little incident between ourselves, all right? No need to worry Sarah about it." He winked and started for the kitchen.

But Blue had the feeling Ben was concerned. Very concerned.

Still wide-awake, Blue stepped out onto the front porch and sucked in the cool night air. In the silvery moonlight, he scanned the yard, taking in the barn, fences and corrals, everything that made up White Oaks. He took another deep breath and hugged himself, embracing it all.

"Mother," he whispered to the wind, "you were right to bring me here. These are good people who treat me as their own. I love it here and never want to leave. This is home."

He left the porch and climbed the stairs to his room. Settled in his bed, the twittering crickets and hooting owls lulled him to sleep.

Horses hooves pounding up the drive and men shouting jerked Blue from his slumber. He was about to jump out of bed when his door burst open and Ben stood in the frame.

"What's going on?" Blue asked.

"I don't know. Get your pants on and let's go."

Running toward the staircase moments later they passed Sarah, clutching her robe, unable to mask her fear.

"What is it? What's going on?"

"Stay inside," Ben commanded. "And away from the windows."

Sarah stepped forward, ready to protest.

"Don't argue, Sarah!" Ben shouted. He raced down the stairs, Blue close behind him. "Just do it!"

They reached the landing as an explosion of gunfire erupted the quiet night. Glass shattered and Sarah screamed. Ben and Blue tore back up the stairs just as she came into view, white-knuckled, gripping her robe as though it could protect her from stray bullets.

"I'm all right," she assured them. "They shot out a window. Go on, I'm fine. Just be careful." She squeezed the collar of her robe tighter.

Two more shots exploded from outside, followed by shouts Blue couldn't understand.

With Blue behind him, Ben cracked the front door open enough to see outside.

"How many are there?" Blue asked.

"Just two."

Blue peeked out from behind Ben and spotted the riders at the end of the lane, their horses prancing with excitement.

"Stay here," Ben commanded. He pulled open the door, stepped onto the porch, and fired two rounds from his rifle into the night sky.

"Get off my land," Ben shouted. "The next shot I fire will have a distinct target." He leveled the rifle on his hip. "I won't tell you again."

Blue peered past Ben toward the riders. He sucked in a deep breath as he watched a silent figure creep around the barn toward the men. Mr. Hawkins! No, his mind screamed as he watched the shadow make its way toward the lane.

Blue reached out and yanked Ben's shirt. "Mr. Hawkins. He's trying to get a jump on the riders. Don't let him, Ben. He'll get killed," Blue whispered as fear gripped him.

Ben nodded almost imperceptibly then stepped forward.

"I'm going to give you to the count of three. When I'm finished, I'd better see the backsides of your horses heading out of here!"

Blue held his breath. He couldn't see the men's faces, but he recognized their horses. It was Hollister and Rosen.

Emotions of every kind assaulted Blue. Guilt, fear and anger. These men were here because of him. And Ben or Sarah, or even Mr. Hawkins, could get hurt because of it.

You want to be treated like a man, he berated himself, *but you cower behind Ben like a child and let him take care of your mess.* He drew up his back, tightened his grip on the rifle he'd grabbed from beside the fireplace and stepped out beside Ben.

"Two...three!" Ben shouted.

One horse was turned away from the ranch, but the other wasn't. The man jerked on the reins and the animal reared.

"Indian lovers, you haven't seen the last of us!" the man shouted. He fired one last shot into the air before he whirled his mount around and the two men raced away into the darkness.

The words hit Blue like a punch. When Ben turned to face him, his surprise must have shown and Ben draped his arm across Blue's shoulder.

"We've heard it all before, Blue. Don't let it spook you."

But it was too late. It already had.

Chapter Seven

"How can you be so sure it was the same man Blue tangled with at the depot?" the sheriff asked Ben. "He's a drifter. Nobody'd ever seen him before he showed up yesterday in town."

"It was him." Blue stepped forward. I recognized their horses.

The sheriff ignored Blue and looked at Ben. "I don't mean no disrespect, Walters, but you can't accuse somebody without proof."

"He shouted 'Indian lover'", Blue cried. "I recognized their horses. Isn't that proof enough?"

Again the sheriff ignored Blue and spoke only to Ben. "That could've been anybody. Lots of horses look the same, especially in the dark. I need more than just the boy's say so." The sheriff removed his hat and scratched his head.

"What more proof do you want?" Ben shot back. "Someone dead? Sarah maybe? Blue's word is good enough for me!" He turned and stalked toward the door.

"Come on, Blue. Let's get the hell out of here. He's not going to be any help."

Ben slammed through the jailhouse door, Blue on his heels.

Blue knew the sheriff wasn't going to do anything. It was Blue's word against Hollister's. A 'breed against a white man. Even a no-good drifter's word was worth more than a 'breed's. Hell, the sheriff wouldn't even believe Ben.

But Ben had never seen Hollister, Blue reminded himself. So it came back to Blue's word alone. "The sheriff won't take the word of an Indian," Blue berated bitterly.

He and Ben mounted and headed for home, the sheriff's words buzzing in his head: *"Well, that could've been anybody."*

Blue mulled over the words. *Could it be that Ben and Sarah had few friends because they'd given Blue a home? Because they cared enough to take in a 'breed? Were they*

60

considered "Indian lovers" by doing so and thereby shunned by "proper" white society?

He shook his head and tried to dispel the unpleasant thoughts from his mind. But they wouldn't go away. No matter how hard he wished the sheriff's words weren't the truth, deep in his heart, he knew they were.

Ben and Sarah were outcasts, too. Because of him.

Blue sat on the porch, a rifle across his lap, and waited, as he'd done the last two nights. But all was quiet.

Was it over? Could he hope? Or was Hollister toying with them? Letting them get comfortable before he struck again?

Blue pushed the unwanted thoughts from his head and gazed across the yard. The leaves of the huge white oaks that lined the drive rippled and snapped in the breeze.

His mind returned to the bitter lesson he was dealing with. "This is my home," Blue whispered to the wind. "And after all my searching, some stranger wants to take it away from me because of what I am." He studied the buildings, his surroundings giving him strength. "Not while I'm around to stop it," Blue said to no one.

Anxiety wrapped around his heart like a claw. It had happened the past two nights since the first attack. He'd laid in bed that first night, breathing hard, trying to put the incident out of his head. But he couldn't. Hollister's words danced around and around his brain, taunting, as painful as any punch. The only way he could deal with the anger and fear that coursed through him was to wait and be ready.

But every morning he woke with a stiff neck and every muscle in his body aching from sleeping in the rocker on the porch.

But it was worth it, he told himself. He was ready for them. He wouldn't be caught unawares again.

The next morning at breakfast, Ben pulled up a chair beside Blue.

"It looks like the cowards aren't coming back." Ben took a sip of his coffee.

"I'll be ready if they do," Blue said.

"It's over, Blue. Forget about it. He's had his fun, now. Don't let it spook you. That's what he wants."

Blue shrugged. He'd humiliated the man in front of the whole town and Hollister didn't seem like the forgiving, or the forgetting type.

But after another night of a stiff neck and aching back, Blue decided Ben was right and gave up his nightly vigil.

Arriving in town the next day, he dropped Sarah off at the general store, then headed toward the livery. He wanted to make sure he was square with Mr. Jackson about what happened.

Blue entered the stable. Old man Jackson ambled toward him, a crooked smile on his face.

"Well, son, see you don't look no worse for wear after your little altercation." Jackson spit a stream of tobacco juice.

Blue felt his face redden. "No, sir. I'm sorry about what happened."

Jackson raised his hand. "Got no cause to be sorry, son. Them two are like too many others I've met in my lifetime. Worthless two-bit hoodlums, just fixin' for a fight wherever they go. And findin' it most of the time." He paused and stepped toward Blue. He placed his gnarled hand on the boy's shoulder. "I'm proud of the way you stood up to them two. You done your job and done it well."

Blue couldn't help but smile. "Thank you, sir."

"Is everything settled now?" Jackson asked, his voice wary. "I heard about the ruckus at the ranch. You think it was Hollister?" he asked.

"I'm sure it was. But I can't prove it. It's been a couple of days, though, and they haven't come back, so maybe it's over."

"I hope so, son." He clapped Blue on the back.

"Now that we got that over with, when are you coming back to work? This old back of mine needs a young 'un to do the things I can't anymore. You've spoiled me, son. I need your help. Will you be back to work tomorrow?"

"Yes, sir," Blue said, grateful the old man took his side.

Blue turned and headed for the doors. "See you tomorrow," he called over his shoulder before he got back into the buckboard to go pick up Sarah.

Feeling better than he had in days, Blue stepped into the general store and scanned the large room for Sarah. She was at the front counter completing her purchases. He grabbed the bundle and guided her to the door.

They stepped onto the sidewalk and ran smack into Hollister and Rosen.

"Looky what we've got here." Hollister looked them over like two prize chickens, openly examining Sarah. "An Injun lover and her young buck. Quite a pair," he drawled.

Blue surged forward, but Sarah stopped him with an arm across his chest.

"Don't."

Hollister laughed. "That's right Miz Walters. You keep that buck on a short chain. Else wise he might get hurt."

A rush of heat raced up Blue's face.

Sarah, her back straight, looked Hollister square in the eyes. "I've been insulted by far better men than you. Your words mean nothing to me."

She turned to Blue. "Get in the wagon, Blue. We're leaving."

The smirk left Hollister's face, replaced by a slow spread of red. "You can't talk to me that way!" he shouted. "Come on, Rosen. Let's get that dirty, little breed."

"This is your fight, Hollister. I ain't in it no more, just leave me out of it," Rosen said.

Hollister's face turned a brighter red and his eyes pinched with rage. Blue helped Sarah into the wagon, sat down beside her and headed the mule out of town. A short distance away, he dared to look back. The two men were still standing on the boardwalk, arguing.

When the town was well behind them, he jerked the wagon to a stop.

"Why'd you stop me?" he shouted at Sarah. "I could've taken care of him. I already have, once."

Sarah lifted her chin. "His petty words don't amount to a hill of salt." She raised her hand to keep him from interrupting. "The man isn't worth it, Blue. It's over, let's go home."

"But...."

"Not another word, Blue. Not another word."

63

Blue rode home in silence, his mind spinning. Maybe it was over for today. But what about tomorrow?

Screams that sounded like they came from the bowels of Hades woke Blue, his room illuminated by an eerie orange glow. He scrambled to the window where he saw the barn engulfed by fire. It raged and sputtered like a rabid wildcat. The shrieks of terrified horses echoed across the yard.

Blue raced out of his room and slammed into Ben and Sarah in the hallway. The three ran down the stairs and into the yard, met by a nightshirt-clad Mr. Hawkins.

Flames danced and licked the night sky and the acrid smell of burning wood and hay filled the air. Panicked screams intensified, joined by the frenzied pounding of horse's hooves against stall walls. The hair on Blue's neck stood on edge.

"Midnight!" he screamed.

Ben flung open the double doors and thick, black smoke billowed out.

"Hawkins, you and Sarah gather the horses when they come out," Ben yelled over his shoulder. He charged inside, Blue behind him.

Heat singed the hair on Blue's arms and face, and smoky light surrounded him like a dark cloud. In their haste to escape, several horses ran past almost knocking him over. Others kicked wildly at stall gates and walls.

"Let 'em out!" Ben shouted over the screams of the horses and roaring of the fire.

Blue ran from stall to stall, throwing open the gates. Some of the horses bolted. Others continued to kick, wild in their panic.

"They won't go!" Blue shouted. "I'm going for Midnight."

"No!" Ben grabbed Blue's arm. "I'll get him. Get those last three out. We don't have much time. Cover their eyes if you have to, but get them out!"

Fire popped and crackled all around Blue. His nose and mouth burned from the heat and smoke. His eyes watered. Panicked animals shrieked and kicked. Smoke filled his lungs. He grabbed a lead rope and threw it around one of the horse's neck, then dumped a feed sack and covered its eyes. The animal jerked and tried to pull away, but Blue held tight as he led the animal toward safety. Out of the burning barn, Blue pulled the blindfold off the horse, led the animal toward Mr. Hawkins and ran back for another.

Smoke kept Blue from seeing more than an arm's length in front of him. Using the animal's screams as his guide, he went deeper into the barn. A loud groan echoed above him.

"Ben! We gotta get out of here," he shouted. Raw fear gripped him like a giant vise. "The roof—it's gonna go!"

He hurled himself flat against a wall.

There was another long, loud moan, then an ear-splitting crack. Wood, debris and fire rained down all around him and in front of him, hissing like hundreds of angry snakes. More shrieks melded with his own, and echoed through what remained of the barn.

"Ben!"

With the roof collapsed, sparks caught the dry hay like tinder as the wind whipped in from above and spread the fire even quicker through the open barn.

"Ben, where are you?" Blue shouted, fear sharp in his chest. "Ben!"

Blue heard a faint reply.

He groped his way toward the voice. A smoldering beam pinned Ben's leg. All around hay ignited into smaller fires. Blue glanced up at the gaping hole over Midnight's stall and took a step toward it. He could hear the animal struggling beneath the burning debris that had fallen on top of him.

"Midnight!" He tried to reach his horse, but flames drove him back.

"Blue..." Ben's weak voice brought him back to his senses. He had no choice but to leave the horse and get Ben out of there. Now!

Blue grabbed Ben's arm and tugged. But each time he pulled, Ben cried out in pain. Smoke grew thicker. Flames licked the walls and stalls of the barn.

Blue scanned the fallen debris. He grabbed a board, shoved it under the beam and lifted. The timber moved, but the board snapped in two and the heavy piece of wood dropped back onto Ben's leg.

A bellow of pain tore from Ben's throat. "Leave me," he shouted. "You've got to get out of here!"

Blue ignored him. He wasn't going anywhere without Ben.

Groping around in the eerie darkness Blue laid his hands on a thicker piece of wood.

Searing heat assaulted him; sweat soaked him and ran into his eyes.

"Dammit, Blue! I said leave me. Get the hell out of here while you still can!"

"I won't leave you," Blue yelled back over the roar of the fire.

Blue positioned the larger piece of timber like a lever, took a deep, searing breath and heaved with all his might. The beam groaned and creaked then rose high enough for Ben to slide out.

Blue dropped the wood and the beam fell to the ground. He grabbed Ben around the waist, helped him up and they stumbled through the barn. Fire licked at their arms and legs, singed their hair, as they worked their way to the open doors.

Clearing the doors they dropped to the ground. They coughed and rolled in the dust to smother their clothes, which had caught fire on their way out.

Seconds later there came a final moan and shudder and the remainder of the roof crashed in. Flames reached high into the night sky, illuminating the house and bunkhouse. One last animal cry pierced the air as the walls fell inward and the fire consumed the structure.

Sarah and Mr. Hawkins ran to Ben and Blue. Sarah sobbed and checked each for injuries, while George's father slapped the last of any smoking material away from their clothes.

"Thank God you two are all right. I was so scared," Sarah cried. She touched their sweaty, grime-streaked faces, smoothed back their hair. "I thought I'd lost both of you." Tears streamed down her face and left white streaks through the dust and soot on her cheeks.

The four stumbled to the porch steps and tried to calm their rattled nerves. Sitting down on the top step, with Mr. Hawkins beside him, Ben laid back and allowed Sarah to administer to the lacerations on his leg.

Blue crawled onto the porch and stretched out on his belly. He took deep, gulping breaths to try and fill his singed lungs with fresh air. He lay there, staring at the barn, now a glowing mass of ruins. Smoke continued to spiral at random into the black sky. A pop, a hiss, and more crackling, as the fire ate itself into nothingness.

He turned away, unable to think of what he'd lost.

The devastation was complete. All that remained were the blackened skeletons of what had been two living, breathing animals and the larger skeleton of the barn around them.

Blue stood beyond the perimeter of the smoldering building watching gray-black smoke drift into the clear morning sky.

He kicked at a pile of blackened wood. And another. He kicked anything in his way. Something in the debris glistened in the sunlight. A silver flask. With the toe of his boot, he pushed it out of the rubble, then using his shirttail he picked up the hot container and examined it. He jerked his head away when he sniffed it and the smell of whiskey assaulted his nose. What would a whiskey flask be doing in the barn? Ben never touched the stuff. Mr. Hawkins? No. When he drank it was alone, in the bunkhouse and from a bottle. And certainly neither he nor Sarah...

Realization hit him like a blow. He remembered the flash of Hollister's flask in the sunlight the day he'd humiliated him in front of the town.

Hollister had set this fire!

His mind roared with rage. The bastard had come back! Air issued from his chest in defeat while gooseflesh rose on his arms and neck. *Would this ever stop?* He peered into the ruins.

"Midnight," he whispered, his throat tight. Because of one man's hatred, his beloved Midnight paid the price.

He tried to move one of the large fallen beams. He heaved and pulled. The more he tried, the heavier it became.

With each try, his anger consumed him like the fire had consumed the barn. He screamed, cried out Midnight's name. Tears came and washed away the rage, filling him only with sorrow.

"No one else! Not another living creature will suffer because of me," he vowed to the rising sun.

Chapter Eight

"Damn it, Sheriff. I want that son-of-a-bitch arrested and put in jail where he belongs!" Ben slammed his fist on the desk.

"Hold it, Walters. I can't just go out and arrest a man with no proof," the sheriff said. "I told you that already."

"The hell you can't. Who the hell else could it have been? We've never had trouble with anyone else except that no account drifter. Now, you tell me, Sheriff, who else in this town would do such a thing?"

"Your barn might have caught fire by accident, Walters. I can't say. But I can't just arrest the man on your say so."

"Or mine?" Blue stepped up beside Ben. "I know it was him, Sheriff. No one else wants to hurt us except him. Besides, I found this." He threw the silver flask on the sheriff's desk. "It's the same one I saw him with that day we tangled in town."

"It still doesn't prove anything. Other men carry similar flasks. It doesn't prove Hollister set that fire." He paused. "What about that old fool, Hawkins? Is he still living at your place? Well known fact the man's a drunk. The flask is most likely his." He shrugged his shoulders. "Probably got himself drunk and set the place on fire without even knowin' it."

Blue tried to suppress the anger crushing his chest.

"It wasn't Mr. Hawkins. I know it was Hollister."

Ben placed a hand on Blue's shoulder. "Let me handle this." He leaned forward on the desk.

"I want this taken care of, Sheriff. And soon. I won't put up with another attack on my family. Next time, I won't hesitate to kill the bastard, *whomever* it is. You have my word on it."

"Now, Walters, don't go and get all riled up."

"All riled up!" Ben's face contorted with rage. "My barn was burned to the ground last night, with some of my most prized stock inside. Not to mention the fact, if it weren't for Blue, I could very well have died right along with them. So don't you stand there and tell me not to get riled up!"

"All right, all right." The sheriff remained quiet for a moment before he leaned forward, his chair creaking. "So you're certain the attacks are being made because of the incident in town?"

"Of course we're sure. We didn't have any trouble until that drifter came into town. Now the attacks are getting bolder with dire consequences. I won't have it, Sheriff. I tell you, I won't have anymore." Ben's body shook. "If I have to go out and hire gunslingers to protect us, I will, but I won't allow my family to live in fear of that son-of-a-bitch!"

The sheriff cleared his throat and motioned Blue towards the door. "Like a private word with you Ben."

Ben nodded and Blue stepped out onto the boardwalk, but stayed close enough to listen through the doorjamb.

"Maybe you should consider sending the boy away," the sheriff said.

"And where the hell do you think I'm going to send him?" Ben asked.

"I thought, maybe, you might send him back among his own people. You know, the Lakota. Wait a few months and see if the trouble stops."

"We're his people," Ben said. "Sarah and me. And don't you forget it, Randall. You just do your damn job and arrest the man who burned my barn and killed my stock."

Blue scooted away from the door, his mind a cyclone of thoughts. *Go back to his people? Was that the only way to get Hollister to stop the attacks on White Oaks? The sheriff wasn't going to do anything. He wanted proof. Or was he just plain scared? And if Blue did leave, would the attacks stop?*

Ben emerged from the jailhouse, his face a mask of concealed rage.

"Come on, Blue, let's get outta here. This weak-livered son-of-a-bitch who calls himself a sheriff isn't going to help us one bit." Ben shoved his hat on his head.

Riding into White Oaks later that day the sun's fading light streaked across the ruins of the blackened barn. Blue's insides twisted like a butter churn. If only Hollister would go away. Leave them alone.

Blue thought back over the conversation he'd overheard at the sheriff's office. "We're his people," Ben had said. Warmth spread through Blue as he mulled Ben's words. Ben had stood up to the sheriff. Said he wouldn't send Blue away. "We're his people," Blue repeated under his breath. *But they're my only people,* he reminded himself.

To everyone else, he was just a 'breed.

Blue was in his familiar spot on the porch in the rocker, rifle in his lap when he jumped up and swung the rifle toward a noise.

"Who's there?" he called, his nerves frayed like a busted rope. "I've got a rifle."

An owl hooted again and Blue relaxed his stance.

"Just a barn owl." He sighed, sat back down and rested the rifle across his lap again. Slowly, he set the chair rocking and let it to lull him to sleep like a cradle.

Three days and nights had passed the same way. Blue was anxious, irritable and short-tempered, yet he wouldn't give up his nightly vigil. If Hollister struck again, this time he'd be ready.

Sarah stepped through the front door and wiped her hands on her apron. Worry etched her brow.

"Has Ben come in yet?"

Blue rousted from the rocker. "Not yet."

Sarah wrung her hands together. "He should've been back hours ago." She scanned the perimeter of the yard, the woods behind the house. "I'm worried, Blue. It's not like Ben to miss supper. Something's happened."

Blue stood up and peered into the darkness. "I'll go look for him. He's probably just trying to finish up something before he comes in."

Sarah nodded, her face tight with worry. "Maybe, but I don't think so."

The pounding of horse's hooves drew their attention. Ben's horse raced up the drive and stopped in front of the barn, reins dangling, the saddle empty.

Sarah grabbed Blue's arm. Fear ripped through him. He ran to the horse and slid his hands over the leather of the saddle and down the animal's flank. Everything was as it should be. So where was Ben?

71

He turned back to the porch where Sarah stood with the apron clutched in her hands.

"Did you find anything?"

He shook his head.

"Where is he?" she asked, her voice quaking.

Blue ran back to the porch, cradled her in his arms and led her to the swing. He forced her to sit down.

"I'm sure he's fine, Sarah," he lied, his own fear streaking through him like a cattle stampede. "Maybe something spooked his horse and it took off without him. Why, he's probably hoofing it back home, cursing that dumb animal right now," he said, trying to allay Sarah's fear.

Huge tears filled her eyes and Blue choked down his rising doubts. *Was Ben really all right? Or was he hurt somewhere, waiting for someone to come help him?* Blue's heart thudded in his chest.

"Don't worry, Sarah. I'm going to go find him."

She jumped to her feet. "Oh no you're not. It's dark. You could get hurt out there."

But she suddenly seemed to remember why Blue wanted to go and her expression changed. "Oh, Blue. We have to find him. He has to be all right," she whispered. "Should I saddle up, too?"

"You stay here. I'll go alone. You should be here in case he comes in."

"You'll be careful? Promise me you'll be careful."

Blue nodded and wiped the tears off her face.

She smoothed back his hair. "You're a good boy, Blue. Don't ever let anyone tell you otherwise." She kissed his cheek.

"Thanks, Sarah. You don't know how much those words mean to me."

"I think I do. Please, find Ben."

"I will." He dropped from the porch, ran to the horse and pulled into the saddle.

"I'll be back as soon as I find him. I won't come back alone. I promise."

He sent the animal racing down the drive, into the darkness.

72

He rode for hours, following the fence line Ben was supposed to be working on, and searched the woods and ravines along the way.

"Ben!" he shouted for the thousandth time without response. "Answer me."

Blue called again and again, but each time he called, only night creatures answered.

The horse stumbled in the darkness. Blue got off and walked, continuing to call Ben's name. The moon, barely a sliver in the sky, gave little light. Exhausted, realizing he could pass within five feet of an unconscious Ben and not even see him, he curled up in a pile of leaves and went to sleep.

He was up before the sun to continue his search. He headed to the south side of the ranch where Ben might have been rounding up strays. He crested the top of a hill and called Ben's name.

He heard a faint groan in the distance.

"Ben?" he shouted again. "Where are you?"

"Here. Down here."

Blue scanned the ravine that stretched between the two hills and finally spotted him.

"Ben! Are you all right?"

"My leg's broken. Need help to get up the ridge," came Ben's weak response.

"I'll be right there. Hold on."

Blue slid down the side of the hill until he reached Ben.

"What happened?"

"Damn snake spooked my horse. Threw me before I knew what the hell had happened." Ben's voice was gravelly.

"Let's get you out of here. Can you walk at all?"

"I might be able to with some help. Tried all night to claw my way out of this hole, but it's too steep."

Blue wrapped Ben's arm around his shoulder and took the brunt of the older man's weight upon himself. A few minutes later, both soaked in sweat and exhausted, they flopped down at the top of the hill.

After they'd rested, Blue helped Ben into the saddle. He swung himself up behind the older man and rode for home.

Sarah was pacing the porch when they rode into view. She ran toward the drive to meet them.

"Thank God you're all right!" She reached up for Ben. "Are you hurt? What happened?"

"We'll talk when I get inside," Ben said, his voice weary. "I took a fall, that's all."

That evening after supper Ben excused himself early.

"I'm exhausted. Think I'll turn in." A crude crutch under his arm, he hobbled his way toward the stairs. "Sarah? Can you give me a hand upstairs?"

"I can help," Blue volunteered.

"No thanks," he said. "I'd like Sarah to help me up."

Blue caught the look that passed between them and wondered what was going on. But the look was gone as quickly as it came and he decided he was imagining things.

Slowly they made their way up the stairs. The bedroom door closed gently behind them.

The look between them kept running through Blue's mind. What if there was something he should know about? Curiosity got the better of him. He crept up the stairs and stopped in front of their door.

"You've got to tell the sheriff what happened," Sarah said.

"And just what the hell do you think he's going to tell me?" Ben answered. "I've still got no proof. Just like the last two times. I didn't see who surprised me. To be honest, I don't even know what this son-of-a-bitch looks like up close!"

"Keep your voice down," Sarah hissed. "Blue'll hear you. That's why you dragged me up here, remember? So you wouldn't worry him any more than he already is."

"I'm sorry. I'm just so damned frustrated by all this." Ben stopped talking. Blue realized his hands were in fists at his side.

"You know that bastard had me in his sights. He could've killed me if he wanted. But that isn't what he wants. He's a coward who just wants to torment us. Keep this thing going until God knows what happens." Ben's voice rose and Sarah shushed him again.

74

Blue stepped away from the door and slipped into his room, his mind racing like a runaway stage. Ben was trying to protect him from the knowledge that Hollister, and not a snake, had spooked his horse and sent him rolling into the ravine. Blue shuddered with the realization that the man could have killed Ben at any time.

He fell onto his bed and draped his arm across his face. He fought the tears forcing their way into his eyes, but lost the battle. He hurt. Almost as badly as when his mother died.

He rolled to his side and curled up like a baby.

No matter what, I won't let Ben or Sarah get hurt any further because of me. But what can I do to stop it?

Only one answer came to mind.

Leave.

But I love it here. This is my home. I love Ben and Sarah. And White Oaks.

Which was exactly why he couldn't stay. He punched the bed.

He rolled onto to his back again. *Why does it have to be this way? Why couldn't it just end? Why can't he just leave us alone?*

He lay in the darkness and mulled over the last few weeks. Hollister had torn his world apart and now he threatened Ben and Sarah. There was no question what Blue must do.

"Please, Blue, reconsider," Sarah begged.

Blue shoved his clothes into the saddlebag. "I've made up my mind. I'm leaving."

"No. Whatever happens we'll face it together," Sarah pleaded.

Blue faced her. "I can't stand the thought of Ben being hurt because of me. I care about you both too much to let that happen again." Blue paused. "The next time it could be you." His throat was tight.

"But we love you, Blue. You know that, don't you? We have to stick together to beat this bastard."

Blue took her in his arms. "I know you do. That's why I have to leave. You'll both fight to your last breath to keep me safe, which could get you killed.

75

"Besides, I'll never be happy here, outside of White Oaks that is," he added for clarification. He returned to his packing and shoved the last of his clothing into the saddlebag. "I'll never be anything but a half-breed to everyone but you and Ben and Mr. Hawkins."

He felt Sarah behind him. "Don't try and talk me out of this," he said before Sarah could speak again, his voice harsher than he'd intended.

He put down the bag and turned back to her. He looked into her stricken face and the love he had for her filled him so much, he almost changed his mind. He knew this would hurt her, but he couldn't back down. It could be hers or Ben's life if he stayed.

He knew the people in town talked about Sarah behind her back. They openly wondered whether she was really Blue's mother when they spoke about it in hushed tones when they thought Blue didn't see or hear.

The children at school had let him know their parent's ideas of what Sarah was. But he'd ignored it and learned to live with their taunts. But this was different.

He couldn't deal with this. Hollister had left him no choice. He couldn't risk Ben or Sarah being injured—he loved them and White Oaks too much. And it was because he loved them he had to leave.

"Where will you go?" Sarah broke into his thoughts. "Please, just stay here. We'll work it out together. What will you do?"

Blue took her hands. "I'll find my mother's people. I was happy there as a child. They treated me well. And you and Ben will be safe. With me gone Hollister won't have a reason to bother you anymore. You'll see. It'll be all right once I'm gone." He threw his hairbrush inside the bag.

"Besides, maybe I'll find I belong there. You know I've always wondered where my future is. Maybe it's with them." He paused. "George went to find his destiny, maybe I have to do this to find mine." He sighed. "Anyway, the sheriff won't do anything as far as Hollister's concerned without proof. We don't have the proof he needs. We never will. Hollister's a sneak and a coward like Ben said. He'll attack by night and leave no trace.

76

There's no telling when, or where, he'll strike again." Blue placed his hands on her shoulders. "I can't risk yours and Ben's safety. Not Mr. Hawkins, either. I won't."

"I'm afraid for you, Blue," Sarah said. "There's so much unrest with the Indians right now. You don't know what you'll be walking into. They may treat you worse than the people in town do. Then what?"

"I have to go, Sarah. I have to find out. I can't hide at White Oaks forever. There's got to be something else out there for me. There has to be."

Blue looked into Sarah's pain-filled eyes. He wished he could make her understand.

Sarah wrapped her arms around him.

"Oh, Blue, I'll miss you so." Blue felt the wetness of her tears as their cheeks touched. She took a deep breath and stepped back. "I do understand." She wiped her nose on the end of her apron.

"You know you're the son Ben and I never had. And you know this ranch will be yours someday." She touched his cheek. "Don't go to the Lakota. Your mother didn't want you there. She had her reasons for bringing you to us. She knew your future is in the white world." Sarah paused and Blue felt her pain-filled eyes look deep into his heart.

"Don't throw away what you have here to chase ghosts. You might not even be accepted by your mother's people."

Blue knew she hurt. He didn't like being the cause of her pain. But things could get worse. So much worse.

"I have to go, Sarah."

She pulled him into another embrace. "When you come home, we'll be here."

Sarah wiped her face and left the room.

Blue felt as though his insides were being twisted in knots. He finished packing and went into the living room where Sarah and Ben waited.

"I guess this is goodbye." He stepped up to Ben.

"We can handle this, son," Ben said, his eyes betraying sorrow mixed with anger.

"I have to do this, Ben."

"No you don't!" the older man exploded. "We can take care of this. As long as we stick together, we can handle it."

Blue's heart swelled with love for this man and once again he almost backed down. But the sight of Ben's broken leg strengthened his resolve.

"This is the only way," Blue answered, his throat tight. "I'll be back when things settle down." But he knew he wouldn't return to this town.

"Damn it. I won't let you leave," Ben said.

Blue held his temper, understanding why Ben forbid him.

"I'm sorry, Ben, but you can't stop me. I'm full-grown now and I can say what I will or won't do."

Ben seemed to shrink in defeat. "Please reconsider?"

"No, sir."

"But you haven't even thought this thing all the way through. How do you intend to even find the Lakota, let alone your mother's people?"

Ben was right. Blue hadn't thought that far ahead.

"I, I don't know," he stammered. "I'll find them somehow." He shouldered his bags.

"I can't even begin to thank you for all you've done." His voice cracked, betraying his emotions.

Ben drew Blue into his arms.

"I love you, son," Ben whispered before he released him.

Blue met Sarah's eyes. Tears streaked her cheeks. She enfolded him in a motherly hug that shattered his weak facade of strength. He wanted nothing more than to throw down his belongings and say he'd stay.

"Sarah," he managed as his tears came.

She held him closer, her warmth and love enveloping him. She was his mother. She pulled away and smoothed his hair off his forehead.

"We'll always be here for you, Blue." Her eyes glistened with tears. "Remember that. And we love you."

"I love you, too." The words tumbled from his mouth before he even thought.

"Be safe," she whispered and ran upstairs.

78

Blue stepped onto the porch, Ben beside him. The sky swirled and churned overhead, mirroring the turmoil in his heart. How he wanted to stay here and be happy with these two people who had, indeed, become his parents.

"You'd better get started if you want to make any distance before nightfall." Ben looked up at the boiling sky.

Blue nodded, unable to speak.

"Be safe and, like Sarah said, if you ever need us, we'll be here." Ben clapped Blue on the back one last time before he limped back into the house.

Blue watched him disappear through the door. Sadness settled over him, but mingled with a strange feeling of excitement. With excitement and anticipation coursing through his body he saddled the horse Ben had told him to take and he started down the long drive.

At the gate he paused and looked back at the house. His home.

"Why does it have to be like this?" he whispered to the wind. "I don't want to go. But I have no choice."

Rain began to fall, mixing with the tears that ran down his face.

Blue rode toward town, determined to let Hollister know he was leaving.

The sky churned overhead as he rode up the main street, fat raindrops spattering on the road around him. He rode slowly and searched for Hollister or Sheriff Randall.

In the middle of town he spotted a familiar silhouette in the shadows of one of the saloon doors. Rosen.

With his saddlebags in plain sight, a bedroll tied to his saddle, it was easy for anyone to see Blue was setting out. Hopefully, plain enough for Rosen to figure out, who would then tell Hollister.

Riding past, Blue stared at the shadowed figure. As though understanding Blue's thoughts, Rosen inclined his head.

"Now, it'll end," Blue whispered as he rode in silence out of town.

79

Chapter Nine

Blue turned his horse toward a stand of scrub oaks just off the trail. *How long had it been since he passed the town of St. Joseph or the Nebraska border?* He wasn't sure.

Reaching the spindly trees, Blue dismounted and unrolled his pack. He took a biscuit and dried meat from his food supply and settled on the bedroll. He chewed without tasting and surveyed the land around him. Wide open and almost treeless, the tall grass looked like a green-brown ocean that reached far into forever. Early in his journey he'd passed several wagon trains, but nothing else for weeks. He felt alone searching for an unknown something. Was he chasing ghosts, as Sarah suggested?

He closed his eyes. Sated for the moment, exhausted from days in the saddle, he lay back and allowed sleep to claim him.

Faces laughed at him through a gray fog. He tried to run, but his feet wouldn't move. Flowing figures came closer and the masks over their faces took form. Horns sprouted from their heads. Eyes cried black tears. Lips curled into silent laughter.

The ghosts began to dance, their voices rising in a feral chant. Blue stared, he didn't understand. A fire sputtered and reached for the sky as its sparks floated up and disappeared into the darkness.

One figure moved away from the rest. A buffalo's head covered its face. Blue saw the gleam in its eyes through the mask and fear rose sharp in his stomach. He raised his hand to shield his heart as the figure raised a lance.

Blue woke with a start, crickets singing and the moon full in the sky. He was shaking. The dream haunted him. *Was it an image of things that might be? Or would be?*

Two more weeks of riding and the land became gently rolling hills. Miles of yellow and purple wildflowers grew in the low crags and between layers of rock covering the peaks of the hills. Tall trees now lined the river he followed, along with short pines and bushes. The river fed small ponds, scattered here and there and the dark red earth outlined watering holes of the elk and antelope.

Blue's horse was trotting through a dense patch of grass and flowers when the hairs on the back of his neck rose like hackles on a dog. He whirled around in his saddle, but saw only the gentle swirl of the river and the skittering of birds in the trees.

He took a deep breath and tried to settle his jittery nerves. *How much longer would it be before I meet up with my mother's people? Any people?* A chill raced along his spine. *What will they be like? Will they be as I remembered? Will they remember me?*

He left the open country behind him and ventured deeper into thick woods, hoping he was near the Black Hills. Again, the feeling someone was near prickled his skin. But as before, he neither saw nor heard anyone.

Giant trees loomed above him. Their tops reached into a crystalline blue sky so overwhelming it took his breath away. Huge white clouds floated through the azure sea and birds swooped between the treetops. A breeze drifted through the woods to offer slight relief from the heat trapped inside the forest. More birds sang lilting songs as hidden creatures skittered through the underbrush as he passed.

Rocks clattered under his horse's hooves. The animal inhaled a deep breath, blew it out through his nose then shook its head to dislodge the flies on its head and neck.

Blue wiped his forehead with his sleeve, sweat leaving a wet stain on his shirt. He was uneasy. This had to be Indian territory. But when, and how, would he find the people he sought?

High-pitched shrieks shattered the quiet forest. Four painted Indian warriors on horseback exploded through the trees and circled Blue. Blue jerked his horse to a stop. His knees and hands shaking, he thought his heart would explode.

The Indians circled, their mounts rearing when they jerked on the reins. They looked Blue over with open hostility.

"Wait!" He raised his hands. "I'm a friend. Don't hurt me." His heart pounded a thunderous beat.

81

One warrior raised a tomahawk in a threatening manner. Blue cringed.

The Indians laughed and continued to circle, their horses snorting and prancing.

Blue's wits returned. "Iyokipi, please," he shouted in Lakota, the word barely remembered. "I come in peace. I am Shoon Henah Toh Cante Nupa." His Lakota name tumbled from his mouth, awkward and clipped, from somewhere deep in his memory. "Kola. Friend."

The Indians stopped their ponies and stared, surprise evident in their eyes.

He repeated his name. "I am the son of Hinhanna Wanahca Win, Morning Flower Woman, sister-by-marriage to Wicasa Wan Duzahan, Man-Who-Runs, of the Lakota." He spoke half in English and half in Lakota. Fear stabbed at him as the braves started shouting between themselves.

Blue searched his mind for something, anything he could remember that might make them realize he was a friend.

The warriors continued to yell and his horse pranced uneasily. Terror ripped through him as another brave raised his tomahawk.

"Wait!" Sarah's face flashed into his mind and he fumbled with the words.

"Wi Tapeta Yuha Win, Wi Tapeta Yuha Win," he shouted.

The riders jerked their horses still and glared. He waited, body tense, his fingers white-knuckled around the reins.

One of the riders prodded his mount forward. "Wi Tapeta Yuha Win?" He pointed at Blue.

Blue nodded. "Wi Tapeta Yuha Win," he repeated Sarah's Lakota name. "My aunt." He touched his chest, not knowing what else to do.

The brave continued to glare, his face a mixture of questions and anger. The Indian leaned forward and grabbed Blue's horse's reins. Shouting to the others, he led them into the trees.

Blue inhaled deeply, but tried not to show his fear. All his muscles clenched tight and his hands balled into fists, the nails digging into the palms of his hands. But more than fear coursed through him. He was exhilarated, excited. He'd found what he'd been looking for. He hoped. Rather, they'd found him. *Now what?*

The brave led his horse deeper into Lakota country.

This wasn't exactly what he'd envisioned. But what had he expected? he berated himself. *A welcoming committee?*

Blue rode into camp with the four braves. He scanned the village nestled at the base of several hills with a winding river lining the eastern slopes. What looked like a hundred or more conical tipis were arranged around a central common area. Children stopped playing and walked toward the returning men to see what was going on. Dogs yapped at their heels. Women left sewing and the scraping of hides and stepped toward Blue and the other riders, along with the men of the village. Their sun-darkened faces were curious. Blue understood exactly what Sarah must have felt the day she rode into Man-Who-Runs's camp. Anxiety. Uncertainty. Terror.

An older Indian with waist-length, pitch-colored hair streaked with gray, stepped up and grabbed Blue's bridle. The man's black, penetrating eyes peered out from leathery dark skin and examined him, the scowl on his face so stiff it seemed frozen on his face.

The man released Blue's horse and stepped back. His arms crossed over his bare chest and his feet spread apart in authority. Blue noticed long, horizontal scars just above his crossed arms, white in contrast to his bronzed skin.

The warrior spoke, his words too quick for Blue to understand. Until he heard Sarah's Lakota name spoken.

Blue nodded several times and tried to tell the man about Sarah and Man-Who-Runs. He pounded his chest and said Sarah's Lakota name over and over. "Wi Tapeta Yuha Wi. My aunt." The brave pondered his words.

"Man-Who-Runs?" the warrior asked in halting English.

Blue couldn't help but grin. "Han. Yes, he was my uncle." Unable to stop the excitement that suddenly flowed through him, he continued in a rush. "Morning Flower Woman was my mother and Woman With Fire Like the Sun is my aunt."

"Slow. You must speak the white words slow." The brave waved his hand.

Blue nodded, his heart racing at the recognition. "I have come to find my mother's people. I wish to live among them."

"What are you called?" the warrior asked.

"I am Blue Fox with Two Hearts, Shoon Henah Toh Cante Nupa." He raised his chin.

"A good name," the warrior said. "Come. I have many questions."

Blue dismounted. This was more than he had dared hope for. He'd found someone who knew his mother. He followed the grizzled warrior to a lodge.

Blue pushed through a hide flap and found himself in a large, airy, circular room. At the center was a fire pit, dug deep into the earth with rocks built two and three high in a circle around it. Heavy buffalo hides covered the floor. A sleeping pallet of more hides lay on the other side of the pit.

The warrior turned and pointed Blue toward a pile of furs. Blue sat down and sank into their softness. The Indian sat beside him and spoke in halting English.

"You seek the people of Hinhanna Wanahca Win and Wicasa Wan Duzahan?" he asked.

The words were spoken quickly and Blue wasn't certain what the question was.

"Morning Flower Woman and Man-Who-Runs-Swiftly. You seek their people?" the Indian asked again.

"Yes."

"Why?"

"To live with them."

"Why?" the Indian asked again. Blue searched his mind for some way to explain so the man would understand.

"I lived as a child with my mother among The People. But she became sick and left me with Wi Tapeta Yuha Win."

"Wi Tapeta Yuha Win is a strong, brave woman," the warrior said. "Why do you leave her?"

"I was not accepted among her people." Blue looked away from the open scrutiny of the brave's eyes.

"And you believe you will be accepted here?"

Blue turned back to face him. "That's my hope."

84

The warrior shook his head and his lips curled into a frown. "You hope for much."

Blue sighed and nodded, disheartened by the expression on the older man's face.

"These people, your mother's people, must learn to accept you, Blue Fox with Two Hearts. You cannot just come into their village and be welcomed openly. My people are wary. You are half white. You must prove yourself among them."

Blue couldn't believe what he was hearing. He wasn't accepted among the whites because he was Indian. Now he wouldn't be accepted among The People because he was white! Several moments of heavy silence passed before Blue said, "You know my name. What's yours?"

"Mato P'see P'see Cha. I am Jumping Bear."

"Jumping Bear," Blue repeated, nodding his head. "And how do you know of Sarah and my mother?"

"I come from the same tribe as Morning Flower Woman, your uncle and Sarah. That of Little Thunder. Your uncle was a brave man, and Wi Tapeta Yuha Win had great courage for a white woman. Her story among our people is still sung. For this reason she is greatly respected among The People."

"Tell me this story, iyokipi," please. Blue settled deeper into the comfort of the furs. It helped him to hear about Sarah.

"The day the Bluecoats attacked Little Thunder's village, Wi Tapeta Yuha Win was among them with your uncle," Jumping Bear said. "He tried to send her away. But she would not go. He turned his horse toward the approaching soldiers to show his defiance of their coming. He was killed before he reached them.

"Seeing his fate, Wi Tapeta Yuha Win raced after him, into the soldier line of gunfire. But her courage was rewarded, for she reached her fallen husband without injury, to cradle him in her arms and cry over his dead body." Jumping Bear sighed.

"Husband?" Blue asked, shocked at the revelation he knew nothing about.

Jumping Bear nodded. "Among our people, she was his wife for she lived in his lodge." He took a breath and continued his story.

"Few of our people survived that day, but some, including your mother, lived that day because of Sarah. Those who did survive scattered across the plains and hills. They sought distant relatives and made new lives. That is how I am here, among these people."

Blue said nothing, but pride washed over him for Sarah. Relieved to have finally reached his destination, he allowed himself to relax with a long exhale.

Jumping Bear sprang to his feet. "You are weary and I am a sorry host. I will bring food and drink and you will rest." The man stopped, pondered something, then added, "And you shall remain in my lodge, if you wish, until you set up one of your own." Jumping Bear strode from the tipi.

Gratitude and hope washed over Blue. This was more than he could have imagined. He'd found someone who knew his family, who would take him in and give him food and shelter. He lay back on the soft furs, tucked his arms under his head and smiled. Before Jumping Bear returned with refreshments Blue was sound asleep.

That evening a great fire reached to the sky from the center of the tipi village, its light reflecting on the dancers that twirled around it. They worked themselves to a fevered pitch, while others ate and drank.

Blue's chest swelled with pride. This celebration was for him.

He watched The People and knew a great task was before him. He must prove he belonged here. To do so he would have to relearn their language and their ways. He was a good student. He'd proven that in the white school. He would learn fast and well.

Blue scanned the wraith-like figures around him. Some drank, some danced in the firelight, but even though this celebration was supposed to be in his honor, he realized few even noticed him. Except one.

Undisguised hatred in the eyes of one young brave bore into Blue like a wedge. A chill ripped up his spine.

He turned away but was drawn back to the hard face of the warrior. Pinched eyes continued to stare at him.

Blue's attention was drawn by shouting and the loud banging of drums. More dancers ran into the circle around the fire, chanting and shaking turtle shell rattles. Blue tried to enjoy the spectacle, but still felt the warrior's angry gaze boring into him like a knife.

Minutes later, unable to keep himself from looking back, he turned to the brave. The Indian's eyes met his and Blue's heart swelled with fear. The warrior's nostrils flared and his hands clenched in and out of fists at his side, his hatred unmistakable.

Why? Blue asked himself. *What had he done?* He'd only been here a short time and the only one he'd had any contact with was Jumping Bear.

Ignore him. Just ignore him.

But before Blue was able to pull his gaze away, the brave's unspoken hatred tore through him like a silent arrow.

Chapter Ten

Below Blue the camp sparkled like the clear river that flowed through the rocky land along its border. Beyond, crystal blue sky stopped only where it met the lush green of the land. Children splashed in the river, horses grazed and women bustled about.

He'd been with The People for two days. Many of the elders seemed to accept his presence, if only by ignoring him. But the younger braves watched him with caution. Especially the one called Sunkmanitu Tanka Watogla, Wild Wolf, the brave who'd been glaring at him the night of his arrival.

Wild Wolf said nothing. He only watched. Wary, Blue stayed with Jumping Bear as much as possible. But today, the older warrior had left him alone.

Blue continued to survey the camp, surprised at the peacefulness of the village. Mothers worked outside their lodges, tended fires, taught their daughters to cook or make clothing from the pelts of animals. Other women worked with bone scrapers, stripping skins and packing meat and berries in hide pouches.

Men sat in clusters playing games or smoking pipes, loud and boisterous in their leisure. Children ran and played, just like he had as a child, carefree and happy.

He ambled down the hillside where, tethered to a tree, was a pure black stallion with a white blaze on its nose. The horse snorted and stomped its foot.

Unable to resist, Blue touched the animal's flank. "Shhh, I won't hurt you." He caressed the smooth silkiness of the horse's coat. "You're beautiful." The memory of another black stallion ripped through him and caused a pang of regret.

He ran his hands over the horse's back and slid up to stroke its neck and chest until he felt a presence behind him. He turned to find Wild Wolf standing only a few feet away.

The Indian shouted, but Blue didn't understand his words. The angry brave pointed at the horse.

88

"He's beautiful." Blue tried not to let the brave see his fear; tried only to let the brave see his regard for the animal. "I was only admiring him."

Wild Wolf stepped closer and shouted again. The muscles in his neck bulged. Blue stepped back, but was up against the side of the horse.

"I didn't mean any harm," he shouted, his own irritation beginning to rise. Several young braves gathered around him and Wild Wolf. He looked over the group and was reminded of Harvey and his followers. *Had he, for whatever reason, traded one bully for another? How could such rotten luck follow him wherever he went?*

Again, he tried to placate the angry brave, but his words only made Wild Wolf angrier. A moment later, Blue was on his stomach on the ground, the laughter of the others echoing in his ears.

Blue hadn't seen the punch coming. He pushed himself up, spit dirt out of his mouth and tried to clear the dust from his eyes. But Wild Wolf's foot crashed onto his back and sent him back to the ground.

Although Wild Wolf was about the same age as Blue, the young brave stood taller and looked stronger. But Blue had had enough. He jumped to his feet and whirled on the Indian. Surprise showed on Wild Wolf's face.

"Okay, Wild Wolf, if it's a fight you want, a fight you'll get. Come on!" he shouted. He stood his ground, curled his hands into fists in front of him. Cheers exploded from the crowd.

Wild Wolf charged into Blue's belly and they landed hard on the ground, Blue gulping in air.

Wild Wolf pushed himself up and stepped to the side. But Blue saw the kick coming and rolled away. He sucked in some air and jumped to his feet.

The other braves goaded them on, but no others joined the fight.

"Okay, so you want to play rough? Let's go!" Blue yelled.

Wild Wolf charged again, but this time Blue was ready. He sidestepped the rushing Indian, curled his hands in a tight fist, and slammed Wild Wolf in the back as he ran past. The brave went to his knees.

"There!" Blue shouted. "How does it feel?"

His chest heaved from exertion and the adrenaline racing through his body. He scanned the faces around him and knew he had to stand up to Wild Wolf. He had to give a good fight or be considered weak in their eyes.

With a loud bellow Wild Wolf ran at Blue again. He grabbed him around the waist and drove him backward. Blue clawed at the brave's arms, trying to pry himself free.

Blue mustered enough strength to halt his backward motion before he broke free of Wild Wolf's grip. He threw a quick right punch and caught the Indian in the jaw. Wild Wolf stepped backward from the force of the blow with a look of surprise. Blue drove his left fist into Wild Wolf's stomach then threw his right again into the brave's face.

Wild Wolf howled with rage and charged. He caught Blue around the waist again and shoved him to the ground, the impact crushing the breath out of him.

Wild Wolf was standing over a gasping Blue, ready to strike again, when a sharp, stern voice sliced through the air. Wild Wolf immediately stepped back and became quiet.

Blue sat up gulping for air. A stocky older man Blue guessed to be a chief, approached them. With a few quick words the crowd dispersed. The older man went to Wild Wolf. He spoke harshly then turned and walked away without even a backward glance at Blue.

Wild Wolf stalked off, but not before he gave Blue a look that could curl leather.

The summer passed quickly. Jumping Bear's lessons began early in the morning with the rising of the sun and daily prayers to *Wakan Tanka,* the Great Spirit. After prayers, Jumping Bear took Blue hunting to teach him the bow and arrow. Or they walked through the forest, the older man explaining plants and animals as they went. They spent afternoons talking about The People, speaking the Lakota language as much as possible, while Jumping Bear instructed Blue in how to string a bow or build a fire. Patient and thorough, the older man taught Blue all he needed to know.

"Tatanka, the sacred buffalo, tacha, our brother the deer, and hehaka, the elk, give us all we need to clothe and feed ourselves," Jumping Bear said. Blue slipped on a deer hide shirt with several tufts of buffalo tail hairs woven into thin braids and tied below the scooping neck as the older man spoke.

"Tatanka supplies us with food and clothing for the winter. Everything from this sacred animal is used, from its hide to its tail and hooves. Deer and elk give us clothing for the summer months, softer and more pliant in texture," Jumping Bear explained, one of many lessons to follow.

Blue pulled on a pair of elk skin pants noting the fringes that ran down the sides of each leg and the tough buffalo sinew that held them together. He slid deerskin moccasins with circles of colored beads on the top on his feet. He marveled at the intricacies of each of the garments.

In the afternoon sun, Blue listened to the older man speak of The People and their ways.

"Part of being a Lakota warrior my young friend, is to count coup." Jumping Bear produced a club about three feet long with a large, round stone attached to the end.

"It shows more courage to strike an enemy close with your coup stick than to kill him easily from a distance with an arrow or rifle." Jumping Bear raised the club in the air and showed Blue how to strike.

Blue took the weapon and imagined the dull thud it would make when it struck a man's head. The idea sickened him, but he didn't let Jumping Bear see it in his face. He handed it back to the older warrior, listening as Jumping Bear continued with the lesson.

"You will be given the opportunity to count coup when we raid our Crow enemies. Until that time, you will not be accepted among The People. You are still considered a child, not having proven yourself in battle."

Thoughts tumbled through Blue's mind. *Could he strike another human being with the intent of killing him?* He didn't

91

think he could. Ben and Sarah's faces flashed into his mind. *What would they say if they knew?*

Months passed. One bright autumn afternoon, after a demoralizing attempt at stripping feathers for arrows, Blue stood up and stretched. Jumping Bear had walked off and Blue couldn't tell if he left in disappointment or to keep from laughing at his ineptitude.

He turned as riders raced into the village, shouting. A herd of buffalo had been spotted.

Cheers erupted throughout camp. Blue knew how important the hunt was to The People. And to him. He would ride with Jumping Bear and show his worth and help fill the food stores for the coming winter. Yes, he'd show them.

The next morning the village was struck. Amidst the swirl of dust, the neighs of horses, cries of children, and travois' packed to overflowing with The People's possessions, the village departed to follow the herd.

Blue waited with Jumping Bear on the crest of a hill, which overlooked a seemingly non-ending undulating sea of buffalo.

Gazing at the expanse of lumbering animals, Blue felt blood surge through him. A man could easily be gored by an angry bull's horns or trampled to death by the stampeding animals. Fear, excitement and anticipation washed over him.

This was the way of The People. They hunted for survival, buffalo their mainstay. The meat fed them throughout the long winter. The hides clothed them and covered their lodges against bitter weather. Tough sinew became bowstrings and thread. Bones were used for cooking utensils, meat scrapers and combs. Even the bladders were used to hold water. Without the buffalo to sustain them in their everyday lives, the Indians would die. They killed not for sport as white men did, but to survive. And he would play a part in that survival.

He gazed out over the herd, which must have numbered in the hundreds of thousands, and seemed to stretch all the way into tomorrow. Jumping Bear touched Blue's shoulder as if aware of his uncertain thoughts.

"You will do well, Blue Fox. You're strong and brave. Today you will begin to prove your worth." Jumping Bear looked over the herd. "It is time to prepare."

The warrior crawled back off the ridge, Blue close behind. They gathered with the other men and stripped off all clothing except their breechcloths. They painted pictures of the sun and moon on their horses and their own faces using mud and berry juices.

Blue did as the others did. He filled his quiver and slung it around his left shoulder. Then he mounted his saddleless horse and joined the other hunters riding in silence downwind of the herd.

The warriors and most experienced hunters were first in line, twenty abreast. Then came the best hunters, who rode side-by-side. Behind them, Blue and Jumping Bear rode with the rest of the men of the village. The women and children followed behind. The lines of people moved slow and silent in the hope of getting as close as possible to the herd before they were discovered.

The herd lumbered ahead, unaware they were being stalked. Calves bawled and ran beside their mothers to keep up. Some stopped to graze.

The People moved closer. No one spoke. Even the horses seemed to sense the necessity for silence.

The People drew near and a bull raised its head. It sniffed, slung its head and bellowed a warning. In one fluid motion the herd began to run.

Massive, pounding hooves flung clods of earth into the air. Dust billowed into a thick brown cloud in a swirl around the racing animals.

The hunters thundered toward the herd, reins gripped between their teeth. Their legs hugged the sides of their well-trained ponies and left hands free to load and aim weapons.

Blue attempted to copy the other riders, but found it impossible to use only his legs to guide his horse. He tried to load his bow without holding on and almost toppled off the animal's back.

He watched Jumping Bear guide his horse toward a racing cow with barely the touch of his knee. The Indian raised

93

his bow and fired, striking the buffalo in the hindquarter. She veered away from the rest of the herd and charged Jumping Bear. With the press of his knees, the horse turned and raced out of danger.

Blue released his breath, unaware he'd been holding it.

Trying to imitate his friend, Blue turned toward the herd and loaded his bow while balancing on his horse. He raised the bow and fired. The arrow missed. A cow veered toward him. Blue grabbed the reins and jerked his horse away from the beast, his heart racing like the animals he chased.

Terrified, yet exhilarated, Blue felt charged like a lightning bolt. Again he guided his horse beside the pounding herd. Again he steadied himself, loaded his bow and fired. Again he missed and turned his horse away.

He searched the other riders for Jumping Bear, anxious to be near him. He found him and rode in behind his friend.

The brave again raised his bow and fired. The arrow struck an animal just behind its left shoulder, the arrow imbedded to the feathers. The buffalo's knees buckled and it tumbled to the ground in a heap. Blue had been told it sometimes took two, three, even four arrows to drop one of these huge beasts. Jumping Bear had done it with one.

Blue began to slow, but Jumping Bear raced on in search of another kill. Blue followed. Determined to add to the tribe's meat supply for the winter, Blue zeroed in on a small cow.

Guiding his horse beside her the two animals raced side by side while Blue steadied himself. He drew an arrow from his quiver, raised the bow and placed the cow in his sight. Squeezing his legs to stay steady, he took a deep breath and released the silent death.

The animal bellowed as the arrow pierced its neck and stumbled to its knees. Blue bounded past, but watched the animal try to get up. Its legs buckled and wobbled until it fell to the ground, still.

They rode for hours. The hunters stopped only to restock their arrows, carried by women on horseback behind them.

After hours of riding and hundreds of buffalo killed, the hunt finally ended. Blue reined in with the other men and looked back.

Carcasses stretched for miles behind him. Women worked quickly to strip the hides and cut out the meat they would haul back to the village. Blue surveyed the carnage, but felt no revulsion. Only pride. This winter The People wouldn't be hungry. And he had played a part in their survival.

Jumping Bear rode up beside him. A smile played around the corners of his mouth.

"You have done well, my young friend. You will join in the feast of celebration. But first..." He motioned for Blue to follow. They rode to a fallen buffalo and dismounted. Jumping Bear drew his knife and sliced open the underside of the downed beast.

A sickening smell assaulted Blue's senses. He wanted to vomit.

Jumping Bear reached inside the animal, yanked out one of the organs and offered it to Blue. Blue backed away.

Jumping Bear offered it again.

"What?" Blue asked. "I don't know what you want me to do." His insides churned.

"This was your first hunt. You must take the soul of this animal as your own. Eat." Jumping Bear again offered the organ to Blue.

Blue barely kept the bile in his throat. His mind screamed in revulsion. *Eat it? How could he eat this animal's heart or whatever it was Jumping Bear offered?* He backed away again, but Jumping Bear followed.

"You wish to be one of The People?" Jumping Bear asked. "Is this not true?"

Blue nodded while he tried not to inhale the awful odor.

"You know I do, Jumping Bear. More than anything," he managed.

"Then prove it. Eat." Jumping Bear shoved the bloody thing under Blue's nose. "Eat!"

Trembling, Blue took what he realized was the animal's still warm heart into his hands. His skin crawled. Jumping Bear pushed Blue's hands closer to his face. Warm blood smeared on his face and chin.

"Eat!"

95

Blue forced the repulsive thing to his lips. The smell made him gag. He moved it away.

Jumping Bear pushed it toward him again, his eyes hard.

Blue opened his mouth and felt the heat coming off the heart. He closed his eyes, held his breath, and forced a bit into his mouth.

He took a small bite, swallowed quickly then opened his eyes. Jumping Bear shook his head. The brave grabbed the organ, shoved it into his mouth and tore off a huge chunk of meat. Blood dripped in big clots down his chin and neck. It streaked his chest red. Jumping Bear chewed with great satisfaction before he shoved the heart back at Blue.

"That way!"

Mustering every ounce of determination he possessed, Blue grabbed the organ and shoved it into his mouth. Without allowing himself time to think or smell or feel, he tore off a hunk as the animal's blood rolled down his chin and chest.

Jumping Bear grinned and nodded approval.

Blue chewed fast while he tried to forget what he ate. He hoped to force it down before his stomach revolted and he threw it all up in disgrace.

Blue swallowed hard and gave the bloody organ back to Jumping Bear. With the back of his hand, he swiped at the blood that dripped down his chin and neck. His chest swelled from the look of pride on Jumping Bear's face. He'd proven he could hunt and bring down game with the others. Proven he was willing to take the spirit of the animal as any Lakota warrior would.

"I am of The People."

Chapter Eleven

The People followed the buffalo herd for two more days. They gathered as much food as they could carry for their stores. Now, on the evening of the third day, melodious chanting reverberated through the cool night air in celebration. Dancers swayed to the music of drums while others raised their voices in song.

Blue surveyed those around him. He reveled in their joy. In *his* joy. He searched their faces and noticed one young woman watching him.

He turned his attention to her long, black hair, plaited in one braid that hung down her back. Almond-shaped eyes crinkled at the corners when she smiled and her face lit with the dancing light of the fire.

Blue examined her face, her high cheeks, straight nose and thin lips. But as he gazed at her, he felt nothing. He thought of Karen and remembered the rush of heat that had raced through his body when she looked at him. He felt nothing remotely close to that excitement, even though this young girl was attractive and clearly interested in him.

She rose. Hips swaying, she strode toward him. A slight smile curled her lips. Her breasts moved beneath her dress. Still, he felt nothing.

She stopped in front of him and dropped to her knees.

"I am Tipiziwin. Yellow Lodge Woman. I have watched you since you came to our village, but you do not see me. I saw you with the men today. You were very brave."

"Thank you." He was still unmoved as the drums and chanting continued around him.

"What is your name?" she asked.

"Blue Fox with Two Hearts."

Yellow Lodge Woman stared into his face, and it made him uncomfortable. "It is a good name. A Lakota name. But I'm told you are half white."

"I am," he said. "My father was a white man." He examined Yellow Lodge Woman's face and for one moment, he

97

was proud of that fact. But the old taunts quickly echoed in his mind.

Tipiziwin's soft voice penetrated his thoughts.

"It is a good name," she said again. She opened her mouth to say something, but snapped it shut. Her eyes darted behind Blue. He heard a footstep and knew Wild Wolf was there even before he turned around.

"Leave here," Wild Wolf commanded Yellow Lodge Woman.

Blue watched her eyes cloud with anger. She glared at Wild Wolf and stood up.

"You do not own me, Wild Wolf. You have offered for me, but my father has not accepted because I have not accepted. Therefore I am not yours."

"You are mine, Yellow Lodge Woman. All the village knows this." Wild Wolf's voice was hard. "Why do you think no one else has spoken for you?"

Yellow Lodge Woman's nostrils flared and her eyes gleamed in the firelight. Blue heard Wild Wolf step closer and he tensed, ready to deflect any blow the Indian might throw.

"You would choose to speak with this...boy, over me?" Wild Wolf's voice dripped with sarcasm. "Do you see the scars of manhood across his chest?" Wild Wolf pounded his chest with his fist. "You toy with a child. You'd do better to seek out a man."

Yellow Lodge Woman's jaw worked, but she kept her temper. She jerked around and strode away, her hands in fists at her side, her braid swaying with her hips.

Blue stood and faced Wild Wolf, his own anger carefully checked.

"Perhaps I haven't proven myself in the test of manhood, Wild Wolf. Yet. But that doesn't make me any less a man." He released his fists. "And, if Yellow Lodge Woman is, indeed, your woman, why does she keep refusing when you offer for her?"

Wild Wolf's face turned crimson. He took a threatening step toward Blue but halted.

"I won't strike you, for we celebrate the good hunt," the brave said. "Another time you will not be so lucky. Yellow Lodge Woman is mine. Don't forget it."

The brave turned and stalked away. Blue watched after him and wondered if he'd ever understand Wild Wolf's hatred of him.

Later in Jumping Bear's lodge, Blue lay down on his pallet of furs, his arm crooked behind his head. A small fire burned in the middle of the room, its smoke spiraling upward to the hole at the top of the tipi. Jumping Bear was still celebrating so he was alone.

Certainly he had gained some degree of acceptance among The People, hadn't he? At least with Jumping Bear? Or was he merely tolerated by the elders out of respect for his dead family? And what of the braves his own age who mocked and provoked him at every opportunity? And what about Yellow Lodge Woman? Did she play him for a fool to anger Wild Wolf like Karen had Harvey? Or was she sincere in her interest in him as a man?

And what about his manhood? If he didn't celebrate the ritual of wiwongwaci, the Sun Dance, he would never be considered a man by these people.

He closed his eyes and remembered Jumping Bear's words the evening of the first day of the hunt.

"You are far from being one of The People, my young friend. Yes, you have proven yourself a hunter, but you must still count coup. Then you must show your courage in wiwongwaci. Until that time you will be considered a boy, without a voice. Invisible."

Blue knew some of the details of the Sun Dance ritual from his mother. He knew it was a brutal test of physical endurance. Although he'd gained some respect in the hunt, *would he be strong enough to pass the test of the Sun Dance?*

He turned on his side on the pallet, closed his eyes and tried to force sleep to come. But it eluded him. Visions of Wild Wolf and Yellow Lodge Woman floated through his mind, mingled with the faces of Hollister and Harvey.

He pounded the ground. *Could no one in this miserable world look at him and see him for what he was? A man who only wants to belong? Somewhere. Anywhere.*

He thought of Sarah's smiling, caring face. She loved him. So did Ben. He rolled onto his back, his arm slung across his eyes.

And George. His friend's face swept into his thoughts and he felt a bitter pang of loneliness. *Where was George now? Did he still remember the good times they'd shared? Did he recall their vow? Or had he forgotten it in his quest to become the soldier of his dreams?*

Blue's heart ached for all he missed. *Would it ever be different?*

Blue hunted and took lessons from Jumping Bear when he could, but the rest of the time, he was alone. Winter loomed and The People ignored him as if he were invisible. He didn't dare try and make friends, for fear of reprisal by Wild Wolf, who seemed to control the young braves with an iron grip.

Although Blue stayed mostly with Jumping Bear, he still heard the endless gossip that circulated throughout camp that white men were coming. And as the days and weeks passed, the stories became wilder and more intense.

Prospectors had invaded *Paha Sapa,* The Black Hills, seeking the yellow metal they held so precious. Like the ring that circled Blue's finger. The cavalry was in the Hills, led by Pahuska, the Long Hair, George Armstrong Custer. The man who'd ordered the raid against Black Kettle and his Cheyenne at the Washita River where many innocents had died.

The promise of winter hung in the air, along with the promise that white men would soon invade their lands in search of the precious yellow gold in the Black Hills.

Gathered around a brightly-burning fire, Blue listened as the men compared the numbers of whites in *Paha Sapa* to the leaves that fall from the trees before the winter wind blows.

Rage simmered in his stomach. The white man. Always the white man. Always destroying. Now they'd try to drive The People from their sacred lands for gold.

Many warriors wanted to attack, but the old ones told them they must wait. *For what?* Blue wondered. *Until the whites came and destroyed The People as they had at Bluewater Creek, where his uncle, Man-Who-Runs, had died and his father had found his mother, barely alive, in the aftermath?*

In his mind, he heard and saw the screams of the women and children as they ran to save their lives. He saw the warriors of the village try to protect their families. He watched his uncle cut down by the soldier's bullets, Sarah crying over his lifeless body.

He shook his head to clear the ugly thoughts. He got up and headed toward his lodge, thoughts of the council meeting on his mind. The meeting to which he wasn't invited.

But he had to talk to them. Had to make them understand.

He stopped and watched the men file into the lodge, his heart aching for all he needed to tell them. Unable to sit idly by without doing something, he waited until all the men were inside then asked permission to speak to those gathered.

Admitted entrance, he waited. His heart thrummed until he was recognized by a nod of the old chief's gray head. He sucked in a deep breath.

"You know who I am and you know I have lived among the whites. I know how they think." He scanned the faces inside the room. "The elders say not to fight, but if we don't, the whites will come and take until there is nothing left. Our gold. Our land. Our respect."

No one spoke. No one moved. Blue felt his face burn with heat. *Did they even hear his words?*

"Listen to me! I know what I'm talking about."

He glanced around the room and his eyes fell on Wild Wolf. A smirk of satisfaction covered the brave's face. Blue knew his words were insignificant. Unheard.

One of the elders, Red Squirrel, held up his hand. "We have heard your words, Blue Fox. We will speak of it." With a wave of his gnarled hand, he dismissed Blue.

Blue shoved out of the lodge. He summoned everything in his power to keep from yelling at the old fools to listen to him. Didn't they understand what was happening? Didn't they realize

101

the white man would stop at nothing to get what they wanted? Gold.

Outside the lodge, Blue kicked at dirt and stones in his path. He jerked to a stop. They had heard his words. But they didn't take him seriously. *Why?*

The answer reverberated like an arrow through his body.

He wasn't considered a man. He was eighteen years old, taller and stronger than most of the men in the village. But he was still a child in their eyes.

A cold chill swept over him. *Was the Sun Dance the only way to be heard? The only way they'd listen to his words?*

He turned and stalked back to the council tent. Re-entering, he drew little notice from the men who spoke together, except Red Squirrel. Blue waited for the old man to recognize him. Finally, with a sigh of reluctance, Red Squirrel waved him to speak. Blue again scanned the blank faces of those around him.

"I'm Blue Fox with Two Hearts, son of Morning Flower Woman, sister-by-marriage to Man-Who-Runs, Dog Society Chief of the Brule. The words I tell you, you refuse to hear. Is it because you still see me as a child?"

He looked around the room. All eyes rested on him, a few heads nodded.

"If you don't hear my words because I'm not a man in your eyes, then it's time for me to become one. In six months during the Moon When the Cherries are Ripe, I will join in the annual Sun Dance to prove I'm worthy. Perhaps then, I can show The People my heart wants to be among them. Will you hear my words then?" He looked into the faces of the men around him, hoping it wouldn't be too late.

He waited for a response. Finally, Red Squirrel forced himself to his feet.

"You, Blue Fox with Two Hearts, shall become a man. But first, you must prepare. When the green grass again pushes out from Mother Earth, you will seek *hanblechyapi,* your vision. You will fast alone and wait for your spirit guide to reveal itself. Then you will join the others in the dance."

Blue nodded to Red Squirrel and those assembled. His glance fell on Wild Wolf. The brave sat rigid, his lips drawn tight. Blue turned and left the lodge, new purpose in his step. Heading toward his lodge, Blue's mind raced and fear washed over him. He stumbled. *Was he strong enough to find his spirit guide? Could he prove himself worthy in their eyes?*

Chapter Twelve

Bitter cold and long weeks of deep, swirling snow, exhausted the tribe's winter supplies sooner than expected.

"How many will make up the hunting party, Jumping Bear?" Blue asked, anxious to be included.

The grizzled warrior faced Blue. "Most of the men will go," he said, his voice gruff. "Some will remain behind to protect the women, children and old ones."

"Against what? It's winter. Surely we're safe from attack now." But the look in his friend's eyes told him otherwise.

"We do not seek animal prey. We go to raid a Crow village many miles away."

Blue suddenly couldn't breathe. Crow! They intended to raid another village. To strip the Crow of their winter stores, leaving them to starve.

"But Jumping Bear..."

Jumping Bear raised his hand. "We have raided back and forth between our two peoples for all memory. It is our way."

"You'll take what they've hunted and foraged and leave them with nothing?" Blue asked, incredulous.

The older man nodded. "There you will count coup, again show The People you want to be accepted. That you are willing to prove you belong here."

Blue hung his head. Fear washed over him. "But I don't know if I can, Jumping Bear. I was taught it is wrong to steal from others. That you work for what you get."

"But this is the way of things among The People, Blue Fox. It will always be like this. You must accept that, or never become one with The People. I will tell you a tale handed down for generations. Sit," Jumping Bear commanded.

"Long ago on a dark, starless night, a young Crow brave, anxious to prove himself among his people, crept into the village of my grandfathers. He cut the thick buffalo hide covering of one of the lodges, then slipped into the tipi of the sleeping family. One by one he slit the throats of all who slept, even the children.

Since then we have been bitter enemies. We raid them and they raid us. It has been this way for time remembered."

Blue shuddered at the mental picture, but still didn't understand why the Lakota and Crow couldn't live together peacefully.

"Isn't there some other way Jumping Bear? That was a long time ago. Couldn't you talk it over and work it out?"

Jumping Bear shook his head. "That is not to be. We have come too far. Too many raids and too many deaths have taken place to change our feelings of hatred."

Blue stared at his hands. *Perhaps it was the way, but would he be able to steal food that would keep other people from starving? Could he kill?*

He wanted to become one with The People, he reminded himself. But if he refused to join the attack on the Crow village, he would be scorned, rejected.

"Rest," he heard Jumping Bear say through his musing. "Think of these things I've spoken of. We will speak of it tomorrow." Jumping Bear left the lodge, leaving Blue alone with his thoughts. And doubts.

The raiding party, including a wary Blue, gathered in the still morning and prepared to depart for the Crow village. Apprehension flowed through him. Never as a child living in his mother's village had he been aware these raids took place. Men would die, possibly women and children. The idea turned his blood to ice.

He joined the others with a heavy heart, but remembered Jumping Bear's words.

"We will enter the village as they sleep," he'd said. "You will gather as much as you can carry before leaving the village. And if you encounter one of their warriors, you must kill him—or he will kill you." Jumping Bear swung the coup stick in the air then smacked it into the palm of his hand.

Blue felt sick.

"What if I stay behind to protect the women and old ones," he offered, anxious not to participate.

Jumping Bear shook his head, disappointment on his face. "You do not want to become a man in the eyes of The People? Do not want to count coup?"

Blue's mind whirled with mixed emotions. He loathed the idea of what he knew they were about to do. Yet he yearned to be accepted among these people.

"You know I do, Jumping Bear. It's just that..." he broke off, unable to voice all he feared.

The party mounted and rode out of camp. Blue joined them, but lagged behind. He spoke to no one, not even Jumping Bear.

After a silent all-day ride, the raiding party stopped and made camp in a forest a few miles from the unsuspecting Crow village.

Blue unrolled his pallet far from the others, unable to join in their preparations. The thought of what was to come made his stomach turn.

He couldn't sleep. His mind whirled with questions. He'd left a comfortable home and loving parents because of the intolerance of white men. He'd believed he could learn to live among his mother's people. But what he was learning of those people gave him cause to question himself and them. They would soon ride down on a sleeping village and strip them of all they had. Kill any warrior who tried to stop them. Possibly kill women and children. How were they any different than the white men who rode across the Black Hills, killing and taking gold that wasn't theirs?

After a sleepless night Blue joined the others. In the early gray light the braves painted their faces with red mud and berry juice and readied their bows, quivers, and clubs. In silence they walked their horses to the edge of the forest and rode toward the still slumbering village.

With the village a dark outline against the morning sky, Jumping Bear laid a comforting hand on Blue's back.

"You must get close, Blue Fox. Count coup. Prove you are worthy of riding with the men of this village."

Blue shook his head, his conscience overpowering him. "I can't do this, Jumping Bear. I didn't grow up this way. I can't go with you." Blue glanced at Jumping Bear's weathered face.

106

The older brave sighed, closed his eyes and nodded understanding. "I was afraid you would not. You'll remain here, protected by the cover of trees until we return." Disappointment etched his features.

Blue knew in his heart he was doing the right thing. He couldn't plunder this village. Possibly do murder. It wasn't in his nature, not in his blood, even though that blood was part Lakota.

A horse snorted and he looked up to see Wild Wolf on his mount beside him.

"I see you do not ride with us, Blue Fox. Are you too much a child or too much a woman?" Wild Wolf's voice dripped with scorn.

Before Blue could respond, Wild Wolf sent his horse to join the others racing toward the unsuspecting camp.

Moments later screams of terror and cries for help shattered the quiet morning.

Blue watched from his vantage point in the trees. Men scrambled from their lodges, coup sticks and arrows cutting them down as they tried desperately to protect their families. Women and children screamed and cried. Horses squealed and warriors whooped. Jumping Bear rode into the center of the village and struck a Crow brave with his coup stick. The brave fell in a heap. A woman ran from her lodge, a child tucked protectively beneath her arm. She spotted her fallen husband and ran toward Jumping Bear yelling and pounding at his legs. Jumping Bear kicked her away. She scrambled out from the horse's prancing hooves, aided by another child, and the three cowered beside their lodge watching the destruction of their home and loved ones.

Blue's stomach twisted as the Lakota warriors continued the attack. He watched in horror as men, women, children, and old people were assaulted by lances, tomahawks, or coup sticks.

He spotted Wild Wolf gathering furs from beside a tipi and noticed two Crow braves creeping around another lodge to the rear of where Wild Wolf gathered his booty.

Blue's mind raced. Wild Wolf didn't know they were there and if he weren't warned, he would surely be killed. For an instant, Blue considered not warning the brave of the danger that stalked him. In the next, he sent his horse racing toward the village.

He shouted at Wild Wolf, raised his bow and aimed. Wild Wolf stopped his gathering and straightened, defiant in his stance as Blue thundered toward him.

"Behind you!" But the upheaval around Wild Wolf swallowed Blue's words. Wild Wolf grabbed an arrow, loaded his bow, and aimed. At Blue!

"No!" Blue shouted, his heart pounding like the horse's hooves beneath him. "Behind you!"

Blue aimed and fired.

The Crow warrior behind Wild Wolf screamed a strangled cry and fell to his knees, Blue's arrow protruding from his chest.

Wild Wolf whirled in time to stop the other Indian's tomahawk from imbedding itself in his skull. When Blue reached striking distance of the two men, he grabbed his coup stick and sent it crashing into the Crow's head. The warrior staggered, but didn't fall until Wild Wolf swung a tomahawk into his chest.

Wild Wolf looked down on the fallen braves. His muscular chest heaved as he turned surprised eyes to Blue. And for a moment Blue saw gratitude there. In the next instant, Wild Wolf snatched up the furs and disappeared around the lodge.

Blue stared down at the two dead Crow, his heart like a lead weight in his chest, revulsion rising in his throat.

A movement between two lodges caught his eye. A young white woman with long, crimson hair, her face wild with fear, was scooting between the lodges.

Blue followed, careful to stay out of sight. She dodged Indians, children and animals. At the perimeter of the village she grabbed up her skirt and raced for the cover of trees.

She ran across the open field and Blue sent his horse after her.

She'd almost reached the tree line when Blue rode up beside her. She yelped with surprise when she spotted him and ran faster. Blue raced after her.

"Stop!" he shouted in English. She jerked to a halt and whirled, her eyes wide.

Blue bent over and scooped her onto his horse.

She pounded his legs and arms. "Let go of me," she screeched.

"Stop so I can talk to you," Blue said in her ear.

She stopped fighting and slowly turned to look at him with eyes as deep green as the forest around them. "Who, who are you?"

His chest tightened as if a giant claw had him in its grip. His heart stopped and started like it'd forgotten how to beat.

"My name is Blue," he said, regaining his wits.

"You speak English?"

Blue nodded.

"But you're an Indian!" She started to squirm again, tried to unseat herself. Blue clamped his arm tighter around her.

"Will you hold on a minute! I'm trying to help you." He drew up his horse in a thicket of trees.

"Help me? How are you doing that? I was doing just fine by myself until you plucked me off the ground." The intensity of her hateful glare unsettled him. She wiggled again. Tried to jump free. Blue squeezed tighter.

"I'm keeping you from getting yourself killed is what I'm doing. And you're damn lucky it was me who spotted you and not one of the others." He jerked his head toward the village and felt her shiver.

"Now calm down and let me talk to you."

She closed her eyes, drew in a breath, and nodded. He eased his grip on her. She rammed her elbow into his stomach.

He doubled over.

She slid down and sprinted into the woods.

"Damn it," Blue cursed. He sucked in a big gulp of air, dismounted and took off after her. She ran between the trees, her ankles showing from under her gathered skirt.

"It's no use, miss. I'm right behind you and I'm not letting you get away," he shouted. He couldn't let her escape.

She ran faster.

"You have no idea what dangers are out here. Other Indians, wild animals." He let the words hang, but she didn't slow down.

"Leave me alone," she shouted.

"Afraid I can't do that. You're coming with me, and that's that."

He dove toward her and managed to grab her around the waist. They fell to the ground. She screamed obscenities at him as they tumbled to a halt.

"Quiet, you little she-cat! I'm trying to save your life."

"You have a funny way of doing so," she managed. "Could you do so without throwing me into the dirt and crushing the life out of me in the process?"

Blue rolled off her. She pushed herself to her knees then stood, her back to him, smacking dirt off her skirt. She was a slender girl who stood almost a foot shorter than Blue. A mass of fiery red hair was thrown over her shoulder and fell in waves to the middle of her back.

She turned around, her lips tight with worry, her cheeks red from exertion, her breath tightening her dress across her breasts.

"Are you finished?" Her annoyance was obvious at his rude perusal.

He looked back at her oval face and her creamy skin. He noticed her small, upturned nose and the smattering of freckles that ran across it. She sniffed at his bold gaze, but he was helpless to stop. His breath caught as he settled on her eyes, which glittered like green emeralds in the morning sunlight.

"Well?" she snapped. "What now?"

Blue had thought no further than keeping her alive. He couldn't let the others harm her. He had to keep her safe.

She set her hands on her hips, tapped her toe.

"Well?"

"Listen to me you little hellion," Blue said with all the sternness he could muster. "If you want to see tomorrow, you'll do as I tell you now."

"What are you, anyway? How is it you speak English so well?"

"There's no time for that now. Just do as I tell you and you'll keep that pretty red hair attached to that head of yours."

His words seemed to penetrate her facade and her eyes reflected her fear.

He grabbed her hand. "Come on."

"Let go of me you heathen! Let me go!"

She kicked at him, but he dragged her forward.

110

He lifted her onto the horse's back, still kicking and yelling, then mounted behind her.

"Damn you," she shouted. "Let me go!"

But holding her close, feeling the soft curve of her body, he knew that was something he'd never do.

Chapter Thirteen

Blue and his captive rode into the raiding party's temporary encampment later that morning. He was exhausted. She was still yelling, still trying to get away from him. Some of the warriors nodded and grinned while others simply glared.

"This woman is mine," Blue shouted. "I've found her and no one will take her from me."

While the others returned to preparing for their departure, one brave stepped forward. The warrior was stocky, his muscles taught, sleek. He was Tall Bull, well known among the warriors. He was a troublemaker and had a reputation as a dirty fighter.

"I challenge you for the woman!" Tall Bull shouted.

Blue went rigid. He knew Indian law allowed anyone to challenge him.

"It's your right, Tall Bull. But I will kill you to keep her."

Tall Bull wavered a second. "I want the woman. I will take her."

"What's he saying?" the woman whispered to Blue. Her voice shook and her body pressed against him.

"I've been challenged."

"For what?"

"You."

He heard her sharp intake of breath, felt her go stiff. Her hand flew to her throat and her bravado dissipated like water on a fire.

They dismounted. Blue stared at the frightened girl. He wanted to tell her he'd protect her, but Tall Bull shouted again.

"The woman—fight for her or give her to me."

The Indian charged. He caught Blue in the chest and they landed with a thud.

Tall Bull pulled a knife from his belt. Blue rolled a split-second before the knife embedded in the ground beside his shoulder.

112

Blue jumped to his feet and pulled his own knife. He surged forward and felt the knife slice Tall Bull's arm, a second before he heard a bellow of rage erupt from the brave's throat.

Tall Bull rushed again and Blue barely sidestepped his weapon. They whirled and faced-off again, their knives glinting in the sunlight.

The girl screamed, reminding Blue he had to win this fight or he'd lose her and, most likely, his life.

Tall Bull advanced. Blue feinted right then left. An opening. Blue drove his knife into the soft tissue of the brave's belly. Tall Bull grunted and staggered backward. His hands covered his stomach. Blood seeped through his fingers.

"I don't want to kill you Tall Bull. But this woman is mine. You can't have her."

Tall Bull dropped to his knees. "She is already yours, Blue Fox with Two Hearts." The warrior fell to the ground and didn't move.

Blue stared at the still form. The others gathered around and congratulated him on his victory. But Blue only felt empty.

He looked for his prize. She wasn't standing where he'd left her. His eyes swept the area. Panic gripped him. She was nowhere in sight.

"The girl! Where is she?"

"She ran away." Jumping Bear laughed and pointed. "That way." In the distance Blue saw her billowing skirt churning up dust as she ran.

He jumped onto his horse and raced after her. He rode up beside her, scooped her up in his arm and dropped her in front of him.

She kicked and pounded, and shouted obscenities. But he held tight.

"Let go of me you heathen!" she shrieked.

He ignored her protests and headed back toward the others wondering what, exactly, he *would* do with her.

Blue eyed his captive. He thought she had been a hellion yesterday during their first encounter. She'd done nothing this morning to discourage that perception.

She'd spat and sputtered curses at him last night until he finally tied a gag over her mouth. She continued her tirade, gag and all, until he turned his back on her. It wasn't two minutes before he felt a jerk on the rope wrapped around her wrists.

"You're not going anywhere," he said without turning around. "You might as well accept it and go to sleep."

She kicked a few more times. But exhaustion must have finally claimed her, for she stilled and her breathing grew faint and even.

When the sun rose he removed the gag and she'd started all over again.

"Damn you, whoever you are! Whatever you are," she sputtered, spitting the rag taste from her mouth. "Why are you keeping me here? You and your Indian friends are as bad as..."

She clamped her mouth shut and her eyes became angry. Or sad? Blue couldn't tell.

"As bad as what?"

"Nothing. Just leave me alone."

Blue wondered how she'd come to be in the Crow village. *How long had she been there and what humiliations had she suffered?* But he didn't have time to ask. The others were ready to leave.

He tossed her onto his horse and tied her wrists around the horse's neck. He mounted behind her, but not before he saw the stubborn anger on her face.

A rider came up beside him.

"Come to gloat I'm still a child, Wild Wolf?" He glared at the brave and waited for the expected insult.

Wild Wolf's hand clamped down on Blue's forearm.

"You are no child and you are no woman," Wild Wolf said. "Yesterday you were a warrior, made so to save my life." He paused as if searching for words, frowned, then slammed his heels into his pony and rode away.

Blue watched the Indian join the others ahead. Reflecting on Wild Wolf's words, he decided he'd gotten as much of a thank you as he was going to get.

Blue pulled the woman close. Her hair brushed his face when she straightened in defiance. She stared straight ahead, tried her best to ignore him. Good, he thought. At least she's quiet.

His mind returned to the taking of the village. The men he rode with laughed and joked about the devastation of the other's lives. But he felt no joy in what they'd done, only ambivalence. Aside from saving the girl, he'd done nothing to be proud of. Even the extra stores and horses they carried with them to make the winter easier couldn't displace the nagging guilt and shame that had settled into his brain.

Unable to dispel the memories of the raid, he became lost in a sea of strange feelings. He recalled the dull thud of his coup stick when he hit the Crow brave and the vision of his arrow protruding from the chest of the other. He shuddered. He wanted so much to be one of The People, but would it cost him his soul?

The daylong ride home was trying. Throughout the journey the woman spat curses and threats at Blue. Each time he tried to soothe her she began another tirade. She wouldn't even tell him her name. Blue let her rave and decided it was her right, after all, for all she'd already endured.

Cheers greeted the braves when they entered their village—and wails for the dead, as the families of those few warriors killed learned the fate of their loved ones.

Tall Bull's family pulled the brave from his horse and turned vengeful eyes toward Blue. He watched Wild Wolf speak to the father of what had happened and expected the worst. But moments later, the man turned sad eyes toward Blue and nodded before shuffling away, carrying his dead son.

The warriors trotted into camp and Blue felt his captive melt closer and closer to him. Her eyes darted around, wide with fear. Few of the villagers paid her any attention, most celebrated only the successful raid. But some glared in open contempt. The girl shifted uneasily and slid as close to Blue as she could.

"Don't worry," he whispered in her ear. "I won't let anyone hurt you. Trust me."

She nodded almost imperceptibly.

115

He noticed Yellow Lodge Woman staring at the woman in front of him. His captive. She looked at him, then turned away, but not before Blue saw hurt on her face.

At his lodge he dismounted and reached up to help the woman down.

"I'm quite capable," she snarled sliding from the horse to land squarely on her feet. "I've been riding since I was knee-high to a toadstool."

"Is that a fact?" He untied her hands.

Their eyes locked. Blue's insides constricted. God, she was lovely. Never before had he seen such fire and beauty in one woman.

"And where do I go?" she asked.

He pointed to his lodge. She threw up the flap and stalked inside.

Blue marveled at her gumption. She was going to be a handful, but he'd taken on the burden and he intended to see it through. He almost chuckled out loud as he stepped into the lodge behind her.

She stood beside the blackened fired pit, her back to him, her shoulders shaking.

He touched her arm and she stiffened.

"Don't cry," he said gently.

She whirled on him as though he'd branded her with a hot poker.

"Why not?" she shouted, her eyes wet with tears. "Are you some kind of dolt? Don't I have a right to cry? I've been abducted by savages. Twice! I don't know if I'm going to be killed, ill used, or what! And, and...," she broke into sobs.

Blue didn't know what to do. He didn't want to see her cry. She'd seemed so tough a moment before, but now she wept like a child. He laid his hand on her shoulder. She jerked away.

"Don't touch me!"

"I won't hurt you," Blue said. "Can't you believe that?"

She searched his face and he felt her eyes reach into his soul.

"You're not like them," she whispered. "You're different. You don't belong here. And neither do I."

Her words pierced him like a well-placed arrow. *Was it that obvious, even to her?* He remembered Karen's false kind words. Remembered her betrayal.

He grabbed her elbow and led her to his pallet.

"Sit down," he commanded.

Would this woman betray him, too? Could he blame her if she did? She only wanted to go home.

He looked into her face, into her tear-filled green eyes. His heart lurched at the need he felt to hold her, console her. Prove to her he'd take care of her. If only she'd let him.

"Please, sit down," he said again. "You're probably exhausted." He squatted and patted the soft furs. "Everything's going to be all right," he said when she didn't move. "How many times do I have to tell you that?"

He saw some of her tension drain away. Hesitantly, she sat in front of him on the pallet.

"Are you of a mind to tell me what's going to happen to me? Or do you intend to keep me guessing?" she asked, her voice curt again. But Blue knew she was terrified, trying to make him believe otherwise.

"Miss, every time I've opened my mouth to talk to you, you lash out at me. How can I tell you what's going to happen when you won't let me speak?"

She stiffened. "Very well. You may speak." Her voice held the hint of a southern accent.

"I may speak?" Blue repeated.

"Yes. I'd like you to tell me what you intend for me?"

She took a deep breath, held it as she awaited his answer.

"It's certain I can't just let you go. You wouldn't last a week. If wild animals didn't get you, you'd starve, freeze to death, or wind up captured by the Crow again." He looked deep into her eyes. "No. You won't be leaving right away."

"When, then?" she asked, her voice childlike.

He hesitated, couldn't tell her he had no intention of letting her go. Ever. That he meant for her to be his.

"Well?"

"I don't know. Don't ask any more questions. Just rest."

"But..."

"Rest," he commanded. He pushed up and walked across the room.

"You're not going to leave me, are you?"

He turned back to her. "I'm just going to get some wood for the fire. I'll be right back."

He stepped outside and grabbed some kindling from a pile beside the lodge.

His arms full, he reentered the lodge. He couldn't help but smile. The girl lay on his pallet curled into a ball, sound asleep.

The next morning after he'd tended to his horse, Blue watched his lodge from a distance.

The girl still hadn't told him her name or how she'd been captured by the Crow. The things he wanted to know, she wouldn't tell him, but the things he didn't want to hear, she spoke enough for ten women.

Her head popped out of the lodge flap and she looked around the empty village. He knew what she was thinking and his heart skipped a beat at the thought of her escaping.

She stepped away from the lodge to get a better view of the village. Most of the villagers were still sleeping, exhausted from the long night of celebration.

Blue watched her work her way behind his lodge. He followed her.

He caught sight of her again when she was running full tilt, slipping here and there on the snow-blanketed ground. She had to make it across an open expanse before she reached the cover of trees and was almost there when he took off.

A fast little sprite, he thought racing after her. She disappeared into the trees. But Blue knew this forest well. Knew the places she could hide.

He entered the line of trees and stopped. Only slightly winded from his run, he listened intently to the woods around him. In the distance he heard the cracking and snapping of twigs and leaves. He sprinted off.

He couldn't lose her. He admitted she had captured his heart. And if he didn't find her, she would die in this unfamiliar land. It took without warning and gave nothing back if you didn't know how to take it first. She was a kitten alone in a world of rabid dogs.

Blue skidded to a stop. She stood hunched over, bathed in the sunlight streaming through the trees. Her hands were on her knees and she sucked in huge gulps of air. The light sparkled on the snow around her feet and surrounded her in a surreal glow. She looked up, her breath issuing from her mouth in little white clouds.

Blue was in full view if she looked to her left. He didn't move. Just waited. Slowly, she straightened, took a step then jerked her head and froze, her eyes wide. She grabbed her skirt, turned and fled.

"It's useless to run. I can catch you, even if you have a head start. I've already proven that." Blue started after her at an easy lope.

"Leave me alone!" she shouted, out of breath. "I just want to go home."

"Home?"

She stopped and let him catch up.

"And where is home?" Blue asked, coming up beside her.

"I, I don't know," she muttered.

Her eyes softened and glistened with welling tears. Her lower lip trembled. But she drew up her back and ground out the threatening wetness with her fists.

"It's none of your damn business!"

"Whoa." Blue took hold of her arm to keep her from running again. "I'm not your enemy. What do I have to do to make you understand that?"

"Not my enemy? Well, what are you then? You're holding me against my will. Stopping me from leaving. What would you call yourself?"

She broke into sobs, then forced them back into her chest. She swiped at her nose with the back of her hand, then stalked back toward the village.

Blue wanted some answers. He grabbed her arm and stopped her in mid-stride.

"How did you come to be with the Crow?"

119

Her chin rose and she licked her lips. "I was with a small party of prospectors when the Crow attacked our wagons three days ago. They killed everyone, except me." Her eyes welled again with tears, but she blinked them back.

"One of those men was my father."

"I didn't have anything to do with the death of your father," Blue said, understanding her sorrow, "yet you seem to hold me responsible."

"Who else should I hold responsible? If you'd just left me alone when you raided the Crow camp, I'd be safe by now."

"Or dead," he reminded her.

Her eyes closed and her head dropped, conceding only a little. "Or dead. But we don't know that, do we? So all I choose to believe is that I'd be gone by now if you hadn't interfered."

"What the hell were you doing with prospectors? Didn't your father know the dangers here? You could have been killed along with the rest of them."

Blue felt suddenly angry at the picture in his mind. *How could the man have been so stupid as to bring a grown, young woman into this kind of territory? For gold. What else?* Blue's insides constricted. He remembered Hollister and Rosen and their bold talk of getting their fair share of gold out of the Black Hills. It was men like them that came looking for gold. Men that wanted something for nothing. His anger boiled to the surface.

"What kind of man was your father? To bring you to a place like this?"

He glared at her bent head. Slowly, she raised her eyes to his.

"He was a foolish, broken man. But he was a good man, a kind man who only wanted something for his daughter other than pain and hardship. He had dreams—and hopes."

Tears welled in her eyes and before she could crush them away, they spilled over her cheeks.

Afraid to touch her, Blue let her cry until she'd had enough. Moments later, her tears spent, she took a deep breath.

"I'm ready to go back now. But understand this isn't the last time I'll try to escape. You've been warned."

She grabbed her skirt and stomped toward camp. He followed behind her, his head shaking in amazement. "Somehow

120

I knew that," he said aloud, unable to stop the smile that came to his lips.

Chapter Fourteen

Blue stared at the woman sleeping across the room from him and reflected back over the events of the past few days. He'd proven himself a warrior—and won an incredible prize.

He recalled the journey home and puzzled at Wild Wolf's lack of antagonism during the trip. Maybe, just maybe, Blue had proven himself enough for the brave to put aside whatever hatred he had for him. But Blue wasn't overly hopeful. Given a few days, he supposed things would be back to normal, Wild Wolf and the others taunting him as usual.

Unable to sleep, he threw on a heavy fur and stepped outside into the frigid air. A walk would help clear some of the dust from his mind.

Lost in reflection he ran right into the subject of his musing. Moonlight played across the brave's hard features.

Forget a few days, Blue thought. He drew up his back, ready for an assault.

"We would speak," Wild Wolf said.

Wary, Blue followed Wild Wolf to his lodge and entered at the brave's insistence. When the flap closed behind them, Wild Wolf motioned for Blue to sit on a pallet beside the glowing fire at the center of the lodge.

Seated, Wild Wolf offered food and drink. Blue refused. "Why have you brought me here?"

Wild Wolf focused solemn eyes on Blue. "I have brought you to ask understanding," he began, his voice unsteady.

Blue stayed tense, but nodded.

"Two days ago you saved my life. This act I will not forget, Blue Fox. But I asked you here tonight to seek understanding for my mistreatment of you since you came to The People."

Blue watched the Indian speak and saw something in the warrior's eyes he'd never seen before. Vulnerability?

"There's a reason for my hatred, Blue Fox." Wild Wolf stopped, searched the fire as if the words he sought could be found there and swallowed hard.

"I have hated the whites for many years. All whites. Since I was a small child." Again he stopped, his eyes drifting to another time, another place.

After a long pause, Wild Wolf returned to the present, and Blue saw pain in his features.

"I was about ten summers and lived in a small village with my family," Wild Wolf began. "Perhaps only twenty warriors and their families. We were peaceful, happy to live amongst ourselves to hunt and move our village with the change of the weather and migration of the buffalo.

"During that time, other tribes attacked the white men's forts. This made the Bluecoats angry and they wanted revenge. But to them, one Indian is the same as another."

The brave's eyes clouded and Blue saw an inner battle being fought.

"Early one morning as my village slept, soldiers came. They swarmed over our people like bees on honey. They were too many to fight off and they killed all the old men and warriors. With the men dead, the women and children were chased down and captured."

Blue shifted, unsettled by the developing story. Visions flashed into his mind of screaming, terrified women and children. Of men fighting desperately to save their loved ones. Of Sarah, his uncle and mother at Bluewater Creek.

Wild Wolf continued, his voice thick with pain. "The children, perhaps twenty-five of us, were gathered, tied together and left outside without protection." He shivered.

"All the women were taken to the council lodge. From inside I heard their screams, their pleas for a quick death. But I was a child and didn't know then what the soldiers did to our mothers and sisters." He lifted tortured eyes to Blue. "I know now. When the soldiers were through with them, they slit their throats and left them on the floor of the lodge.

"The soldiers rode away and left the children tied together, at the mercy of the weather and the beasts of the forest. Many of the children died quickly. From the cold, or fear, I don't know.

"Then the wolves came. I still hear their snarling in my dreams. They came closer, closer, their white teeth bared and shining in the moonlight. Even in my waking hours I still see their yellow eyes seeking their victims."

Wild Wolf shuddered again.

"I hid under one of the children who had already died, while others around me tried in desperation to break the ropes that held them. I hear their screams even now."

He looked away and drew a ragged breath.

"Wolves like fresh meat and were happy to tear the flesh of those who still lived. I remained still and waited for them to reach me. I tried to block out the screaming of the others, to die a good death. But the Great Spirit was watching over me and it was not my day to die.

"Blood from the others made my ropes slick, and I was able to wiggle my hands free. But I couldn't outrun the beasts and if I remained they would soon know I was there, hidden among the dead." He wrapped his arms around his chest, a haunted look on his face.

"I looked for a weapon and spotted a hatchet not far from me. I jumped up, ran and grabbed it; turned and flung the weapon in front of me. A wolf yelped and backed away. Blood dripped from a long tear in its shoulder where the hatchet had struck. The others behind him stopped, their mouths dripping with the blood of the children.

"But the pack was no longer hungry, had already gorged themselves. I remember shouting, then charging, and they scattered into the forest.

"From that day I have been Sunkmanitu Tanka Watogla. Wild Wolf. A reminder of my past." He let out a short, rattled breath and looked up at Blue.

"For weeks, that child buried the dead of his village in the Lakota fashion, on scaffolds built to honor the dead. And as he built those scaffolds, his hatred of the white man grew. Until today, I have hated all whites."

Blue tried to calm his trembling body. *Now he understood Wild Wolf's bitter hatred.* He stared at the brave. *How could he not accept Wild Wolf's plea for understanding? Had it been him, would he have hated any less?*

He nodded and stood. Wild Wolf waited. The pain and expectation in his eyes tugged at Blue's soul. Blue extended his hand. Wild Wolf hesitated then grabbed it. The two men stared at each other, uncertain. Wild Wolf broke the tenuous silence.

"It is good."

The following morning by the light of the dying fire, Blue again watched his captive sleep. She looked like a contented child, her long, dark lashes closed over her emerald eyes.

Each time he looked at her he wanted to scoop her into his arms and kiss the breath out of her. He wanted to taste her lips and feel her body pressed close to his. Although it was his right by Lakota law to take her as he wanted, he wouldn't force himself on her. Couldn't. Another way he was so different from those he lived with, he berated himself.

He gazed at her and imagined her giving herself to him willingly. His mind drifted to a picture of her mouth curled in laughter, of her eyes bright with joy, her heart filled with love. Children, running happily about, finished the picture. He sighed. *Would he ever be completely fulfilled with a wife and children? Would he ever know true happiness?* His vision drifted back to the delicate creature nestled in the furs across from him.

He froze. Her eyes were open and she was staring back at him.

"Daydreaming?"

"Thinking."

"About what?"

"Nothing of importance." He pushed himself up from the pallet. "Hungry? You've slept well into the morning."

"Yes, some." Her perusal of him never wavered.

He turned his back, unnerved by her continued examination. It reminded him of another girl and how she'd led him down a fool's path. *Would this slip of a girl do the same thing?* Angrily, he dished out gruel and handed her the bowl.

She sat up and dipped her fingers into the mixture, but continued to gaze at him as they slid in and out of her mouth. Blue stared back, captured by her face. By her whole being.

"Are you ready to tell me your name?"

She finished the gruel and put the bowl aside. She licked the last of the food from her fingers and nodded.

"Since it appears I may be here a while, I suppose it will do no harm." Blue didn't miss the condescending tone in her voice. "My name is Amy Ross. And yours?"

"Blue Fox with Two Hearts."

"Hmm, Blue Fox with Two Hearts. Two hearts," she repeated. "A half-breed." Her words sounded dirty and cold.

"Yes, a half-breed," he snarled back.

"But why are you here? You've obviously lived with civilized people, you know our language perfectly."

"I'm here because of people like you, who judge me because of what I am, not because of what's inside me. You said it the other day. I don't belong here. I've never belonged anywhere." His words tasted bitter in his mouth and he felt he'd said too much.

He looked into her face and saw it had softened.

"Feeling sorry for the little breed?" he spat.

"No, I don't," Amy answered. "You feel sorry enough for yourself for the both of us."

Blue jumped to his feet. He stood across from her and the smug look on her face told him she knew she'd hit a nerve.

"You see, I'm right. I didn't judge you. You judged yourself. I could care less what you are. I won't be around long enough for it to make a difference, anyway. But," she leaned forward, "it obviously makes a difference to you."

Blue calmed himself and sat down again. "And what if you were going to be here a while?" he asked. "Would it make a difference then?"

She pursed her lips as she pondered his question. "No. I should think not. I would judge you on what type of person you are. If you are kind or giving, witty or slow." A small smile played on her lips. A smile that made her even more striking. Blue imagined seeing her face filled with laughter, certain it would light his heart like a torch.

"We've strayed from the subject, Blue Fox. Tell me about yourself. Your parents."

His parents, Blue thought. His birth parents that made him a person of mixed blood? Or the parents who took him in and tried to help him become a man? Who loved him as they would their own son. A pang of regret shot through him and he wondered how Ben and Sarah fared. He missed them and wished he could let them know he was well.

"Well?"

"My father, a trapper, died when I was very young. My mother, a Lakota, died when I was thirteen. I lived in the white man's world after that."

"Where?" she asked, her face soft.

"I lived outside the City of Kansas with Ben and Sarah Walters. Sort of relatives of my mother. That's a story in itself. They cared for me, but no one else in town accepted me. Except for George, that is."

His mind wandered to his friend. *Where was he and how was he doing?* The only other regret he had by being with The People was that he had no way to contact George. He had no idea what his friend's life was like. And he missed him. He opened his hand and stared down at the hair-thin scar that ran across his palm. *George had seen him for what he was and accepted him. Could Amy Ross?*

Amy touched his hand. Compassion filled her eyes and he felt drawn to kiss her, but knew he couldn't. He must go slow or she'd run away like a frightened rabbit.

"You've heard all about me, now it's your turn," Blue said.

She sighed. "A sad story much like yours, I'm afraid." She lifted sorrowful eyes.

"Tell me," Blue prompted, fascinated by the woman across from him.

"Once upon a time," she began in a lilting, southern accent, "there was a little girl who lived with her momma and daddy in a world full of happiness. Happiness that didn't last. The Civil War came and tore her world to shreds.

"In the beginning everyone was so jubilant, so certain we'd stomp the Yankees into the dirt in a matter of weeks. Instead we were overrun with the vermin. My father somehow managed to keep food in our bellies, but there was little else.

"And then came Sherman. What little was left was taken or torched by the thieves who called themselves soldiers." Her eyes flashed with unconcealed hatred.

"Papa began to drink. Mama fought to keep us together. I learned to make do with what I had, but by the time I was fifteen, I knew there wouldn't be much of anything ever again." Her eyes grew misty, her voice soft. Her pain seemed to bubble up from the depths of her soul and Blue understood what she felt all too clearly.

"Then, on a moonless night, Papa came home well into his cups. He fell asleep with a lit cigar in his hand. The tiny two-roomed house we called home went up like a tinderbox. Mama ran back inside to try and save what few precious memories she'd managed to keep through the war. But she never came back out."

Amy stopped, her fingers twisted together in her lap.

"Papa never drank again after that night. And he never forgave himself for her death." She looked up, tears glistening in her eyes.

"For years he tried to get back on his feet, but never succeeded. He heard rumors of gold in the Black Hills and decided it was the only way for us to start over. He had no choice. We had no choice. We had nothing."

"But you're fully grown. You could have told him no. You could've married and had a life of your own," Blue protested.

Amy shook her head and snorted. "There were no gentlemen in Charleston. And the men who had survived the war were broken and bitter." She looked away. "Then the dirty Yankees came. The ones who'd save you from the tax man, then turn around and take your home or farm or daughter in the blink of an eye when you couldn't repay them." Her voice was hard, her body trembling when she turned back to face Blue.

"No, I had little more choice than Papa did. And he was determined. He was going whether I went or not. I couldn't let him go alone. And although we knew the dangers we faced, the possibility of starting over drew us like moths to a flame." She paused. "So here I am and Papa's dead, and all his dreams with him."

The lodge grew silent. Blue watched a tear slip unchecked down Amy's cheek. Her hands remained entwined in her lap, her knuckles white.

128

"And what about *your* dreams, Amy?" Blue asked.

Her head lifted and hard eyes stared at him.

"I don't have any."

Chapter Fifteen

Buds burst from the trees and tiny sprouts of green were everywhere. Small animals darted between trees, skittered beneath bushes. A stream trickled beside the trail, its water so clear small fish were visible near the stony bottom. They'd traveled two days to reach this valley, rich with wildlife, to replenish the village stores depleted during the long, bitter winter.

Blue, Jumping Bear, Wild Wolf and the hunting party drew their mounts to a halt. Blue scanned the vast countryside and sighed, content with how his life among the Lakota progressed.

Blue spotted a dark cloud of smoke floating over the countryside and into the clear azure sky, casting a gray pall.

"What do you think it is?" Blue asked. Jumping Bear sat motionless atop his horse studying the cloud, the rest of the hunting party already headed toward the smoke.

"We will find out." He clucked his mount forward.

Blue reined his horse up behind Jumping Bear and Wild Wolf fell in behind him. They entered a dense forest, everything eerily silent around them, as though suffocated by the smoke, which hung overhead.

The forest opened into a valley and Blue drew his mount to a halt beside Jumping Bear.

He couldn't speak, had to breathe deep to keep from screaming. And when he did breathe, he wanted to gag. He couldn't look at Wild Wolf or the others, able to feel the rage that pulsed from them.

Jumping Bear dismounted. Blue jumped to the ground after him. He looked at Wild Wolf who remained mounted, his knuckles white around his reins. Small trickles of blood ran from the palm of his left hand where his nails dug into his flesh.

"Who would do this?" Blue whispered. His eyes swept over the remains of the village.

Jumping Bear knelt beside the still form of a young woman. Her clothes were torn away, her breasts cut from her body, her hair wild about her face and head. Blood streaked her thighs and left Blue no doubt she'd been ill used.

Bile rose in his throat. Rage bubbled in his stomach. Women, warriors and old ones were strewn all around, their bodies mutilated. Small children lay beside their dead mothers, their tiny skulls crushed.

"Can't you tell who did this?" Wild Wolf shouted and jumped from his mount. "Do you see any arrows? Any hatchets or coup sticks left behind by the attackers? Bullets killed them. White men came upon this sleeping village and murdered its people."

He knelt down and pushed back the bloodied hair of a small boy. He cradled the limp child in his arms. And screamed. His body shook with rage and Blue wanted to run away. He knew where Wild Wolf was, what he saw in his mind. His own village. His own mother and father.

The other braves joined in Wild Wolf's wailing, their high-pitched keen echoing among the trees, the birds and other creatures of the forest silent from the warriors' song. Blue's skin pricked. He felt sick. Never had he seen such brutality.

Wild Wolf sang for long minutes, held the small child in his arms and rocked him. Neither Jumping Bear nor Blue attempted to touch him. Finally, Wild Wolf lowered the boy to the ground, went into the trees and returned with an armful of tree branches. He dropped them to the ground and went back for more. He did this again and again. The others joined his search for wood, piling it in the center of what remained of the village. Blue soon realized their intent. They would build burial scaffolds for the dead, to prepare them for their journey to the spirit world. Using various weeds and grasses the warriors would bind the branches to make the platforms. Wild Wolf bent to the task, never looking away, always singing.

Blue was ashamed of the white blood that coursed through him and was unable to speak to any of the others. Too ashamed to offer assistance in preparation of the dead, other than to gather more limbs. He was afraid of Wild Wolf. Afraid the brave's hatred would return to include him because of his white blood.

"Give him time my friend." Jumping Bear laid his hand on Blue's shoulder. "He carries many scars on his heart. What has happened here is too close to his own pain."

"I know." Blue looked at his friend wrapping grass around the pieces of wood to form a scaffold.

Blue couldn't stay among these people. He felt as though they all, living and dead, held him responsible.

"I must go, Jumping Bear. I can't stay here. I'm too ashamed."

"Don't be foolish. They know it wasn't you who killed these people."

Blue looked at the men, all busy building, singing softly. None looked at him.

"Maybe that's so. But I still can't stay." He mounted his horse, but Jumping Bear stayed him with a hand on his leg.

"I know what's in your heart my young friend. And Wild Wolf knows, too. Perhaps he will forget for a time, but he'll remember what your friendship is to him."

"I hope you're right." Blue sent his horse racing from the village. His head spun, his heart raced like the animal under him.

How could men kill so easily? Women...children? He gave the horse his head and let him run for miles, but no answers came to him.

Uncertain of the way back to the village, he doubled back to where the hunting party camped. He laid his bedroll a short distance from camp, unable to join them. He was too confused to talk with anyone about what he felt. Only a short time ago he was content to live among the Lakota, to learn their ways and enjoy their friendship. In a heartbeat that had changed. He felt distant, ashamed of what he was. Part white. And although he knew Jumping Bear understood his confusion, he had to sort through this on his own.

He looked up at the stars twinkling in the sky and realized he'd never felt so alone in his life. Not even when he'd first traveled to this country. Then there'd been a goal. To find The People. And he'd achieved that goal. He knew Jumping Bear and Wild Wolf's friendship. He was part of a society where everyone depended upon one another for their survival. He'd learned the ways of the Lakota. Now that he had all those things, it had been ripped away in one senseless act of violence. He somehow felt as though he'd betrayed them by the blood that coursed through his body.

He threw his arm across his forehead. Until now, he'd only seen the treachery of one white man, Sam Hollister. But it had been enough to drive him from his family and his home. Today he'd seen what many cruel white men could do. It made him sick and ashamed.

But what about the Indian? Hadn't they been just as savage when they raided the Crow village? When they'd killed their own kind to steal food, weapons and horses? Jumping Bear said they'd done it for centuries. Did that make it right? Any more right than what these men had done here today? Were the Indians or the white men different from one other?

No.

Blue avoided Wild Wolf in the days following their return. Whenever he ran into the warrior, Wild Wolf still seemed distant and angry. He didn't speak to Blue, although he acted as though he wanted to say something.

One mild afternoon two weeks later, among many warriors in another hunting party, Wild Wolf rode up beside Blue. He breathed deep, as though gathering the right words. He sighed and turned to Blue.

"What happened in that village was a bad thing. My heart aches for the dead, but it is no longer hard against you." He laid his hand on Blue's shoulder. "It is finished. We have sent the dead to the spirit world and mourned them. We will not speak of it again."

And he didn't.

Blue was thankful, for he had other things to think about. It was time to prepare for the Sun Dance.

He was resting in his lodge, thinking of the impending dance, when Amy entered. Her fingers were splayed across her hips, a telling sign she was angry.

"I just found out you're going to participate in some heathen ceremony. Is that true?"

"Yes. Even now I've begun to prepare myself."

133

"For?"

"Hanblechyapi."

"Which is?" Her fingers drummed her hips and her toe tapped the ground.

"It's time for me to seek my vision and purify my body. When a boy is ready to prove himself a man, he seeks his vision by going off by himself for four days. When his spirit guide has revealed itself to him, he returns for purification. And then the dance." Her face tightened.

"And, exactly, what kind of dance is that?" Her head cocked with curiosity and her fingers continued to drum her hips.

Blue sighed.

"It's called the Sun Dance in which young men participate to pass into manhood."

She stood before him, her face a mask, her body stiff.

"And?"

"The dance begins with the piercing..."

"Piercing?" The blood drained from her face and her arms fell to her sides.

He nodded. "A small bone attached to a long thong and hung from a cottonwood post is passed through the flesh in each boy's chest. Once both sides are pierced, he must dance, pray and sing to the Great Spirit, asking for guidance of his life. The ceremony usually lasts for days, without food or water being taken by those who dance."

Her face told him nothing. He couldn't tell if she was frightened, angry or concerned.

"You mean to tell me you're going to participate in this heathen ritual? You're going to let them stick bones through your chest, then dance and sing to some Great Spirit?"

He nodded again. He hadn't even told her the worst of it.

"Well?"

"Well, what? I'm going to be a part of the ceremony, and that's that." He glared at her as hard as she was glaring at him.

She turned and stalked from the lodge. "Heathen rituals. And I thought you were different," she shouted before she disappeared.

Fear ran up his spine. *Could his desperate need to become a part of The People drive Amy away?* He shook his

134

head and sighed. No matter what he did, acceptance seemed to elude him.

Blue scanned the cliffs around him. Jagged rock walls reached into the bright blue, cloudless sky. He shifted on the smooth ledge and stared into the ravine below. He shivered. It was deep enough to kill a man if he fell.

He leaned back. Sweat dripped into his eyes. He wiped it away and wished his vision would come so he could leave this desolate place.

He'd been alone for four days on the ridge, the sweltering sun cooking him in the daytime, cold winds chilling him to the bone at night.

Thirst burdened him. But he fought the urge to seek water. He must prove his worthiness. Prove he belonged here with his mother's people. His people.

A low growl came from behind him. The hair on his neck stood up.

Slowly, he turned. A slavering red fox stood only a few feet away, its teeth bared behind curled lips. Blue wanted to run, but knew he couldn't outdistance this quick, vicious animal.

The fox stepped closer. Its eyes gleamed with anticipation. Blue was certain he'd lived his last day.

A second menacing growl, a few feet to his right, drew his attention. There stood a gray fox, its coat so dark it shimmered blue in the sunlight.

Teeth also bared, the gray fox stepped closer to the red. Another growl rumbled from its throat. Blue watched the two animals work their way toward each other and away from him. Eyes glittered in the sunlight, teeth flashed through snarling lips. Blue's heart raced. He knew he should run when the two clashed, but he felt imbedded in the ground.

Growls exploded into fierce snarling. The foxes charged and collided. Teeth met flesh, ripping and tearing. The animals broke apart and circled, each eyeing the other's throat. Blue watched the gray fox back away and draw the red fox in, then charge for the soft skin at its neck. He did this again and again.

They fought for long minutes, Blue held rapt in their clash of death. Suddenly, their low, menacing snarls turned to high-pitched yelps of agony as the gray fox tore through the neck of the red. Blood gushed from the animal, a huge gap open just above its chest. The red fox staggered then fell. Its belly rose and fell with each ragged breath until it became still.

Blue was as rigid as the rock ledge he sat on, unable to move, realizing he'd waited too long to act. The gray fox turned dark, penetrating eyes on him. He understood. The animals had fought for a prize. Him.

The fox stepped closer and Blue was certain he would die. On the edge of a ridge, he was unable to go backward, unable to go forward.

The fox stalked him, his coat no longer sleek, but matted with the blood of his dead opponent. The animal moved within five feet of Blue. Desperate, Blue looked for a stick or rock, anything he could use to protect himself from the creature stalking him. There was nothing but smooth ledge.

The animal came within two feet. Blue threw up his arms to protect his face and throat, the first place the animal would strike.

The attack didn't come.

Puzzled, Blue lowered his arms enough to peek at the animal. The fox sat on its haunches, its head cocked to one side, as if in question, with eyes so blue they penetrated Blue's consciousness.

"Do not fear me," the fox spoke to his mind. "Accept me. Use my knowledge to help your people."

Blue could only stare. He was unable to move, unable to speak.

The animal stood, turned and loped away.

Blue remained where he was, stunned. He closed his eyes and shook his head, realizing he'd just seen his vision.

But what did it mean?

Chapter Sixteen

It was the Moon When the Cherries are Ripe. June of the white man's calendar. And it was time.

The night before the Sun Dance Blue prepared for *Inipi*-- the purification ceremony.

Jumping Bear led Blue to the *Ini ti,* the purification lodge, a small, domed structure erected just outside the circular area where the Sun Dance would take place.

Blue crawled through the small opening into the foggy chamber, naked except for his breechcloth. Two other young men were already inside, sitting cross-legged on the sage-covered floor. From the rear of the room steam rose hot and steady as Lone Dog Binder of Wounds, the medicine man, poured water over rocks taken from a glowing fire. Blue began to pray and sing, to cleanse his spirit-self in preparation for the sacred *Wiwongwaci.*

Time stretched on forever. He had no idea how long he'd been in the lodge. A day, a week, two? His mind wandered the traces of his life. From the life he'd lived as a boy with his mother among these same people, to the one he'd spent with Ben, Sarah and George. Faces flashed before him. They taunted, shouted and called him names. He felt like a child, wanting only to cry into his mother's arms. Over and over, burning anger ripped through him at the injustices he'd faced throughout his life.

He was a misfit. An outcast. Trying so hard to become a part of something. Anything.

Where was his destiny? He prayed to *Wakan Tanka* for strength and guidance.

Sweat poured down his face and body, pooled at his bent knees and elbows. Still he prayed and sang for direction as to where and what his life would be.

Finally, the flap at the other end of the lodge lifted. Soft, pale, early morning light filtered into the room. Blue and the others crawled out.

Wild Wolf and Jumping Bear met him outside the exit of the purification lodge and drenched him with cool water. Once Blue could breathe again after the shock, his final preparation for the ceremony began. His long hair was left unbraided and unbound, free to flow down his back. As Wild Wolf and Jumping Bear attended him, Blue studied the sacred circle where the dance would take place.

In the center of a roughly built, circular structure stood the *wakan,* the sacred post cut from a cottonwood tree. Blue studied the post, hung with the crude replica of a rawhide man painted red, a plume of feathers adorning its head. The sides of the post were painted to the four winds. Below it, on a blanket of leaves, laid the sacred buffalo skull.

Carefully, Wild Wolf and Jumping Bear painted Blue's face, neck, arms and torso white before they added black stripes atop the white. His feet were left bare to touch the holy earth on which he would dance and pray.

The sun rose higher and Blue shielded his face from the bright rays that burned his eyes and skin. Soon he would become a man among the Lakota. Respected. Accepted.

The preparation of his physical appearance complete, Blue began the customary exchange of gifts.

He stopped at the entrance to the sacred circle and took Wild Wolf's hand in his.

"This gift I give you, Wild Wolf, my friend." He removed the gold ring that circled his pinky finger and slid it onto Wild Wolf's. "This is my most treasured possession. I give it to you for safekeeping."

Wild Wolf raised stunned eyes to Blue. He inspected the ring.

"I take this ring as a symbol of our friendship, Blue Fox. I'll wear it with pride."

The two clasped their arms up to the elbow before Blue turned to Jumping Bear.

"For my wise friend, Jumping Bear, I give my only other possession." He stepped to the man's side, put his hand on his shoulder, then pointed in the distance toward his lodge. "There. See my gift? My horse is yours. Treat him well."

138

"By giving this gift, it's clear what is in your soul, Blue Fox with Two Hearts." The older man grabbed Blue's shoulders and nodded.

Jumping Bear stepped back and announced, "It is time."

The grizzled warrior led Blue the last few steps inside the sacred circle. Entering from the east, Blue joined the other two young men who would participate in the ceremony. All three stood quiet. The people of the village gathered in a circle and awaited the arrival of the medicine man.

Blue scanned the faces of those in the circle for Amy. She'd openly shown her contempt for this 'heathen ritual.' He didn't expect to see her among the crowd.

But there she stood, her face a mask of worry. He smiled. She smiled back, but the corners of her mouth trembled.

Blue turned back to his friends. Jumping Bear stood beside Wild Wolf, his face awash with pride. Wild Wolf crossed his arms over his well-muscled chest, his own scars of the pending ritual proudly displayed above his forearms. Wild Wolf gazed at Blue. Their eyes met. The brave nodded slightly, then smiled, changing his face from one of a fearless, frightening warrior, to the friend he'd become.

Blue smiled back.

Blue forced his mind to the task at hand. He studied the *wakan* tree. From the top of the pole dangled six leather lines. The end of each line hung just above the leaf-covered ground. Tied to the end of each line was a straight bone about five inches long and filed to a spiked point on both ends.

Gooseflesh tore up Blue's body at the thought of those bones piercing his chest.

The crowd stood silent. Lone Dog approached, his face painted yellow and red, a cap of beads and feathers on his head. In his hand he gripped a rattlesnake tail rattle, the shaft garnished with more feathers.

Lone Dog stepped into the circle and walked to the young men. He stopped at each one and shook the rattle along their bodies. He stepped to the *wakan* tree and picked up two lines, then strode to the first boy. With a sharp knife, Lone Dog opened a small entry point in the boy's chest and attached the line. The boy's face twisted. He tried to contain the scream that wanted to erupt from his throat. The second line was attached and the boy lost his inner battle and cried out. Tears streaked his face and blood stained his painted chest.

Lone Dog went to the next boy and repeated the same steps. The second boy gritted his teeth against the pain and his eyes shut. When the second line was attached, he, too, lost his battle to remain silent.

Blue listened as the others cried out and vowed he wouldn't do the same.

Lone Dog stepped in front of him.

"You, Blue Fox with Two Hearts, came to us as a boy. Now you will become a man."

Blue nodded and lowered his head. The medicine man stepped away and retrieved the lines. Seconds later, the sharp bite of the knife sliced the flesh of his chest. His breath surged from his lungs and his eyes clamped shut against the explosive pain. His teeth ground inside his mouth and he bit down to keep from crying out as the others had.

Roughly, the medicine man passed the skewer through his left breast. Blue thought he would pass out, but forced himself to stay upright. He felt blood run down his chest. He continued to grit his teeth against the pain and breathed deeply through his nose. He was trembling, but felt the second knife prick, then his other breast sliced for entry of the bone spike. Still he didn't cry out. He thought he'd grind his teeth into dust, he bit down so hard. The second bone passed through his chest. Nausea washed over him. He thought he'd black out. By sheer strength of will he managed to stay upright. Spittle seeped from his mouth in his effort not to scream.

Suddenly the pain lessened and he realized the piercing was over. He opened his eyes and looked down to steady his weak legs.

Blood trickled down his chest and left bright, red streaks amidst the black and white paint. A dull ache raced through every fiber of his being. His breath came short and quick. He felt dizzy, as if all the skin on his body was being ripped off in one piece. Tears stung his eyes, but he held them back.

In the deep recesses of his mind, Blue heard the rattle shake and the melodious song Lone Dog Binder of Wounds sang as he danced and chanted in the circle with the boys.

Beside him, the others had already begun to dance and sing. He had to join in. Slowly, teeth still grinding, he forced his feet to move. He danced and sang the learned songs with the others, hoping to drive the blinding pain from his mind. Each jarring step brought him closer to falling over the precipice into a black abyss of nothingness. But then, his body went blessedly numb.

The heat scorched him. Sweat poured into his eyes and mouth, down to the wounds in his chest, burning. Still he sang and danced. He sang for strength. For wisdom.

The crowd chanted of love and honor.

"Look at that young man. He is feeling good. Because his sweetheart. Is watching him."

He searched through blurred eyes to find Amy. She was sitting on the ground, her knees pulled up to her chest, her chin resting on her knees.

As though sensing him, she lifted her head and he saw her tears. They streamed down her cheeks. They streaked her face and plopped on her dress to leave big, wet blotches.

His heart ached. *Could she be crying for him? For the pain he endured? Or did she cry because she now saw him more as a brother of the Lakota than a man she might someday care for?*

Blessed numbness took over his body. His legs shook, but still he danced. He tried to smile at Amy, but couldn't force his lips to do as his mind commanded. He watched her lower her head back to her knees. Her shoulders shook.

He danced and chanted the sacred words through the night and into the next day. Thirst taunted him. He prayed to *Wakan Tanka,* The Great Spirit, for strength to survive this test. To prove he belonged.

The hours passed one into another, each a blur of prayer, dancing and chanting. Blue prayed for a good hunt, for a mild winter, and before he realized it, he prayed for Amy to come to him as a woman comes to a man.

He turned to where she'd been watching. She was gone. He searched the crowd, but couldn't find her. His heart sank. *Was she waiting for him in their lodge? Or had she run away again and Blue unable to stop her?*

It was near sundown. Uncertain how many days had passed, beyond exhaustion and only wanting the ceremony to end, Blue heard Lone Dog stop singing. Those gathered grew quiet and Blue knew it was time for the completion of the ritual. Now he would prove he was a brother of the Lakota.

Lone Dog began to chant, his voice rising with each second that passed. Suddenly, Blue felt the leather thongs attached to his chest tighten. His heart raced. His teeth clamped together and his eyes squeezed shut. He was jerked off his feet and dangling in the air. A scream ripped from his throat before he could stop it as the bones tore out of his flesh. He fell to the ground in a quivering heap. Blood gushed from his shredded flesh onto the dirt and leaves. He lay silent, dazed, and unable to move.

Minutes later, his vision and mind cleared and he forced himself to his feet. He shook uncontrollably, barely able to stand. The crowd surged around him. They congratulated him and the others, now on their feet, too.

Pride washed over him. He'd done it. Now he'd have a voice among The People.

Wild Wolf stepped up beside Blue, a grin on his face.

"Here." He handed Blue a gourd of water. Blue put it to his lips and drank until Wild Wolf jerked it away.

"Not so much so fast, my friend. This will help." He poured the rest of the water over Blue's head. He gasped when the water hit his skin, but he quickly recovered, happy for the cold wetness that drenched him.

"Where's Amy?" he asked Wild Wolf when he could talk again.

Wild Wolf looked at Blue with concerned eyes.

"I watched her throughout the ceremony. She's strong, but she's not familiar with our ways. She tried to stay, but when the thongs were tightened..."

"Where is she?" Blue's heart pounded. "Did she go to our lodge?"

Jumping Bear laid his hand on Blue's shoulder.

"She is here and safe," he assured him. "She asked me to take her to your lodge." He chuckled under his breath then added. "All the while she mumbled about our heathen ritual. Go to her. She is waiting."

Blue left his friends behind and staggered from the Sun Dance circle, his legs as weak as a babes, even though adrenaline rushed through him like a raging river.

He pushed open the lodge flap, stepped inside and scanned the interior for Amy, anxious only to make sure she was safe. Then he would sleep.

She was curled up on her pallet. She jerked upright and wiped her face with her hands, but not before Blue saw her tears.

Cautious, he walked toward her. She looked at him, her eyes glimmering with more unshed tears.

He sat down beside her, every muscle in his body screaming at the movement. He reached out to touch her.

"Don't, Blue Fox. I can't bear to look at you, let alone allow you to touch me. You look so—so barbaric. I really thought you'd change your mind. Thought you'd come to your senses. Instead you let them tear your body apart. For what?"

"For what?" he asked, incredulous. "What I've been trying to do since I came here. Become a part of them. Today I proved I'm worthy. And I'm damn proud of it." He took a deep breath. Dried blood tore at his skin and pain raced through his body.

He looked at Amy's face. She was staring at him, looking at him like she'd never seen him before. Like the sight of him repulsed her. In finally realizing his dream to be accepted, Amy now saw him as a savage.

Anger surged through him. "Fine," he shouted. "If you loathe the sight of me so much, then leave me alone. I'm tired and I'm going to sleep. Go stay with Yellow Lodge Woman, I'm too tired and sore to care right now."

Her face pinched with anger. She shot up from the pallet, her hair wild around her face.

143

"All right, then. If that's what you want, I'm leaving." She stomped out of the lodge.

Blue knew he should go after her. Make her understand. But he was too tired and too weak. Exhaustion swept over him. Within seconds, he was asleep.

Blue slept throughout the night and into the next day. He woke groggy, sore and stiff, dried blood biting into his wounds. But none of that mattered. All that mattered was he find Amy.

He pushed up from the pallet and went outside. He found Wild Wolf a few minutes later.

"You are awake," his friend called. Laughter teased around his lips. "You look like a bear has dragged you from the forest for his supper."

"Where's Amy?" Blue asked, unmoved by his friend's joke.

Wild Wolf raised his hands. "She is fine, Blue Fox. She has not run away as you fear." He snickered and shook his head. "She is a wild one, that white woman. Stormed from your lodge last night shouting and raging like a hyena. Stomped around the village for hours before she finally asked Yellow Lodge Woman if she could sleep in her lodge. She does not approve of our ways, eh?" he asked, the teasing tone back in his voice.

Blue glared at Wild Wolf, in no mood for his jokes. He wanted to find Amy and throttle her. Make her understand the importance of what he'd done.

Wild Wolf clapped him on the back, which drew a long hiss from Blue when he jerked away.

He swayed on his feet, as he tried to get his bearings.

"Come, my friend. We will find Jumping Bear. We have something for you."

"But I need to find Amy."

"Pah. She will wait. Let her boil in her own anger. Perhaps Yellow Lodge Woman can help her understand why you danced."

"Maybe," Blue answered, uncertain he would ever understand Amy Ross or her fiery nature. "Maybe you're right. Let her worry about it for a while. Yes!" he shouted, suddenly puffed with male pride and ready to take on Amy and her unpredictable emotions.

"Let's go find Jumping Bear. I need to celebrate!"

Blue headed toward his mentor's lodge, a new feeling of pride guiding him.

Jumping Bear met them at the door and embraced Blue, who gasped and jerked away.

"The pain will pass, my friend," Jumping Bear said. "Soon you will display your scars with great pride."

"Soon won't be soon enough," Blue hissed through clenched teeth.

The two other men became serious.

"We wish to congratulate you on your accomplishment." Jumping Bear turned to Wild Wolf. They grinned at each other like a pair of weasels.

"What are you two up to?"

"I wish to give you a gift," Jumping Bear said. He disappeared around the side of the lodge, Wild Wolf smiled after him.

Blue caught his breath as Jumping Bear stepped to the front of the lodge, the reins of a horse in his hand.

"As you gave me one of your most precious gifts, I now return it to you as a symbol of my great respect." Seconds later, Blue's horse was in front of him, nudging him with his soft nose.

Stunned, Blue swallowed and tried to speak.

"Thank you, Jumping Bear. This gift I'll not forget."

"Ah, but that's not all," Jumping Bear continued, his tone solemn. "As you have come to The People and proven yourself to all, I now take you as my son, Blue Fox with Two Hearts."

Blue stared at his friend, unable to form the words to what he felt. Slowly, he stepped to the man who would claim him as a son. A Lakota warrior who accepted Blue for the man he was. Emotion raced through him. He ignored the hot pain that tore at his skin and threw his arms around Jumping Bear.

The discomfort of someone pounding on his back reminded him Wild Wolf was with them. He pushed away, ground at his misty eyes with a fist.

Wild Wolf beamed. "And I, Wild Wolf, take you as my brother-friend." The warrior reached his hand out to Blue.

Again, Blue was stunned into silence. He knew what a great honor Wild Wolf gave him. Someone who would be loyal beyond all others. Closer than brothers by blood. A brother by choice.

Again Blue disregarded the pain that tore through his chest and yanked Wild Wolf to him. He held him there while trying to regain his composure and form the words of gratitude.

Blue took a huge breath and pushed back from Wild Wolf. He smiled.

"These gifts I accept with a full heart, my father and my brother-friend. I'll protect them, and you, with my life."

They locked their arms together to form their own sacred circle.

In spite of his happiness, sadness washed over Blue. A new circle had been created. But it was incomplete without Amy.

Chapter Seventeen

Blue's wounds healed well. It'd been several weeks since the Sun Dance, and with Lone Dog's attention, the scabs on Blue's chest were more itchy than painful. He often mulled over the vision he'd seen before the dance, still uncertain what it meant.

Although he wanted Amy by his side, she remained distant. Every time he tried to touch her she shrank from him as if his hands were burning sticks. She'd done it again that morning. With clipped words and the turn of her back, she'd made him feel the gaping distance between them. So now he rode fast and far into the hills trying to get her soft skin and expressive eyes out of his mind.

He turned his horse between two narrow outcroppings of rock and entered a boxed canyon. It extended only about a half mile, but an outcropping of rocks at the far end caught his attention. Buzzards flew low above it. He rode toward them.

The dark rocks turned into four bloated bodies sprawled on the ground. Blue dismounted and put his hand over his nose and mouth to stifle the sickening smell of the decaying corpses. He batted at the ugly green flies scavenging the mounds of dead flesh.

White men. Scalped with various parts of their bodies mutilated. His attention was drawn to one form, vaguely familiar. The big man was lying face down, the arms and legs thrust away from his body. A dirty, cream-colored duster flapped at his ankles in the stiff wind. The size and thickness of his hands drew Blue's gaze.

He worked his way around the man, unable to touch or disturb any of them in their death rest. But he had to see for himself. *Could it be?* He stopped just above the man's head, bent down and looked at the face. Bile rose in his throat and he scrambled away as fast as he could. The eyes had been gouged out, but it was plain to see it was what remained of Sam Hollister.

Blue flopped down on a nearby rock and wiped the sweat that had beaded on his forehead and composed himself.

Vindication swept through him. He couldn't stop the yell bubbling up inside him from bursting out. He raised his fists in triumph.

"Got what you deserved you son-of-a-bitch!" he shouted. "Do you think I feel sorry for you? Not me. You got what you deserved."

He stared at the rotting carcass. Memories of what this man had done to him and his family raced through his mind. The smell and flies brought him back to reality. He mounted his horse and rode from the canyon—and never looked back.

His mind began to whirl. Now he could go home.

But where was home?

He thought of Ben and Sarah, of White Oaks and George, and what it had meant to him long ago. *Was that home? Or was home with the Lakota?* He felt the absence of his mother's gold ring on his finger. The same kind of gold that had brought people like Hollister to invade *Paha Sapa.*

Blue stopped his horse, confusion scrambling his thoughts. *Where do I belong? Among the whites, who take with no regard for others? Or among the Lakota, who will go to any lengths to protect what is theirs?*

His mind flashed to the Sun Dance and all he'd endured to prove he belonged among The People. As if in response to his thoughts, the wounds on his chest began to tingle.

He lifted his hands to the sky.

"Hear me, Great Spirit, I am To Shoon Henah Toh Cante Nupa, Blue Fox with Two Hearts, and I am Lakota. This is my home." He rode for the village. *His* village.

Blue rode into camp and wanted nothing more than to go straight to his lodge and eat, but tension in the air around camp gave him a feeling something had happened in his absence. Instead of the lazy time of the afternoon when people rested and ate, they stood in small groups and talked excitedly. Blue stopped his horse beside Jumping Bear's lodge, anxious to learn the reason for the tension around camp.

"There you are." Jumping Bear pushed out of his lodge. "I've been looking for you. Spotted Tail has sent for you."

"Why would a chief like Spotted Tail ask for me?"

"A great council between The People and the whites has been called on the White River. Spotted Tail sent a runner to our village today while you were away. He asked our chief if there was a warrior among us who could speak the white man's words. You were chosen, Blue Fox."

Blue was dumbfounded. This was a great honor. One bestowed only on a true warrior of the Lakota. His chest puffed with pride.

"I am honored to do this thing for Spotted Tail and the Lakota."

"We leave in the morning."

"I don't understand." Amy watched Blue roll his pack. "Why do you have to go?" She paused then threw out, "Besides...they should just sell the land and be done with it." Her tone was flip, as though speaking of something of little or no value.

Blue whirled on her. "You can't mean that? The land is everything to them. It's their life. Everything they have comes from the land. Whether it's food, shelter or clothing, the land provides it."

She sighed and crossed her arms under her breasts.

"I only know that if they don't sell it, there'll be trouble. You can bet on it. They might as well just sell it and finish it before there's bloodshed." She plopped down on the fur pallet and shook her head, her mass of red curls glittering in the firelight.

"You know if there's gold here, no amount of talking is going to keep white men out," she added.

Blue nodded. She knew what she was talking about regarding the white man and his gold. She voiced his concerns quite accurately. Amy wasn't an empty-headed female who didn't know a lick about life.

Blue sat down beside her. He heard her quick intake of breath. Anger ripped through him. She was still afraid of him. Or repulsed by him—he didn't know. Hadn't she learned yet he had no intention of harming her or going to her as a man until she was ready?

He pushed his anger aside.

"What you say is true, Amy. I feel the same way, to a certain extent. But the land is their life. They won't just give it away. Unfortunately, it may come to blood being spilled before this is over."

"And if your blood is shed, who will you bleed for? The Indian or the white man?" Her tone was hard, her eyes accusing.

Blue couldn't answer her question. He didn't know the answer. He couldn't choose, but knew he was going to do whatever it took to keep it from happening. And that was why he was going now to the council.

Blue reached out to touch Amy's arm, but stopped and let his hand fall into his lap.

"I'll be back soon. Maybe this meeting will solve some problems."

"Is that possible?"

Silence filled the lodge.

Thousands of Lakota, Cheyenne and Arapaho awaited the arrival of United States government representatives to discuss the problem in the Black Hills.

Blue surveyed the different tribes clustered together along the Smoky Earth River, known to the whites as the White River, the chosen site for the meeting between the Indians and Bluecoats. The headmen of many tribes had banded together to formally protest the invasion of *Paha Sapa,* their sacred land, to the Great Father, the president of the United States. After being turned away many times, a council was finally called so their protests could be heard.

From his vantage point beneath the huge tent erected to shield the representatives from the hot rays of the sun, Blue scanned the crowd. Earlier in the day most of the Indians gathered had expressed, in absolute terms, they would not give up *Paha Sapa.* It was as simple as that. They were angry the treaty of 1868 was being broken and many were willing to fight to retain their land.

Blue watched dust swirl high into the September sky as the commissioners arrived. Their escort, a hundred or more cavalrymen, all rode in on snow-white horses. Blue shielded his

150

eyes against the sun as the soldiers dismounted and stood at attention beside their mounts to the rear of the canopy. A conveyance pulled to the front of the structure. Several men in long-tailed suits and top hats stepped into the tent and greeted the chiefs who waited there.

Blue stood beside Chief Spotted Tail, elected spokesman for all the tribes.

Before the meeting could begin, Blue heard the thunder of hooves in the distance. From the crest of a hill not far away, a great cloud of dust rose into the clear blue sky. Out of the cloud emerged a band of warriors, all dressed for war. Their ponies raced toward the council tent, the rider's rifles raised, their black hair whipping around bronzed shoulders. Blue held his breath, uncertain of their intent. He turned to the waiting soldiers. All stood ready, their eyes fixed on the approaching Indians, hands ready on their weapons.

The warriors reached the tent and circled. Blue jumped as the warriors fired their rifles into the sky. The braves taunted the commissioners for several minutes until with one final, ear-shattering war whoop, they gathered behind the cavalrymen to the rear of the commissioners.

A larger band of Indians appeared from the other side of the hill and headed toward the tent, circling as the others had done.

Then came another.

Blue realized what was happening. He relaxed and chuckled under his breath. The chiefs were giving the Bluecoats a united show of strength.

He scanned the restless soldiers and his heart thrummed as he looked for one face. George. Where else would they send a trained soldier but to Indian Territory?

Blue didn't spot his friend and he exhaled the breath he'd been holding.

Reminded of where he was by the arrival of more warriors, Blue scanned the area around the tent. The commissioners and cavalrymen were surrounded by thousands of Indians. With great ceremony the last of the chiefs joined Spotted Tail in a semi-circle in front of the sweaty, shaking white men.

One commissioner mopped his brow with a handkerchief; another glanced from one side to the other and eyed the Indians surrounding them. Soldiers moved from foot to foot, sweat beading their foreheads.

Several minutes of strained silence passed. Finally, one of the government representatives stood and stepped forward. He cleared his throat and spoke, his words translated by Blue.

"We have come to ask if you are willing to give our people the right to mine for minerals in the Black Hills." The commissioner stroked his chin, nervous. "As long as gold or other valuable minerals are found, we will pay a fair and just sum. If you are so willing, we will make a bargain with you for this right. When the gold or other valuable minerals are taken away, the country will again be yours to dispose of in any manner you may wish."

Blue couldn't believe his ears. This had to be a joke. Could they actually be asking the Indians to rent them the Black Hills and when they were through stripping the gold and other valuable minerals, they'd give them back?

He watched Spotted Tail's face as he translated the words for him. The chief showed no emotion. He pondered a moment then spoke.

"Would you lend me a mule on such terms?" he asked the commissioner through Blue.

The white man's chest puffed up and he straightened his back.

"It will be hard for the government to keep the whites out of the hills," the man said. "To try to do so will give you and our government great trouble, because the whites that may wish to go there are very numerous."

The commissioner pointed west. "There is another country lying far toward the setting sun, over which you roam and hunt, and which territory is yet unceded, extending to the summit of the Bighorn Mountains. It does not seem to be of very great value or use to you, and our people think they would like to have a portion of it."

Blue grew angrier as each word was translated. These people offered to rent the land, strip it, then give it back when they were through. But that wasn't enough. Now, they wanted the Bighorn Mountains, too.

By the time Blue finished his translation he was furious. The representative's words rushed through the crowd of braves assembled and the air grew charged with energy.

An Indian rider approached and jerked his mount to a halt before the assemblage of commissioners. He dismounted and pushed his way through the assembled braves toward the commissioner who spoke.

"I come with a message from the great Lakota Chief, Red Cloud, Blue translated. He seeks a week for our chiefs to hold their own councils and discuss terms offered by the Bluecoats."

The representatives conferred. Their heads bobbed up and down and back and forth, voices raised one moment and hushed the next.

"We grant three days," the speaker said with a flourish of self-importance. He wrapped his fingers around the lapels of his jacket.

The chiefs discussed his offer and accepted. The council would resume in three days.

Blue rode back to camp with a bad feeling in the pit of his stomach. They asked too much, these white men.

At the Red Cloud Agency where the chiefs had gathered to discuss the situation, Blue listened to them argue about what was to become of their land. They shouted, one chief trying to be heard above the other. Most swore they wouldn't give up a single pinch of dust or blade of grass within their territory without a fight. Blue's skin pricked with foreboding.

"We will not give our last hunting grounds to the whites!" one angry elder shouted with a raised fist.

"When will they stop?" asked another. "When all that was once ours is theirs?"

More shouting erupted. Spotted Tail raised his hand for silence.

"We will not allow *Paha Sapa* to be taken by the whites. This we have already decided. It will be discussed no further. But, we must choose whether to allow them to mine the precious metal that has been found in *Paha Sapa*. They will pay us four hundred thousand of their dollars for each year they mine our land. Shall we take their offer?"

"No!" most shouted in unison. "We will not sell our land or allow them to use it for any price."

Another of the headmen spoke. "If the white man is going to come on our land anyway, and we cannot prevent it without the spilling of blood, why not allow them to take what it is they seek and profit from it?" He looked around the room. "But we must make them pay to take their precious yellow gold."

More yelling erupted as those who wanted to fight argued with those who tried to make them see reason in accepting the offer.

Blue watched in silence as the men argued, understanding hard lines were being drawn. Finally, he stood and sought recognition to speak.

"I am Blue Fox with Two Hearts, son of Morning Flower Woman and nephew of Man-Who-Runs, Dog Society chief of the Brule. Before I came to The People, I lived among the whites. I've seen how they are." He stopped to study the faces around him, watched them harden and watched them nod.

"I've proven myself worthy of being called a brother of the Lakota, so now you must listen to me. If we do not give the whites access to our land, they'll come and take it anyway. Many more will follow. Like the locust, they'll bring a famine on the land. And they'll never leave."

Chiefs and headmen jumped to their feet and shook their fists at him. Others sadly nodded agreement.

"For this reason, I say we should accept the commissioners' offer. If we make them pay to mine the gold, at least the blood of our warriors won't stain the land. And we'll be able to use the great wealth we receive to feed and clothe our people."

"With white man's food and clothing!" an angry chief shouted.

"But at least we won't starve or freeze to death when we're driven farther and farther north into the cold country. Because that's what will happen, no matter what we do." Blue hoped to make them understand it was fruitless to go against the will of the United States government.

He scanned the angry faces and added, "And when the gold is gone, they'll leave our land. It'll no longer interest them."

Men shouted to be heard above the din. Blue's heart raced. He had to make them understand. If they chose to fight it would mean their destruction. There were too few warriors and too much gold to turn the white man away.

Blue turned to speak to Spotted Tail, but the chief's raised hand stopped the words in Blue's throat.

"I have heard your words, Blue Fox with Two Hearts. They are wise words. We will discuss them further." The old chief waved his hand and left the council. The other elders followed in silence.

Three days later, the Indians and commissioners returned to the council tent on the river. But this time, the white representatives were escorted by a much larger contingency of cavalrymen.

Tension rode the air as the chiefs, now including the great Lakota Chief Red Cloud, gathered before the commissioners. Red Cloud stood to address the white men, but before he got a chance to speak, rifle fire resounded from the rear of the gathering.

Blue tried to see what was happening. Several hundred Oglala braves had broken away from the crowd and trotted their ponies toward the council tent. They lowered their guns and began to chant.

"The Black Hills is my land and I love it; And whoever interferes; Will hear this gun." They raised their rifles for everyone to see.

Blue's mind churned with warning. The soldiers stood at attention beside their mounts, their fingers tight around their gun stocks. But Blue saw their uneasiness. All it would take was one wrong move and this meeting would erupt in devastating chaos.

The Oglala stopped several hundred yards beyond the tent. A rider broke away and raced his horse toward the chiefs and commissioners beneath the tarpaulin. He was stripped to the waist for battle and wore a revolver on each hip.

"I am Little Big Man! I speak these words for the great chief Tashunka Witko, Crazy Horse." He scanned those around him, disdain on his face. "I will kill the first chief who speaks for selling the Black Hills!" He jerked on the reins of his prancing horse. The animal reared and Little Big Man raised his lance in the air.

Other warriors surged from the crowd and surrounded Little Big Man, forcing him away from the chiefs and commissioners. Before he rode away he shouted, "Do not forget. By Crazy Horse's decree, I will kill the first chief who agrees to sell the Black Hills!"

He jerked the reins and the horse reared again. Little Big Man whirled the animal around and raced away, the other Oglala behind him.

Blue realized the commissioners had no idea what the Indian had shouted and he quickly translated. The chiefs were already milling around with uncertainty, and now the commissioners joined them.

After a heated discussion between the white representatives and the soldiers, the commissioners' conveyances were called to return them to the safety of Camp Robinson.

They boarded the vehicles and hurried away leaving behind a cloud of churning dust as they disappeared overland, the troops close behind.

Hours later, the Lakota and Cheyenne returned to their own lands, and Blue headed to his village with a heavy heart. Absolutely nothing had been decided between the Lakota and the white men.

Regardless of the course of the day's events, anticipation filled Blue at the thought of seeing Amy. He'd left her in Wild Wolf's protection, but only after extracting her solemn vow she wouldn't try to run away. And Wild Wolf, through a barely concealed smile, had sworn he'd watch her like the cunning wolf he was.

He entered his lodge and scanned the interior. She wasn't there. Panic seized him. He ran into the village in search of Wild Wolf.

Blue found his brother-friend with Yellow Lodge Woman.

"You have returned." Wild Wolf rose.

"Where's Amy?" He nodded briefly to Yellow Lodge Woman before he looked back to Wild Wolf.

"Do not worry over a woman," Wild Wolf chided so Yellow Lodge Woman could hear. "You have more important things to speak of. Tell me of the council."

"Not now. Where's Amy?"

Wild Wolf sighed in exasperation. "She is with Jumping Bear." The brave turned his back on Blue in dismissal.

Blue walked to Jumping Bear's lodge just as Amy was leaving it.

"Amy," he shouted. When she turned to him, joy and relief flashed across her face. But it only lasted a moment before the heavy veil of indignation dropped over her eyes.

"Well, it's about time. If you intend to keep me here, you could at least stay here with me."

He stepped in front of her and gazed at the woman who, with her fire and courage, held him captive as much as he did her. He wanted her near him. Even if her words were like barbs every time she spoke.

"And what are you grinning at?" she asked.

"I missed you." His smile widened. Her eyes softened and for a moment, he felt compelled to kiss her.

"You, you must be hungry," she said, breaking the spell. She headed for his lodge. "And Jumping Bear wants you to tell the elders about the council as soon as you can."

Blue followed her, feeling like a puppy and doing her bidding, but enjoying it nonetheless.

Several days later, Wild Wolf brought a rider to Blue's lodge.

"Spotted Tail has sent word you are to come to the Red Cloud Agency again to speak the words of the white man," the rider said. "The white commissioners wish to parley there, afraid to gather at the river. Will you come?"

"Of course."

"I'll ride with you," Wild Wolf offered. "But first, I will see to this rider's food and shelter." The two men left the lodge and Blue turned to Amy.

Her eyes flashed with green lightning and her face flushed red with anger.

"Why do you have to go running off to translate whenever they ask?" Her hand were splayed on her hips. "Don't they have anyone else?"

Blue shook his head. "I want to do it, it's a great honor to speak for Spotted Tail. I offered him my services at the beginning of all this and I intend to see it through. Besides," he reached for her but she jerked away.

"Besides," he continued, "I might be able to help. I want to stop the bloodshed before it starts if I can. I thought you understood that."

What he couldn't understand was her anger. "Why are you so upset?" She was acting like a wife, yet she couldn't abide his touch.

"Why, you ask? I'll tell you why," she shouted. "Because when you go, I'm left here under someone's protection. I can't even take care of—business, without someone watching over me."

"You know the reason for that."

"I promised when you left last time I wouldn't try and run away. Isn't my word good enough for you?" Her hands were balled in little fists now and reminded him of Sarah when she was angry.

"If I promise not to leave you in Jumping Bear's care, will you promise not to run away?" He held his breath. *Could he trust her? Would she try to run away as soon as he left?* He couldn't bear that thought.

"Yes. I promise. Just come back as fast as you can." Her face flushed redder. "I'm out of place when I'm here alone."

He couldn't stop himself from pulling her into his arms. She was soft against him, but stiffened as he drew her closer. He looked down into her eyes, lowered his head.

She turned her face to the side.

"No," she whispered, breathless.

He pushed her away and strode from the lodge. Spotted Tail and the other chiefs needed him. Amy, obviously, didn't.

"We have listened to your words. I grow tired," Spotted Tail said to the commissioners. "You will make your offer in writing."

The old chief rose and walked from the room, the other chiefs behind him.

"He's being unreasonable," one of the commissioners shouted, the words echoing off the barren walls of the room the chiefs and commissioners were gathered in.

"I told you they wouldn't sell. At any price," yelled another. "We're wasting our time."

"No, we'll make the offer in writing, if that's what he wants. They'll accept it, too, or they'll regret it," the man who spoke for all the commissioners said, his tone menacing.

Blue stepped in front of the three arguing men.

"You heard his words. Give your offer in writing." Blue left the building, Wild Wolf behind him.

Outside Blue stopped. "I can't believe what's happening," he said to his friend.

Wild Wolf nodded. "The elders are wise. They will not sell our sacred land. Maybe they'll allow the white men to come in and mine their gold, but they won't sell *Paha Sapa.* This I promise you."

"But what if they don't accept the offer for mining rights? What then?" Blue didn't really want to hear Wild Wolf's answer.

"Then we will fight."

Blue and Wild Wolf were resting in their assigned room when summoned again. Blue entered the headquarter building and took his place beside Spotted Tail, Wild Wolf beside him.

A paper was placed in front of Blue. Slowly, he translated the words printed on it.

"They have offered four hundred thousand dollars a year for mineral rights or six million dollars for the outright sale of *Paha Sapa.*" Blue waited for Spotted Tail's reaction, his throat tight.

The elder chief stood and faced the commissioners.

"I have heard your offer." He surveyed the anxious faces of the white men in front of him. "The Black Hills are not for sale or lease. I will speak of it no more."

Blue finished translating Spotted Tail's words as the chief exited the building, the other chiefs close behind him.

"You can't just walk out of here," one commissioner yelled.

"We aren't finished," another shouted. "We'll come up with another offer."

The others merely looked on, helpless. Some stroked their beards or slumped back in their chairs, shaking their heads and exhaling in defeat.

Blue thought back over all that had transpired in the last weeks. The great meeting of the two nations; the Indian's display of power and strength. He recalled the words of Little Big Man and the chiefs' absolute final refusal to sell *Paha Sapa.*

He turned to Wild Wolf whose face was tight with concern. Blue forced a smile for his friend.

"What will you do if war comes to our land?" Wild Wolf asked.

"I don't know," Blue muttered. "I just don't know."

How would he fight? With the Lakota or against them? He knew in his heart he couldn't raise a weapon against his brother-friend. *But dear God could he kill whites? George?* He prayed to God and the Great Spirit he wouldn't be forced to make that choice.

All he did know was the ominous feeling in the pit of his belly. If it did come to war, it would be the beginning of the end of the great Lakota nation.

Chapter Eighteen

Blue rode beside Amy at the rear line of horses hauling travois' laden with The People's possessions. Women and children walked in silence, snuggled deep in their furs to ward off the bitter cold.

"Where, exactly, are we going?" Amy drew a fur blanket closer around her neck.

"To our winter camp. There's been talk throughout the village that we'll settle near Crazy Horse and his people at Bear Butte." He watched her face become alarmed with the mention of the war chief's name.

"Don't be afraid, we're only going to camp near his people, not with them. For protection," he added.

"Protection?" she asked. "From what?"

"White men."

Camp was established and soon the village buzzed with excitement. Wild Wolf and Yellow Lodge Woman were to be married. He had offered many horses for her and her father had finally accepted. But everyone in the village knew it was she who had finally accepted, not her father.

Blue shuffled around Wild Wolf's lodge. He inspected his friend, made sure every detail was perfect.

"You're ready." Blue brushed a fleck of dirt from Wild Wolf's buckskin shirt decorated with white quill beads and buffalo hair. Buckskin leggings with fringes along the length of both legs matched his shirt. Knee high moccasins with more porcupine quill beads covered his legs. A lone eagle feather woven into his shoulder-length, raven black hair, completed his attire.

"Yes, my friend. I am ready. I have waited a long time to take Yellow Lodge Woman as my wife."

"I know." Blue could barely hide his humor.

"You laugh at my expense," Wild Wolf teased back. "But now that she has finally agreed, I'll be a good husband to her." He looked at Blue.

"When you first came to our village, Yellow Lodge Woman looked favorably at you." He held up his hand to keep Blue from interrupting. "That is another reason why it was hard for me to accept you. The woman who held my heart had eyes for you."

"But you know I never returned Yellow Lodge Woman's affection. She's always been like any one of the other maidens in the village. She was never more than a friend."

"I know this—now," Wild Wolf admitted. "But then my eyes were too clouded with hatred to see what was really in your heart." He placed his hand on Blue's shoulder. "And it is obvious to everyone who is in *your* heart."

Blue heaved a sigh. "This is true Wild Wolf. Since the second I laid eyes on her. But she doesn't return my affection."

"Perhaps you should just take her, make her yours because you are the first," Wild Wolf said. "And because it is your right as the Lakota brave who took her from the Crow."

"Sure, I'll take her like you did Yellow Lodge Woman?" Blue retorted with a smile.

Wild Wolf chuckled. "You're right. I wanted Yellow Lodge Woman to come to me of her own will. I didn't want to take her and have her hate me. The wait is worth the prize my friend." Wild Wolf clapped Blue on the shoulder.

"But now it is time for us to go. It is my wedding day. My bride waits."

Blue and Wild Wolf met the wedding party outside Wild Wolf's lodge. A small crowd gathered to witness the joining. Wild Wolf took Tipiziwin's hand and listened as Lone Dog spoke to them. During the recitation Blue glanced around for Amy. She was nowhere in sight.

Lone Dog droned on and Yellow Lodge Woman's eyes strayed to Blue. They lingered only a brief second, but long enough for Blue to see the longing there.

Minutes later, the brief ceremony over, the couple disappeared into Wild Wolf's lodge. Gifts were left outside and the feast began.

But Blue didn't feel like celebrating. He was happy for his friend, but Amy's absence at the ceremony made him feel an emptiness he couldn't deny. A part of him was missing. Until Amy became his he wouldn't feel whole.

The next morning a light snow covered the mountains where the village had relocated. Fires blazed constantly to warm the confines of the lodges.

But fire of another kind burned inside Blue. All night he'd been unable to sleep, thinking of Wild Wolf and Yellow Lodge Woman alone in their lodge. Each time his eyes strayed to Amy he envisioned her beside him, beneath him, his lips covering hers.

Morning light filtered into the tipi and he stared at her slumbering face. As though hearing his thoughts, her eyes opened. She held his gaze for a brief second before she turned away, pulled on her moccasins, rose from her pallet, and threw a heavy fur over her shoulders.

Blue watched her every movement, aching to touch her. To lay her down in the soft furs and show her how much he loved her. How much he ached for her. He reached for her as she passed him, but she jerked to a stop and wouldn't look at him before she hurried from the lodge. His hand fell like a stone. He turned away, grabbed an empty bowl and hurled it across the lodge. It thudded against the thick hide wall with a hollow sound. The sound of his heart.

Minutes later Blue stepped outside and found her bundled tight in her furs beside a small creek on the perimeter of the village. She wanted to leave. To go home. He could tell in everything she said and did. And although she hadn't tried to escape in a long time, he knew she wasn't happy. His heart sang with joy whenever she was near. But hers didn't. She avoided him whenever possible.

The few times she did laugh, his heart soared. But as soon as he showed her the least affection, she pulled away, her mood somber and withdrawn again.

He tugged the buffalo hide closer around his neck, walked up and plopped down on a rock beside her.

He listened to the deafening silence around them. Only the trickle of the nearly frozen stream disturbed the tranquility of the countryside. Finally, he couldn't stand the quiet any longer.

"Do you want to leave so badly?" he asked, his heart like a hundred pound weight in his chest.

"Oh, Blue. There's so much you don't understand."

"Then explain it to me."

"I can't." She shrugged deeper into her fur.

"Why not? Why can't you tell me?"

He jumped up from the rock, grabbed her shoulders and jerked her up in front of him.

"Why?" he shouted. "Because I'm a dirty half-breed? Is that it?"

He watched fear creep into her eyes as he drew closer, but ignored it. He was hot with want and need. He needed to taste her, to hold her.

"I've wanted to kiss you into understanding how I feel about you since the moment I saw you." He pressed his lips hungrily against hers. His arms circled her and his loins heated with passion. He wanted her more than he'd wanted anything in his life. His embrace tightened and she seemed to respond. But as always, she began to struggle.

She tore her mouth free, wrenching him back to his senses. Her hands shoved at his chest.

"No. Don't, please don't," she pleaded.

He released her and she ran. Her sobs carried on the air long after she'd gone and left Blue hurt and more confused than ever.

Emotionally confused, Blue returned to his lodge. He didn't care that Amy wasn't there. He didn't care if he never saw her again. He lay down on his pallet and fell asleep. The sun was high in the sky when he woke. A fire burned in the center pit and stew bubbled in a pot over it.

Amy was on her pallet mending her skirt with pieces from the inside hem. The bone needle in her hand was shaking when her eyes darted to his. She looked away when they met.

Blue's stomach tightened. He couldn't keep doing this to himself. She was never going to care for him. He had to accept that fact. They were two different people from two different worlds.

Full realization hit him. He had to take her back to her own people when the weather broke. She would never belong here the way he wanted her to. No matter how much he loved her.

He turned away at the thought of losing her, unable to consider the pain it would bring.

Her soft cry made him look back. She was sucking her finger.

Blue went to her.

"I pricked myself with the needle." She pulled her finger out of her mouth and the blood swelled.

Blue took her hand into his and felt her pulse quicken, but she didn't stiffen as she had before. He watched her face for signs of fear or distrust and raised her finger to his lips. He licked the blood then guided her finger into his mouth while he studied her face. Gently, he sucked.

Her breath became short. Her chest rose and fell. Her eyes grew wide. But still she didn't pull away.

Blue's mind raced. He withdrew her finger from his mouth, but didn't release her hand. Her eyes locked with his, and she made no attempt to draw away from him.

"Thank you," she whispered. "I'm such a dolt."

"No." He shook his head. "No dolt, just beautiful in the firelight. Your eyes dance with its flames."

She looked away, trembling. He had her hand in his grip. With his other hand he guided her face back to his.

He leaned toward her and waited for the first sign of rejection. Her pulse raced, her breath quickened, but she remained steady. Slowly, he moved closer until his lips brushed hers as lightly as a feather.

Her breath caught, but she didn't jerk away. He cupped the back of her neck and drew her close. She melted against him, a short sigh escaping, but she offered no resistance.

Again his lips found hers, gentle but firm. He guided her down on the pallet, cradled her head while his other hand stroked her neck and jaw line. Still she didn't resist, although he felt her chest pound against him with every breath.

He drew away from her mouth and brushed his lips along the side of her face to the lobes of her ear. He felt her stiffen and readied himself for her dismissal, prepared for the anger her rejection would cause. But it didn't come. Instead, she took a deep breath—and relaxed.

He gazed down at her. Her eyes were closed, but she didn't seem frightened. She just waited.

He ran his thumb over her shoulder, up along her neck and down her chin, her skin as soft as the petal of a flower. She shivered. Slowly, he moved his lips back to her mouth. He kissed her gently at first then with the passion he'd withheld for months, forcing her lips open. Warmth exploded through him. The liquid softness of her called to him. He probed and teased her interior. Blue almost shouted with joy when her tongue teased back.

Slowly, her arms circled his shoulders and she drew him closer. A soft sound issued from her throat. He thought he'd go mad with wanting her.

He ravaged her lips with all his pent up emotions. She seemed for a moment to change her mind and Blue held his breath, but at his gentle insistence, she gave in and drew him to her again.

Their mouths and tongues melded until he could stand it no longer, his breechclout swollen with his passion. He moved back and looked into her face. Her eyes were still closed and small tears gathered at the corners. *Tears of joy or regret?* But he was too far gone in his passion to want the answer to that question.

He stripped off his shirt then leaned down to free her of her blouse. She trembled when his hands touched her neck, but she didn't push him away. He undid the buttons and removed the blouse from her shoulders, baring the creamy flesh around her chemise.

"Open your eyes. I want you to look at me." Blue ran his hands over the soft flesh at the hollow of her neck and shoulder.

She shook her head. "I can't." Her voice was feather soft.

"Why?" Fear rose sharp in his belly. *Afraid she couldn't look at his Indian face as he made love to her? Afraid seeing him would bring her to her senses?*

"No questions, please, Blue Fox. Just love me."

166

Her hands drew him to her. Her heat seared his lips as he touched her smooth skin. His tongue laved her shoulders, neck, and face until he could stand the sweet torture no longer.

He stripped off his breechclout and her skirt to expose more of the ivory flesh that curved down her finely shaped thighs to her feet. She exhaled on a soft sigh as his hand roamed the contours of her body and his eyes drank her in.

He unfastened the ribbons of the chemise that held her from him, slowly removing it to expose her bare skin to the firelight.

"You are truly beautiful, Amy," he whispered, his throat tight.

He rose above her and positioned himself between her legs. He must go slow, but his need was almost unbearable. He took a deep breath and forced himself to slow down.

He kissed her stomach and worked his way up. He licked and nipped at her body until the rosy peaks of her breasts stood firm and beckoned him. He took her left breast into his mouth and suckled, while he rolled and fondled the other between his fingers. She arched her back to give him more of herself. She moaned with pleasure and moved beneath him, but not from fear, he was certain. She moaned again and he nearly lost his resolve to be gentle.

He moved to her right breast, bringing it to a rosy, full peak as he sucked and laved and teased.

Her fingers tore at his back and drew him closer. He used his knee to part her legs. Carefully, he positioned himself to enter, aware he would hurt her with the first full thrust, yet hoping he could quickly assuage her pain with pleasure.

She was wet and ready for him, writhing, and her motion drove him crazy. He worked his way inside her soft, yielding body. Deeper and deeper until he was fully imbedded.

Beyond coherent thought, he pounded into her, over and over. She cried out his name and he tried to withdraw, afraid he'd hurt her. But she clawed at his back, drew him closer.

"Please," she whispered.

His resolve snapped. He drove into her with all the passion he'd kept inside these long months. He cried out her

167

name and she answered with his. He'd never felt such joy before in his life.

He withdrew, thrust into her. Withdrew and thrust into her again. He felt the explosion building within him.

Her body tightened around him. She scratched his back.

They reached the pinnacle together, calling each other's names in their sweet ascent to heaven.

His passion spent, he collapsed on top of her, his mind dizzy. She quivered. He looked down at her. Huge tears streamed down her still impassioned cheeks and she turned away.

He rolled off her. Great, gasping sobs erupted from her throat as she curled into a ball beside him.

"Why are you crying?" His heart was breaking. "Talk to me, Amy. Tell me why you're crying."

She wouldn't answer. Just shook her head and cried harder.

He jumped up from the pallet and anger replaced passion. He stalked around the lodge, his fury growing with each stride.

"Are you crying because you gave yourself to a breed?" he accused.

He stalked back to her and rolled her onto her back so he could see her face. Her red, puffed eyes pleaded for understanding. Unable to resist her silent plea he pulled her into his chest. Her arms circled his neck and she clung to him, exhausting her tears.

"Are you ashamed of what we did, Amy?"

She looked up at him and her head shook gently.

"No, Blue. I'm not ashamed. I'm relieved and happy it's finally happened, but I'm not ashamed. Not like the other time." She buried her face in his chest.

"Other time?" he repeated. The words hit him like a blow. "What do you mean? Other time." Only then did he remember he hadn't encountered a barrier when he entered her. Only then did he realize he wasn't the first.

She lifted sad eyes to meet his. "Remember when I first came here how I told you we barely survived after the war? How the Yankees came and took everything?" She swallowed hard. "One thing they took was my innocence."

Blue stared, afraid to hear the rest of the story, afraid of his own emotions.

She sat up, smoothed a fur across her lap and continued.

"When I was thirteen years old the taxes came due on the little house we lived in. Papa was too proud to let Mama know he didn't have the money, so he tried to come up with it by himself. But he couldn't. A Yankee carpetbagger offered to pay the overdue taxes that would save our home and Papa's little remaining honor. But at what cost?" She turned tortured eyes to Blue.

"Me. He traded me for our run down hovel that was lost in a fire along with the only thing I truly loved in this world. Mama." She wiped her cheeks with her fingers.

"Mama never found out, thank the Lord, but since that time, I've not been able to tolerate the stares of men, let alone their touch, without my skin feeling like vermin were crawling all over it. I learned to hate my father for what he'd sold me for. His damnable pride." Her eyes pleaded for understanding.

"That's why when Papa was killed, I didn't grieve overmuch. He'd hurt me more than he ever knew, all for his damnable honor." Her voice sounded flat and Blue felt a tremor of guilt wash through him. Then rage welled in his stomach for the ill use of this girl.

"And me?" he asked, still uncertain of her answer.

"It's never been about what you are, Blue. Not the fact that you're a half-breed, anyway." She touched his hand and looked deep into his eyes. "It's just been about you being a man. Plain and simple."

He held her quietly and wished his arms could take away the hurt she'd experienced.

"If you hated your father so much, why did you go with him to the Black Hills?" he asked.

"What else did I have? No respectable young man would have me. What would he have gotten? No dowry, no land, not even a virgin. Nothing—except a broken old man and a bitter woman to saddle him for the rest of his life. No, I don't think many young men would have taken up that challenge."

169

"I would have," Blue whispered.

Tears sprang to Amy's eyes and she touched Blue's cheek. Willingly and without hesitation, she gave herself to him again.

***

Blue stepped from the warm lodge into the cold winter air, still so happy he felt almost drunk. He flung his arms out to embrace the sun and said his morning prayers to *Wakan Tanka,* thanking him for finally bringing Amy to him. He drifted back to the night before and his insides warmed. His circle was now complete. Amy was within it. *What more could a man ask for?* He had everything he wanted. He was accepted among The People and he could now hold the woman of his heart in his arms.

I'm happy here, he thought looking around him— happier than he'd been, even at White Oaks.

Wild Wolf approached and cocked his head at Blue's obvious good mood, but he quickly became solemn. "We've been summoned to the council lodge."

"Then let's go." Blue threw his arm over the shoulders of an astonished Wild Wolf. Today nothing could dampen his mood. The two headed for the lodge.

The braves filed in, Blue and Wild Wolf behind them.

"Come. Sit." Blue removed his fur covering from his shoulders and sat down beside his chief.

The man turned old eyes to Blue. His dark skin sagged around his cheeks and jaw and his long hair was streaked with gray.

"A runner has come through camp with news from the Great Father. He brings words for those of us who do not stay within the boundaries of the reservations. The Great Father says we must go to the agencies by the end of the Moon When Snow Drifts into the Tepees. That is only days from now." He glanced around the lodge.

"This we cannot do," he continued to nods of agreement from the others gathered. "For the snow and cold would kill our young and old alike. Even if we were to leave on the rising of the next sun, our ponies could not trod through the snow and reach Camp Robinson by then."

170

Mumbling started among those assembled, but Blue remained silent.

"The runner has also spoken these words to Crazy Horse, camped many miles to the north. He told the runner to return to the Great Father and say The People could not come until the cold went away."

Blue felt a sudden sense of urgency. *How would those who didn't reach Camp Robinson by the deadline be punished? They couldn't possibly take their women, children, and old ones, let alone the livestock, into the raging blizzards of winter and be expected to live. What were they to do?*

Everyone spoke at once, the council lodge echoing with angry voices. The old chief raised his hand and silence descended, a heavy silence laden with anger.

"We cannot reach the agency by the time the Great Father has told us. We must wait for the cold to end before we take our people to Camp Robinson. This I have also told the runner to tell the Great Father. This I now tell you. We will wait until the Moon When the Green Grass Is Up and return with Crazy Horse and Sitting Bull. And not before."

The chief pushed himself from the floor, donned his heavy robes and left the lodge.

Shouting erupted among those who remained. *They were on their own land, not bothering anyone. Why had they been ordered to Camp Robinson?* Many shouted to ignore the Great Father's words while others wanted to do as was commanded to preserve the peace. A tenuous peace—at best.

Days later winter turned brutal. Blizzards sent snow and ice swirling across the land, while bitter temperatures forced the villagers to seek refuge inside their lodges. Fires burned constantly and extra hides were worn against the frigid wind and biting cold.

But inside Blue's lodge, a fire burned brighter than sticks or logs could fuel.

Amy dished out the stew she'd prepared, but Blue wasn't interested in food. He wanted only her. Taking the bowl she offered, he set it aside then grabbed her hand to draw her to him.

In the sweetest, most innocent southern drawl she could muster she said, "Why Blue Fox, what on this earth do you have in mind?" Her hand clutched her chest and her lashes fluttered. "I do believe you have a mind to seduce me."

Blue growled deep in his chest before he covered her mouth with his. His tongue swept inside her sweet recesses to tease and joust with hers. But she gave as good as she got as her tongue slashed and mated with his. His body enflamed with desire, he ran a finger across her cheek and down her neck. "I have a mind *and* a body I plan to seduce you with my dear southern belle. And there will be no escaping." Since the day she'd finally let him take her as a woman, she'd been as responsive to his touch as Blue could have ever imagined or hoped for. She'd been worth the wait, as Wild Wolf had predicted on his wedding day.

Hot with desire, Blue rolled her onto the pallet of furs and ravaged her lips and then her earlobes, before he traced sweet kisses down her neck. She shivered beneath his touch, but he knew it was from passion rather than fear.

She made soft, mewling sounds as he slid his lips toward her breast, to capture and suckle like a new babe. Her head moved from side to side and her hands ran up and down his back and through his hair, as though her fingers needed something to do while he continued his assault on her senses.

He worked his way from one breast, across the valley between the two, to take the other in his mouth, to lave and suckle, bringing her back up off the pallet to give him more of her.

He was engorged, but held himself back, wanting Amy to enjoy every moment he could offer and to show her exactly how much he loved her and wanted her happiness.

He trailed kisses down to her navel to lick and suck the sensitive skin on her belly. She writhed beneath him, called his name and dug her hands into his hair.

"Blue!" Her voice sounded strangled, pleasing Blue immensely.

Like a liquid blanket he covered her body with his while he continued to kiss the breath out of her.

"Blue, hurrrry..." she barely breathed.

172

He positioned himself at her beckoning moisture then entered, gasping with the pleasure it brought. She took in all of him, raising her hips to take in more as she moaned his name again. "Blue...please..."

Her pleading for release drove him over the precipice and he exploded inside her, while she reached the pinnacle with him.

Minutes later, breathing hard, he rolled to Amy's side and gazed down at the woman who had captured him body and soul. Who held him captive more so than he could ever hold her.

Sated by their lovemaking, food forgotten, they slept in each other's arms, smiles curling their lips.

Outside, winter could assault the earth as much as it wanted. Inside, the woman who tended Blue's fire spoke only of the promise of spring.

Chapter Nineteen

Gunfire shattered the morning.

Blue rolled Amy out of his arms, waking her with a jolt when he jumped up. He ran to the flap and stared outside, gape-mouthed. Soldiers on familiar white horses raced through the village with sabers, torches and rifles poised for destruction.

He turned back to Amy, on her feet and clutching a hide blanket to her chest.

"Get dressed and get out!" he shouted. "We're under attack."

"By who?" She gathered her clothing in a rush.

"The Bluecoats from Camp Robinson. The ones that were at the White River council."

"What! Why?"

"I guess they think it's their duty to round us up and make us pay for our disobedience in not going to Camp Robinson as we were ordered."

"But how could we obey?" she wailed. "The weather made it impossible..."

"Tell that to them." He jerked his thumb toward the outside. "Come on. We've got to hurry."

Blue shoved his knife into his moccasin and his hatchet into the waist of the buckskin pants he pulled over his hips. He put his hands on Amy's shoulders, held her from him and looked into her frightened eyes.

"You've got to hide. They're burning the village and killing as they go."

In that moment, he realized his worst fear had come true. He would lose her. When she was seen by any of the cavalrymen, she'd be taken away and returned to her own people. With her red hair and creamy skin, she would never be mistaken for one of The People.

He saw the confusion on her face. Grabbing her hand, he pulled her through the opening of the lodge.

"There!" He pointed. "Do you see the other women and children? Follow them," he shouted to be heard over the riot of noise around them.

She jerked away. "No! I won't leave you."

Soldiers raced back and forth between lodges, torching The People's homes as they went, using their rifles as clubs to strike those who tried to flee. Women screamed for their children while men tried to protect their families and possessions. Smoke spiraled in thick black clouds into the sky and soldiers' laughter rode the wind like wraiths.

"You have to go!" Blue shouted. He grabbed her by the shoulders. She shook from the cold and fear. "You can't stay here. Don't you understand what will happen if they see you?"

She stood still as a stone and her eyes grew wide.

"You think that's why I won't leave you?" she accused. "So they'll see me? So I can go home? Damn you, Blue. After what we've finally shared together, you think that's why I don't want to leave you?"

Blue opened his mouth to speak, but the pounding of hooves behind him drew his attention. He lunged at Amy, grabbed her around the waist and hurled her to the ground as a rifle exploded behind him. They landed hard, the earth erupting where they'd stood.

"Run!" He shoved her as she scrambled to her feet. "Go!"

Fear overcame her stubbornness. She ran to catch up with the women and children who fled across the Powder River into the mountains on the other side.

Blue jerked out his knife and threw himself at a soldier on horseback. The horse reared then danced in circles, dragging Blue along the ground. He groped at the rider's legs and torso until he unseated him.

The soldier rolled to his feet and leveled his rifle. But Blue was too quick. Rage drove him. He dove at the man and they crashed to the ground rolling back and forth, each lunging for the rifle. Blue managed to jerk the weapon away. Using it as a club, he slammed it against the man's head and the soldier went limp.

175

The thunder of more hooves caught Blue's attention. The Indians' horse herd, numbering near a thousand or more, was being driven from camp by the soldiers. Blue watched, helpless, as the animals raced away into the slowly dawning morning.

Blue scanned the village and saw it was mostly empty, except for the crazed soldiers, who burned and looted as they went. His eyes swept the hill where the women, children and old ones had run. They were no longer visible and he prayed they were safe. Warriors had taken positions behind huge rocks, holding the soldiers away.

Blue ran toward where the women had gone taking little notice of the destruction being wrought to the village. Hard-packed snow crunched under his feet and the wind howled around him. But he felt none of it, his only thought to reach Amy and make sure she was safe.

He rounded one of the few lodges that hadn't been burned and the world reeled around him when the impact of a rifle stock drove him to the ground. Familiar lights burst in his brain like exploding dynamite. He grabbed his head, tried to stop the pain and heard himself moan with the effort.

"Damn Injun," he heard before he felt the second blow to his back. He crashed to the ground, the throbbing in his head momentarily forgotten as pain tore through his kidney and lower back.

"We'll teach you bastards to respect the United States Government."

Blue knew his life was in the balance and he pulled himself up, jerked the knife from his moccasin and flung it at the soldier a split second before the rifle would have exploded at his chest.

He stared at the lifeless soldier. Sickness threatened him. But within seconds, darkness sucked him down into its depths like a whirlpool.

Blue woke to the flash of lights, each one bringing a new barrage of pain. He grabbed his head, willing it to stop.

"Lie back, my brother," came Wild Wolf's voice, soft with concern. "You took a heavy blow. Give yourself a few minutes to regain your senses."

Blue lay back down on the cold earth. *Why wasn't he inside one of the lodges, a warm fire blazing in the pit, a pallet of soft furs under him?*

Then he remembered.

"Amy?" he managed. "Where is she?" His heart pounded wildly at the thought she might be gone. Or hurt. He grabbed Wild Wolf's forearm.

"I will find her," Wild Wolf soothed. "Not all the women and old ones have come down from the mountain. She will come soon."

"I have to know..." Blinding pain in his head made his eyes water.

"I will search for her," Wild Wolf said again, his voice hard. "Tipiziwin will stay with you until I return with Amy."

Blue tightened his grip on Wild Wolf's arm. "Find her, Wild Wolf. Find her."

Wild Wolf's hand covered Blue's. "I will."

Blue laid his head back, but was unable to stop the blackness from taking him again into its depths.

Fingers glided gently through his hair, stroked his cheek and came to rest on his forehead.

"He's burning up," the familiar voice said. But he couldn't open his eyes to see her.

"Quick, get me some ice or snow. We have to bring his fever down."

He tried again to open his eyes, but the lids felt like they'd been sewn shut and his head felt as though it was held in a metal vice.

He couldn't stop his sharp intake of breath as snow touched his forehead. He started to shiver.

"Don't we have anything to put over him?" she pleaded.

"There is nothing."

Blue concentrated as hard as he could and forced his eyes to open. The world around him spun crazily and he blinked, trying to slow it down.

177

"He's waking up. Blue?"

He blinked again, tried to clear the blur in front of him. Faces came into view. After several moments of uncertainty, his vision finally cleared.

Amy and Wild Wolf knelt over him. Thank God, she was safe. He reached up to touch her and his head reverberated with bright white light.

"Don't," she whispered. She pushed his hand back to the ground. "You've got a bad head injury. Try not to move."

Gingerly, he lifted his hand and touched her cheek.

"Welcome back," she whispered.

"What happened? Why am I outside? It's freezing." The bitter cold stabbed him like a saber.

"The village has been destroyed," Wild Wolf said. "There's nothing left."

Blue tried to focus. The world was still fuzzy, but slowly came into view.

All around gray smoke spiraled into the twilight sky from what remained of smoldering lodges. Women, children and old ones huddled together under one fur, trying to ward off the bitter temperature that cut through Blue like a steel-tipped blade.

Some of The People sifted through the remains of their homes, trying to gather anything that might be left. Many cried. Others wandered, silent, their tears spent, the telltale marks streaking their soot-covered faces like masks.

He looked up at Amy and Wild Wolf and a chill swept over him. He didn't know if it was from the bitter cold or the bitter hatred he suddenly felt for the soldiers who'd destroyed their village. And, very possibly, his future with The People.

Chapter Twenty

The People gathered what little was left for the journey north to join Crazy Horse and his Oglala. They waited for the return of their braves who, using the cover of darkness, had set off to recapture their stolen horses from the soldier camp.

Blue opened his eyes. Amy was beside him. He floated in and out of consciousness, barely heard the sounds of crying children and wailing mothers. He shook from the cold one moment, then felt like the fires of hell burned him the next. Amy's gentle touch forced open his eyes.

"It's time to go," she said.

Slowly, he pushed himself to his elbows, his head spinning like a top.

"You still have a fever," Amy said, "but we can't wait. Everyone's ready to leave now."

"I can ride, just get Wild Wolf or Jumping Bear to help me mount," he groaned.

Amy disappeared for a moment and returned with Jumping Bear, his grizzled face lined with worry.

"You are able, my son?" the older man asked. Gnarled hands reached for Blue's arm.

"As able as I can be." Blue tried not to grimace at the pain that shot through his back and head with every movement.

Jumping Bear pulled Blue to his feet and led him to one of the few remaining horses. Amy steadied the animal while Blue, with great effort and Jumping Bear's help, managed to get seated on the horse's bare back.

Amy pulled herself up behind Blue.

They rode out, bitter wind swirling around them. The sun barely brought the temperature to freezing and the ground crunched beneath hooves and feet.

Blue surveyed the villagers as he rode among them and his heart tightened in his chest. No packs or travois of belongings. No furs or skins for protection against the biting, frigid winds. No food and few horses. The People had nothing but the clothes on their backs and their determination to survive.

And white men were responsible.

He felt Amy shrug deeper into the blanket she'd been clutching when the village was attacked. He sensed her observance of those around her and knew she felt guilty for having it. Children walked with stiff legs, their little arms curled around their small bodies, crying for their mothers to make them warm again. Tears froze on their cheeks and lashes as they cried. Blue's heart ached as women tried to console their children, unable to make the stinging cold go away.

Old men and women were hauled on roughly made travois to keep them from falling behind. Many warriors walked, their backs straight, their eyes forward as they waited for the return of those who went to recapture the herd.

Blue cursed the soldiers for the desecration of the peaceful village. His village.

"I'm ashamed," Amy whispered against his back.

"Why?" Blue asked, surprised by her statement.

"Because I'm white and everyone in this village knows it."

"But they know you're not like the men who did this?"

"Aren't I?"

"No, you're not."

"When you first brought me to The People, wouldn't I have been happy to see the soldiers come? Wouldn't I have run out and screamed for them to find me? But now I understand what they don't. What The People are about, how they live. How they live and love, just like we do."

Her back drew up straight as a lance.

"I'm ashamed for what they've done, Blue. But there's nothing I can do to make it better. Not a damn thing."

Blue noticed a mother walking beside them trying to console her crying child, attempting to warm the little girl with her own cold body. But it wasn't enough. The child cried harder and louder.

Amy stiffened behind him and pulled the blanket from her shoulders. She leaned over and draped it around the desperate mother and her child.

The woman's eyes filled with such gratitude Blue caught his breath. Pride swelled through him. Without thinking of the consequences, Amy had given away her only means to stay warm.

Ignoring the burst of pain that rushed through him, Blue turned and looked into Amy's tear-streaked face.

He touched her hand and she smiled. "I love you," he whispered as he squeezed her fingers.

"It was the only thing I could do. That poor child could freeze to death, and I'd never forgive myself if I allowed that to happen and had the power to stop it." She shivered. "I only hope I don't regret it." She tried to smile when she started to shake.

They rode on in silence. Neither had the words to express their sorrow and fear at what was to come.

Two days later, half-frozen and starving, but with their recaptured horses, The People reached Crazy Horse's village.

The day after Blue and Amy had settled into the Oglala camp a woman came to the lodge they shared with Wild Wolf, Yellow Lodge Woman and Jumping Bear. The woman stepped in front of Amy and took her hands into hers. She looked at Blue and spoke in Lakota.

Blue nodded and stepped forward. "I'm going to translate for her," he said, looking at Amy.

"Three days ago, you gave me and my child your blanket to keep us warm and left yourself with nothing to shield you from the freezing cold. I am certain without your kindness, my daughter would have died." Misty eyes stared hard at Amy. "I am in your debt. My child lives by your generosity."

Amy blushed. "I couldn't *not* give it to her," she answered. "If it were me and my child, I would hope someone would do the same for me."

The woman waved her hand. "There were others who could have given what you gave. But they did not. I know there were few blankets among us, but yours was the one given."

The woman reached inside her dress and withdrew a necklace. She closed her eyes and held it tight in her hand against her heart. She whispered several words then opened her eyes and lifted it over her head. Tears were flowing down her cheeks when she handed the necklace to Amy.

"I give this to you as a token of my gratitude," Blue translated her hoarse words.

Amy took the beaded necklace interspersed with animal claws and tied together on a thick piece of animal sinew. She looked up at the woman.

"I can't take this." She tried to hand back the piece of jewelry and turned to Blue to help the woman understand.

"Blue, tell her I can't take this. It obviously means a great deal to her."

"You must take this," the woman said. "It was your kindness that saved my child from the talons of death. By your hands she lives," she said again through Blue. She pushed the necklace back toward Amy. "You must take it. It is all I have."

"That's why I can't take it," Amy cried. "I can't take the last thing you have. That's not why I helped you and your daughter."

"You have to take it," Blue said. "She'll be offended if you don't."

"But it's the only thing she has."

"Which is why she's giving it to you. She's showing the importance of what you did by giving you the only thing of value she has left other than her daughter."

Amy glanced at the woman who waited for her response. For so long she'd felt like an outsider. Like she'd never be accepted because she was white. That somehow they'd hold her responsible for what the soldiers had done. And now by her act of kindness, she was being offered this precious gift.

She smiled. The woman smiled back.

"I take this gift with a glad heart, happy I could save your child's life."

She lifted the necklace around her head and let it fall to her chest.

The woman squeezed Amy's hands. "Pilamaya. Thank you, Wihpeya Win, Woman Who Gives Things Away," Blue translated as the woman backed out of the lodge.

Amy stared after her. She'd been given a name, something even more precious than the woman's gift. She could hold her head proud among The People.

She was Wihpeya Win, Woman Who Gives Things Away.

Now after all this time, she finally understood what Blue had so desperately sought, for she, too, had found it. Acceptance.

Chapter Twenty-one

The weather warmed and the grasses grew tall again and Blue heard a great deal of disturbing talk among the villagers.

There was talk of war. Many of the Lakota wanted to stay with Crazy Horse and seek revenge against the Bluecoats for the attack on their village. But the chiefs and old ones warned against it.

By spring, the time of the Geese Laying Moon, Crazy Horse led his large band of Lakota and smaller band of Cheyenne to join Sitting Bull and his Hunkpapas at the mouth of the Tongue River.

Blue reveled in the warmth of the sun on his face and Amy next to him as they rode with The People. A cool wind blew through his hair and everyone seemed heartened by the news they would soon join with Sitting Bull. The chiefs had decided the combined number of warriors would make it safer for everyone.

When they reached the mouth of the Tongue River the villagers were joined by a band of Minneconjous, led by Lame Deer, who brought word many Bluecoats were in the area.

Blue listened to the talk as more and more tribes gathered. Oglala, Hunkpapas, Brule, Minneconjou, Cheyenne. The People continued north, their numbers swelling into the thousands.

In the valley of the Rosebud, the men hunted large game so the meat would feed the swelling villages and the hides would become their homes. Lodge poles were cut from the surrounding trees and finally Blue showed Amy how to set up their new lodge. She was a fast learner and they had the framework up quickly. Freshly tanned hides were placed around the poles and staked to the ground. A short time later, Amy stood back and admired her work.

"Not bad, Wihpeya Win." Blue used her new Lakota name and took great joy in watching her eyes sparkle with happiness. "Not bad at all."

All around other lodges were being erected and soon many stretched along the river.

Blue scanned the village that looked more like a city. Hope surged through him. Maybe they would be safe, if only because of their great numbers.

Several days later a runner arrived in camp. Blue joined the chiefs and elders in the council lodge to hear the runner speak.

"Hear what I say, great chiefs. Three Stars Crook comes from the south and the One Who Limps comes from the west. From the east comes One Star Terry and Pahuska, Long Hair Custer."

Braves jumped to their feet and shook their fists in the air, raging for a quick death to the whites invading their land. Blue listened to the runner's words and a cold chill ran up his spine. There could only be one reason the soldiers came—to destroy them.

"We must not rush into war with the whites!" one of the elders said when the room had quieted.

"How can we not?" Wild Wolf shouted. "Must we wait until they descend upon us and destroy all that is ours before we fight?"

The crowd erupted into shouts for war as the elders tried to keep order.

Blue sat beside Wild Wolf and, although Wild Wolf didn't join in the chorus for war, Blue knew where his heart was. His brother wanted to fight.

His mind unsettled, Blue's eyes drifted to Sitting Bull who had made no effort to speak. Finally, the great chief stood.

"We must not run into war with these Bluecoats before we know their strengths and weaknesses," he said.

"Let us attack them first," one brave shouted. "We will surprise them and drive them back to the east where the land is thick with their own kind!"

Many shouted agreement.

"Until it is known how many Bluecoats come we must wait," Sitting Bull said. "We cannot run into war. There are many women, children and old ones to consider. We are not an army of warriors gathered here and there are many who will not survive a war.

"Scouts will be sent out and we will soon know how many soldiers come. Until then we will wait." He scanned the stony faces of the warriors gathered.

"Hetchetu aloh. It is so indeed."

Amy was pacing when Blue returned to the lodge.

"What's going on?" Her face was tight with worry.

"Let's sit down." He took her hands and led her to their pallet.

She jerked away. "I don't want to sit down. I want to know what's going on. Talk is running rampant through the village that soldiers are coming."

Blue heaved a heavy sigh and nodded.

"Sitting Bull's already sent scouts out to determine how many."

"Then we have to go," she said, her voice filled with dread. "You know what'll happen if they come. It'll be the same as the last time they attacked."

"We can't just leave," Blue said. "Where would we go? If we were stopped by an army patrol, they'd probably kill us without asking questions."

"We have to leave," she said again.

He realized what she was asking for. She wanted to return to her own people. The same people who were threatening to destroy an entire culture.

"What about all that noble talk of understanding The People?" he asked. "What about that woman and her child? Was it all a lie?"

Amy shook her head. "No, I meant every word I said. Then. But it's warm now. We can travel without freezing to death. Besides," she rubbed her arms as though suddenly cold, "you and I both know The People can't fight the United States Government and win. They might win a few battles, but in the long run they'll be destroyed."

Blue could only stare at the woman he loved.

"I thought you were happy here. With me," he added, almost afraid to say the words.

186

Her back straightened and her eyes lifted to meet his. "I was willing to give up everything to stay here with you. But things are different now. The soldiers are coming. They're coming to destroy the Indians and us along with them if we stay. I'm not ready to die, Blue. And most certainly not for a cause I know is lost before it even starts."

She touched his face and her voice softened. "I'd continue to be happy here—if they weren't coming. But the Indians are a doomed race. We can only stay and watch it. There's nothing we can do to stop it—or we can leave before it happens. The choice is yours." She strode from the lodge and left Blue watching after her, his mind awhirl with conflicting thoughts.

How could he leave the people he'd come to love and admire? But how could he ask Amy to give up her life for a cause they both knew was doomed to destruction?

He slammed out of the lodge and ran through the village toward the river wishing he could, as easily, run from the questions plaguing him.

187

Chapter Twenty-two

It was June, the Moon When Cherries are Ripe, and time for the annual Sun Dance. The threat of the whites coming was put aside with the preparations for the yearly ritual. But this ceremony was to be different. This time Sitting Bull would dance and pray.

Blue and Amy watched Sitting Bull prepare to seek wisdom from *Wakan Tanka* on how to lead his people in the coming troublesome days.

Blue watched the three boys who would share in the ritual and almost felt the bite of the bone in his chest when the ceremony began. He was glad to be an observer, rather than a participant, as he'd been only a year ago.

The boys began to dance and chant and, although not pierced by the ritual bones, Sitting Bull danced and sang with them.

The group twirled and chanted for hours as the hot sun blazed down on them. The paint on their bodies mingled with blood and sweat as they sang and prayed.

Suddenly, Sitting Bull dropped to his knees. The boys stopped dancing and praying and four braves approached the great chief.

"What're they doing?" Blue asked Jumping Bear.

"Sitting Bull gives his body as a sacrifice to *Wakan Tanka* for his people," his father answered.

Blue held his breath, uncertain what was to come next. The four braves withdrew knives from their belts. Sitting Bull continued to pray as each man sliced and peeled two-inch strips of skin from his body. Blue stared, mesmerized and amazed at Sitting Bull's fortitude, who never once cried out.

Dozens of strips of skin were taken before the men stopped. Sitting Bull stumbled to his feet, blood streaming down his arms and chest, and beseeched the Great Spirit to lead him and his people.

The great chief stared into the blistering sun and, after hours of chanting, stood mute. His eyes remained fixed on the sun and his body remained still as a stone. The People waited, holding their collective breath, and awaited his words.

Blue felt Amy's hand tighten in his, his body rigid with anticipation. She knew the power Sitting Bull's words would carry.

"I have seen many soldiers." Sitting Bull's voice carried out over the crowd. "They fell from the sky like grasshoppers, their heads down, their hats falling from their heads. They had no ears and fell into our camp." He paused, as though seeing the vision again in his head.

"A voice spoke to me. It told me I was given these soldiers because they have no ears."

Whispers raced through the gathering. Blue felt a prickling sensation tear up his spine.

Sitting Bull raised a hand and the crowd quieted. "Because the whites have chosen not to listen to our words, the Great Spirit, *Wakan Tanka,* will give these soldiers to us."

Pandemonium broke out among The People. Warriors shouted and whooped. Women and old ones sang of imminent victory.

Blue's heart pounded. Amy grabbed his arm and pulled him closer.

His mind churned with the implications of what was happening. It would be outright war. The Indians would fight to preserve their land. His land.

If there was one thing he knew about white civilization, they didn't give up. When they wanted something they kept after it until it was theirs, regardless of the destruction it would bring.

Sitting Bull walked through the crowd, stopped in front of Blue and dropped a bloody hand on his shoulder.

"Speak what is in your heart, Blue Fox with Two Hearts. I wish to hear it."

Excitement flowed like a river through Blue's body. *Should he agree with Sitting Bull? Or should he tell them to run for their lives to preserve their heritage for the next generation?*

He stared at the faces of those gathered around him, along with Amy and Sitting Bull. Some he knew as friends, while others looked at him with open hostility. Jumping Bear smiled with encouragement.

Wild Wolf stepped up beside Blue and placed a steadying hand on his other shoulder.

Blue sucked in a deep breath and straightened his back. He looked directly into Sitting Bull's face.

"You know who and what I am. In my heart I know many soldiers will come. Like the leaves that fall from a tree before winter, they'll keep coming until the last of our people is gone or on reservations and they possess what is ours."

Sitting Bull looked out at those assembled then turned back to Blue.

"Your words tell us we will lose our sacred lands whether we fight or flee," he said, his voice somber.

"That's what I fear," Blue answered. "I don't want to see The People fight against an enemy they cannot defeat. Sitting Bull hasn't seen the thousands of people in the white cities. Even if we fight, many more will come. I don't want The People to give their lives for what will be lost anyway."

He looked into the chief's eyes and saw understanding but resolve. Sitting Bull turned and spoke.

"I have heard the words of Blue Fox with Two Hearts and feel his heart is pure. I believe he is afraid for The People. But we cannot allow the Bluecoats to take our land without a fight. We will form war parties and attack as the sun rises. Hetchetu aloh. It is so indeed."

Sitting Bull walked away, his back straight, his knees slightly shaky, and the ceremony began again, the air electrified. *Wakan Tanka* had shown Sitting Bull the destruction of the whites. His words meant a great battle would be fought and won. None of The People doubted. Neither did Blue. But one battle would not win the war. There would be many more and in the end The People would lose.

"I see fear and confusion in your face, Blue Fox," Jumping Bear said. "Is this fear for the soldiers or us?"

"For everyone, Father. What I see is the beginning of the end for The People." He searched Jumping Bear's face.

"I know I must ride with you, but I fear I won't be able to draw a bow against the soldiers. They're my blood, just as The People are my blood. What can I do?"

Jumping Bear shook his head. "I don't know, Blue Fox. It is something you must decide for yourself."

"But this won't stop them," Blue said.

"Then we will kill them all," came Wild Wolf's chilling response. "We will not give them our land. Instead, we'll make them bleed. Or we will die trying."

"And for each white soldier you kill, they'll kill twenty of our people. Even our women and children."

"Then it is so." The glint in Wild Wolf's dark eyes made Blue shiver.

He turned to his father and looked into Jumping Bear's sympathetic face. He felt like weeping. For all he knew was about to happen. And all that was about to be lost.

Alone in their lodge, Amy pulled out of Blue's arms. She opened her mouth to speak, but Blue stopped her.

"Don't even say it, Amy. The soldiers are coming and we're going to fight."

"But you can't, Blue. You're, you're..."

"What? White? Only half Indian? And because I'm half white I shouldn't fight against the soldiers? Even if they're wrong?"

"I don't understand anything anymore," Amy said. "It just scares me to death to think of you riding out to fight. Oh, Blue, all I know is that I love you. Whatever happens, I want you alive."

Tears welled in her eyes and she started to tremble.

"I can't lose you. Not when it's taken my whole life to find you."

Blue pulled her back into his arms and held her against him.

"Then I guess I don't have a choice? I'll have to survive, won't I?"

"Yes, you will. I love you Blue Fox, with all my heart." Her eyes reflected the love she held for him.

Blue's insides tightened. He lowered his lips to hers, tasted the salt of her tears. She sighed and melted against him.

Passion and the fear of losing what he'd found drove him. He laid her down on the pallet, her hair fanning out in waves around her head like a crimson halo. Her cheeks glistened from the tears she'd already shed and new ones sparkled in her eyes.

Her arms encircled Blue's neck. "Love me," she whispered, pulling him down to her.

Again he tasted the salt from her tears as he ran his tongue over her cheek, down her jawbone to her neck.

She whimpered, pulled him closer and ran her fingers through his hair.

Blue moved his mouth up her throat to her lips while he stroked her thigh with his fingertips.

She moaned. Her breath caught as his fingers worked their way to the inside of her leg and reached for the softness he sought. She drew a ragged breath.

No words were spoken; none were needed, as they showed their love with their bodies.

She pulled her hands from his hair and worked at the lacings of his breeches and hide shirt while he fumbled to undo her dress. She moaned when his fingers brushed her breast.

Blue gazed down at the woman who had stolen his heart. Her pulse raced at the base of her neck and her eyes beckoned. He jerked his shirt off and he slid away only long enough to remove his leggings while she slipped out of her dress.

Blue laid down beside her and took her breast into his mouth. She moaned, deep and low in her throat as he suckled and laved. He moved his hand up and down her quivering stomach and stopped at her other breast. He rolled the nipple under his palm then between his fingers, bringing it to a rosy peak.

Amy closed her eyes and licked her lips.

"Look at me."

She opened her eyes. In them he saw no fear as he once had. Now he saw only love. He captured her mouth again in a hot kiss filled with the desire and love he had for her. Their tongues sparred and fought while their hands searched and caressed each other's body.

Blue touched her deep inside and she quivered. He chuckled, buoyant in the knowledge he affected her so. She raised her hips to take in more of him, while she dragged his other hand back to tease and pinch her breasts. She nipped at his shoulder, he sucked the skin at her ribs and flat stomach as he worked his way down.

She stopped breathing and her fingers raked his hair as she bucked and jerked under his administrations.

"Blue!" she cried, losing herself.

He raised himself above her and entered her moist, beckoning body, joining her in flight to the skies. They rocked to the music of love, giving and taking in equal measure.

Amy cried out his name and buried her face in the curve of his neck as she slowly regained her senses, still quivering beneath him.

He, too, had been rocked by their exploding passion, and was still trying to calm his shaking body, when he touched her chin and she raised tear-filled eyes to his.

"What is it?"

"Don't fight, Blue. Please," she begged. "I can't lose you."

Blue wanted to wrench her off the pallet and run for their lives. But he couldn't. Wouldn't.

"Amy, try to understand."

"I don't want to understand! All I want is for us to be together." She pushed him off her and sat up, her back to him, the beauty of their lovemaking forgotten.

"I can't run away." Blue's voice was soft, sad.

"And what if you're killed? What happens to me?"

Blue put his arms around her shoulders and buried his face in her hair, the scent of their lovemaking still on his lips. She fought against him, but he crushed her to him.

"I've lost so many people already, Blue," she cried out in agony to the hide walls of the lodge. "I can't lose you, too. If you must do this, come back. Promise me, you'll come back."

"On my love for you, I'll come back. I promise." He turned her to face him, wiped the tears from her face, and loved her again to seal that promise.

Chapter Twenty-three

The war party of nearly a thousand braves, including Blue, rode throughout the night and stopped only a few hours before daylight to rest. The remaining warriors stayed behind to protect the village.

Blue stood beside Jumping Bear and Wild Wolf and waited in silence for Crazy Horse, the warrior chosen to lead the war party, to speak.

"When the sun rises we will attack the Bluecoats and show them we will not be like sheep led to slaughter," Crazy Horse began.

A murmur of agreement floated to the far reaches of the crowd.

Blue had no desire to race into battle with the morning's first light. He knew the bloodletting was just beginning. If the Lakota were successful in routing these soldiers, it would only provoke the army into sending more in retaliation. Why couldn't he make the Lakota understand? It was a losing battle.

"We have spoken to the Great Father many times," Crazy Horse continued. "Told him we will not give up *Paha Sapa*. But he will not listen." Crazy Horse stepped up on a fallen tree.

"This is the land of our fathers and our father's fathers. And has been since before our memory of time." The chief raised his fist in the air high above his head.

"We will not give up our sacred lands!"

Wild Wolf raised his arms, whooped and yelled at Crazy Horse's statement. His face, tight with anger, his eyes glowing with unconcealed hatred, reflected the excitement and anticipation of the other braves assembled.

All the braves except Blue. He stood silent, his heart thundering and his mind racing like a runaway herd of buffalo. He took a deep breath to compose himself.

Crazy Horse lowered his arm and waited for the cheering voices to fall silent.

"Go now. Rest and be ready."

194

The braves dispersed to prepare themselves for the rising sun.

Blue needed to be alone. Away from the questioning glares of Wild Wolf and the silent understanding of Jumping Bear. He plopped down on a mound of mossy ground in front of a tree.

How foolish they are, he thought. Although he felt The People were justified in their efforts, the United States government wasn't going to capitulate to the wishes of a people who stood in the way of progress. And gold.

He shifted, tried to get comfortable against the tree. He leaned his head back and sighed. Tomorrow would only be the beginning.

All he'd tried to do in these last years was be accepted by these people. Now that he was, he would have to kill men of his father's race to stay among them. If he didn't, he'd be shamed in the eyes of the Lakota.

Dear God in Heaven, how had things gotten so out of control?

Blue closed his eyes and thought of Amy, remembering her touch, her feel. He relaxed, floating in her memories, his only escape from the questions plaguing him.

When the rays of the sun streaked the sky the riders mounted. Blue's horse pranced and snorted as though aware of what the coming day would bring. He reined in the animal and fell in with the rest of the warriors heading toward the soldier camp at the mouth of the Rosebud River.

They rode in silence, the only sound the horses hooves as they plodded the dusty earth beneath them.

Blue's mind spun. Today's outcome would change his life forever. At the top of a hill he pulled his horse to a halt with the others. Beside him, Wild Wolf and Jumping Bear's mounts swung their heads nervously. What he saw below took his breath away.

Down the slope three-dozen Arikara and Crow scouts on horseback were headed straight toward them, unaware the Lakota watched them from the top of the hill.

War cries erupted from the warriors around him when they spotted the approaching scouts. Horses and riders charged, lances raised, tomahawks ready. Wild Wolf raced forward, his coup stick waving like a flag over his head.

Jumping Bear spurred his mount into action and Blue charged down the hill toward their enemies with his father and brother ahead of him.

Surprised and outnumbered, the Crow and Arikara jerked their horses around and fled in different directions.

Three Lakota warriors rode down on one Crow. One of their lances knocked the Indian from his horse, while the others fired their bows. Blue's blood turned to brittle ice as he watched the Lakota warriors pump arrow after arrow into the helpless Crow brave.

Again and again he watched his people overpower the scouts until blue uniforms suddenly exploded into view at the crest of a far hill.

Spread out in pursuit of the Crow and Arikara scouts, Blue knew the Lakota wouldn't stand a chance.

"Back to the hill! Return to the hill," the shout relayed through the warriors.

Blue whirled his horse back in the direction he'd just come from and rejoined the others. He searched frantically for Wild Wolf and Jumping Bear, but found neither in the gathering crowd of warriors. His heart pounded, afraid his friend and father may have been injured.

Crazy Horse rode to the center of the massing braves.

"Ride toward the soldiers!" His mount pranced wildly. "When their lines form—break away and attack from the sides and rear. We will divide their forces, confuse them, and make them weak. Remember," Crazy Horse screamed, "It is a good day to fight! It is a good day to die!"

The chief shook his lance high above his head and shouted. He sent his horse racing toward the approaching Bluecoats. Warriors followed, chanting, "It is a good day to fight. It is a good day to die!

"Hoka hey! Charge!"

Blue gripped his mount's belly with his knees and urged the powerful animal forward. Wind rushed across his face. Blood surged through his body. He charged toward the approaching line of cavalrymen. Fear and excitement gripped him. He had to

196

do this. Had to fight for the rights of the Indian. He couldn't run away. Not now, not ever.

Gunfire popped, metal clanged. Men and horses ran into each other on the rising slopes. All around Blue heard the dull thud of coup sticks striking. Men screamed, arrows whooshed through the air, ripped into flesh. The shattering sound of exploding bullets tore through Blue's ears.

He jerked his horse away from the line of attacking soldiers as rifle fire continued to pop around him. Any moment he expected to feel a bullet pierce his body.

He spotted Wild Wolf and raced toward him. Two soldiers spotted he and Wild Wolf and charged after them—right into the lances and guns of two other waiting warriors. The soldiers ground their horses to a halt when they realized their mistake, tried to turn and run. But it was too late. As Blue and Wild Wolf raced by, the other two braves were on the soldiers before they could escape.

Blue tried not to listen to their screams as he rode farther away. Finally the cries were muffled by the sounds of battle.

Blue and Wild Wolf turned and headed back toward the continuing clash. Drawing near, Blue spotted the two braves scalping the soldiers who had been alive only minutes ago. With a final slice of their knives, they raised their bloodied prizes in the air for Blue and Wild Wolf to see, yelping and shouting.

Wild Wolf whooped and raised his bloody coup stick in response.

Blue's stomach churned and bile rose in his throat. But he forced it down. He had to maintain control. Fighting raged all around him.

Guns exploded. Expended powder floated into the air leaving an acrid smell behind. Men fought on horseback or hand to hand. Bodies lay sprawled in the dirt, their blood staining the earth, their bodies twisted in death.

Blue had no time to dwell on what he saw. An armed cavalryman was headed straight for him. He stared, slack-jawed, for only a second.

The soldier raced forward, his gun raised and ready to fire. Blue pulled an arrow from his quiver and with speed he didn't know he possessed, he loaded and fired.

The same instant the soldier's gun exploded.

The arrow hit its mark and embedded in the soldier's chest. The man fell from his horse with a scream of agony, then screamed no more.

Blue grabbed his leg. Blood gushed from the outer part of his thigh where the soldier's bullet had struck. The damage wasn't severe, only a flesh wound, but it burned like fire.

More horses pounded toward Blue. He turned and looked right into the rifle of another fast approaching Bluecoat. He threw himself off his horse's back, a split second before the rifle roared to life.

He landed on the ground and rolled as his horse raced away. Pain tore through his injured leg, but he ignored it, knowing his life was at stake. He sprang to his feet and drew his knife, his bow lost in the fall. He stood ready, waiting for the soldier to return.

The man rode down on him, his rifle raised again. So close, Blue could see the hate in his eyes. An explosion of sound and Blue's insides constricted into a tight knot. But he didn't feel a bullet rip into his body. Instead the cavalryman slid off his horse and crashed to the ground.

Blue gripped his knife tighter and whirled, ready to face another soldier.

"Get on!" Wild Wolf shouted, slowing his horse only long enough to lean over in the saddle and reach out. Blue grabbed Wild Wolf's outstretched hand and swung up behind his brother-friend as the horse raced by.

Wild Wolf swung his horse toward a riderless Indian pony standing away from the battle.

"Be more careful, my brother," he shouted as Blue threw himself onto the horse's back. Wild Wolf thrust his heels into his pony and raced back into battle.

Blue grabbed the reins. Deafening screams filled his brain.

Without thinking of what he'd survived and what he would ride back into, he rammed his heels into the horse's sides and sent the animal charging back into battle.

For hours under the hot sun the two sides clashed in a bitter fight.

Finally the Lakota eased their attack and, given the chance, the soldiers retreated.

Wild Wolf halted his mount beside Blue and stared after the fleeing Bluecoats. He waved his bloodied coup stick at their backs as they grabbed their wounded and rode away.

"We've shown you," he shouted. "Don't come back or we'll beat you again!"

Blue's chest heaved and his leg burned like the fires of hell. He scanned the battlefield littered with dead and wounded. He wanted to shout. He wanted to scream out to *Wakan Tanka*. He'd survived today's battle.

But the war had just begun.

Chapter Twenty-four

Amidst the feasting and celebration, Sitting Bull stepped forward to speak.

"Although we defeated the Bluecoats yesterday, it was not the fulfillment of my vision. We will meet the soldiers again. When, I do not know." Sitting Bull stopped as though to think, his brow furrowed. "We must be ready. We will leave this place and head toward the valley of the Greasy Grass. There we will find plenty to fill our food stores and feed our horses. We leave with the rising of the sun."

The people cheered and many touched the chief in reverence before they shuffled off to their pallets.

"They'll follow us, won't they?" Amy's frightened eyes sparkled in the firelight. "They'll hunt us down until they find us."

She shivered, despite the warmth from the fire, and Blue wrapped her in his arms.

"We can only hope they don't. Maybe today was enough of a setback they'll think twice about the Hills and leave us alone."

She turned to face him. "You don't believe that any more than I do."

"It's the best we can hope for." He pulled her to her feet and led her to their lodge, his mood for celebration gone.

Wild Wolf fell into step beside them. "You're worried, Blue Fox."

He nodded. "Sitting Bull has no idea what we're up against. The massive strength of the U.S. Army and the determination of a country." He glared at Wild Wolf.

"I'm worried all right."

A week had passed since the battle at the Rosebud and The People had set up camp along the Little Bighorn River. They relaxed and enjoyed the grasslands, the warmth of the sun, and the abundance of wildlife to feed their swelling numbers of various different tribes.

Blue sat outside their lodge watching Amy prepare the afternoon meal. He gazed toward the river where children splashed in the chilly water and women dug for turnips on the opposite side. Men made more weapons and spoke in quiet tones.

He scanned the countryside, noted the rocky, grass-covered slopes that rose in varying levels across the river. Farther south, the terrain sloped more evenly, although deep ravines still cut and sliced at random. The shoreline of the river sloped upward, blending into the hills. Lone trees grew in the valleys between rises.

Blue patted his stomach, anxious for the meal Amy prepared. Game was plentiful. Antelope meat filled their stores and the occasional moose and additional small game gave The People variety. Clear river water cleansed their bodies and cooled them in the hot summer sun.

The People are happy here, Blue thought, deciding he could be content to stay along this river forever.

Across the water someone yelled. Blue raised a hand to shield his eyes against the glare of the noon sun. He spotted one of the women pointing to a huge cloud of dust growing from the direction of the Cheyenne camp several miles upriver.

Blue's heart stopped. He knew, without doubt, what it was.

He turned to Amy who'd also spotted the cloud. Her eyes were wide, her mouth drawn tight in an effort to control her fear.

"They're here," she whispered.

Blue nodded.

They ran to the edge of the river and waited for word. Within minutes, criers raced through the village.

"The chargers are coming! The chargers are coming!"

Blue's blood ran cold. Everything he'd achieved, everything he'd worked for for so long, was about to be wiped away like chalk wiped off a board.

Gunfire exploded in the distance. Blue grabbed Amy's shoulders.

"Find Jumping Bear. Stay with him."

She nodded mutely. "Your promise."

"I promise, Amy. On our love. I'll come back." He kissed her brief and hard on the lips, then ran to capture his horse.

Amidst the confusion of women and children's screams, braves shouting and dust spiraling into the air, Blue managed to find Wild Wolf near the makeshift corral. They mounted and followed the river north toward the Cheyenne camp.

The scene they came upon made Blue's skin crawl. Hundreds of cavalrymen were riding down and firing on the Cheyenne village, killing without regard. A woman and her children lay face down in the water, killed on the first pass. Warriors scrambled for their horses, trying desperately to mount a counter-attack.

Blue and Wild Wolf rode into the village and joined the braves assembling. War cries reverberated through the air and Blue shouted along with the others. The soldiers had attacked a peaceful encampment. They must pay—regardless...

Charged with rage over what he was about to lose, Blue rode hard and fast with the others toward the advancing soldiers.

The warriors exploded from the village and the soldiers halted their advance. They whirled their mounts in confusion as they realized the huge number of swarming, angry braves ready to attack.

Blue's heart raced like the animal under him. All around the sight and sounds of battle deafened him.

Within minutes more braves joined the fight and the soldiers were greatly outnumbered. They tried to run away, but instead found themselves backed against an outcropping of trees that ran along a high bank of the river.

Trying desperately to defend themselves against the swelling number of angry Cheyenne and Lakota joining the battle, the soldiers jumped off their horses and rushed for cover in the trees.

The Indians charged, circled. Rifles popped, arrows hummed through the air, and men died. Warriors picked out a target and waited for the right moment.

"Today you will die, Bluecoats!" Wild Wolf shouted. "It is a good day to die!" He laughed and looked over at Blue, as if looking for approval of his words. Blue nodded.

Rifle shots echoed from the woods.

With the river behind them and Indians surrounding them, the soldiers were at the mercy of the Lakota and Cheyenne. Blue suddenly felt a pang of pity for the men, certain of their fate.

But the men in blue fought on as wave after wave of warriors rushed them.

Sitting Bull rode in among the Indians.

"We must go and protect the rest of our people. Ride to the south before more soldiers come. Ride. Now!"

Blue and Wild Wolf turned their horses and charged toward the Hunkpapa camp where Amy and Yellow Lodge Woman waited.

Potent fear welled up inside Blue. He had to reach camp before the soldiers attacked their village. He rode like a crazed beast, Amy's protection the only thing on his mind.

Blue reached the Hunkpapa camp and spotted the soldiers in the distance, advancing toward the camp in single file. Bloodlust in his veins, he yelled and charged. Wild Wolf followed, as did the other warriors.

They rode down the hills and caught the Bluecoats between slopes. Surprised and confused the soldiers broke formation and ran.

Rifles discharged, smoke filled the air.

Blue fired his bow again and again. Rage drove him. Beside him Wild Wolf used his hatchet and coup stick.

The soldiers retreated and raced toward a hill behind them. The Indians followed.

Suddenly a hundred or more Cheyenne charged from a hidden ravine and surrounded the soldiers.

The Bluecoats dismounted and stood back to back, trying to protect each other from the swelling number of Indians.

Blue halted his horse, held rapt by the unfolding scene.

"Come, we haven't finished yet!" Wild Wolf shouted, bloodlust still in his eyes.

"You go." Blue was suddenly drained of the killing fever.

Wild Wolf glared at him before he rammed his heels into his horse's sides and raced to join the circling Cheyenne. Blue didn't care. A lump rose in his throat as he watched the soldiers fight for their lives within the swirling dust of the Indian ponies. The Lakota and Cheyenne continued to circle—killing at will.

Bitter pleas for mercy rose above the war cries and rifle fire. Through the battle haze, Blue watched the soldiers throw down their weapons and beg for their lives. But their cries went unheard.

Riderless horses bolted away from the soldiers and out of the dust cloud, reins dangling, nostrils flaring, eyes wild.

A sick feeling washed over Blue. The cavalrymen didn't stand a chance. Slowly, their cries for mercy quieted and the dust cloud cleared.

They were all dead. Every soldier. The only thing still alive in the circle of death was one horse.

Blue watched angry Lakota and Cheyenne fall upon the dead and dismember them. He rode closer and dismounted, a sick curiosity propelling him. He scanned the mutilated bodies and reminded himself they did this to keep their enemies from returning in the afterlife to fight again. If a warrior had no eyes or ears or hands, he could not rise up against you to kill you.

He shook his head and stumbled to a naked soldier. Dead eyes faced toward the sky, as though pleading to his Maker.

Bile rose in Blue's throat. He forced it down and staggered forward. An unknown force made him see everything. The stench of guts and blood assailed him with every step. A heavy hand came down on his shoulder.

"It was a good fight!"

Black Crow, a warrior from his village, stood beside him. Blood stained his shirt and leggings. A pair of boots was tucked under his arm along with a pair of blue trousers and a shirt. He displayed them proudly before he sauntered away, searching for more of the dead men's belongings.

Blue wanted to hit Black Crow. *These were men! Men with families. Men who were alive a mere half-hour ago. Now they were only trophies, to be maimed and left on the plains to bloat in the hot sun and become fodder for the buzzards!*

Blue's legs no longer supported him. He sank to the ground. He wanted to weep, while those around him rejoiced.

A shadow blocked the sun and he looked up. Jumping Bear gazed down at him with soft, understanding eyes.

"How could this have happened?" Blue asked his father. "Why did they do it? Why did they come?"

Jumping Bear squatted down beside him. "They were foolish men, Blue Fox."

"You know this won't stop them."

Jumping Bear closed his eyes and nodded. "This is what I see in my heart. But come, let us leave this place."

"Amy? She's all right?"

"Your wife is fine. She tends the wounded. Come."

Blue stood up and scanned the battlefield again. He couldn't go back to the village yet. He had to get away to think. To understand.

"I need to be alone right now. Please take care of Amy a little while longer. Tell her I'll be back soon. I just need...some time."

The older warrior nodded again. He squeezed Blue's shoulder, swung onto his horse and rode away.

Blue mounted and turned his animal away from the scene of the battle. Away from the dead soldiers. Away from The People. All people.

Chapter Twenty-five

Blue slid from his horse's back. He'd ridden a fair distance, the need to be alone overwhelming. His insides were twisted in knots. His body shook and he just couldn't grasp what had happened in his mind.

Hundreds of men were dead. Women and children, too. The Indians had protected the Black Hills for today. But what about tomorrow?

He picked up a rock and threw it as hard and far as he could. Then another. And another.

"Why?" he shouted to God and *Wakan Tanka*. He felt as though one or both of them had deserted him. "Why couldn't you let them live in peace? Instead you gave them this great victory, and now they'll believe they can save their precious Black Hills!" he shouted to the hills.

He dropped to his knees and grabbed a handful of dirt, then flung it away.

"Why? Damn it. Why?"

He climbed to the top of a hill and looked out over the rolling countryside. Near the battle-site roving groups of Indians combed the ravines and crags for straggling soldiers. An eerie haze of dust and smoke hung low in the air. He heard joyous shouts as women and men stripped and disfigured the dead.

God, how could this have happened? He took several gulping breaths to keep from screaming again.

He tried to block out the sounds of the celebrating Indians. There was a noise below him—stones tumbling down the hillside.

Silent as a mountain cat, he crawled to the edge of the hill and peered over. Tiny rocks were settling at the bottom of the ravine. He scanned the side of the hill, but saw nothing.

Curious, Blue worked his way down the hillside. Slow and quiet, he edged along a small ridge that jutted out from the side, groping for something to grab onto.

There was movement a few feet away. He stopped breathing and listened. Something or someone was inside a small indention in the side of the hill. Recalling the layout of the area, he remembered numerous caves were scattered throughout the terrain.

He took a deep breath to slow his racing heart and scooted forward. A piece of the ledge broke away, clattered down the slope and landed with a crash at the bottom.

"I have a gun!" someone shouted.

"I won't hurt you," Blue said in English. "Put your gun down. I can help."

"I don't believe you. Who the hell are you?" came the surprised response.

Blue mulled the question. *Who was he? A red man who would kill this soldier when he showed himself? Or a white man who would help him escape?*

"I can help," he said again.

"Are you a soldier? Are you hiding, too? What unit are you from? Show your face."

Blue shook his head. "I'm not going to stick my head in there for you to blow it off. You're going to have to trust me."

"Trust you? Why should I?"

Blue breathed deeply. "I'm not a soldier. My name is Blue Fox. You have to believe I'm not going to hurt you. If I wanted to do that, all I'd have to do is sound an alert and you'd have a hundred Lakota and Cheyenne here in a heartbeat to kill you."

There was scrambling inside the small shelter and a head poked out. Two wide, questioning eyes stared at him with such wonder, he caught his breath.

Blue could only stare back in shock. Shock that made him mute.

George!

He scooted to the opening, yanked George out of the cave and pulled him into a crushing embrace.

George groaned then threw his arms around Blue.

"Blue? Is it really you?" George choked when he pushed away. Squinting, he eyed Blue from top to bottom.

George's knees gave way and he dropped to his knees. Blue noticed blood on George's shoulder and he dropped down beside him to inspect the wound.

His friend winced. "It's not that bad. Seen a lot worse today." He looked up at the sky. "Saw things today I don't ever want to see again in my whole life."

Blue nodded. "Me, too."

George grabbed Blue's arm. "Sarah wrote me you'd gone. But she had no idea where you were. I can't believe I've found you." His voice cracked with emotion.

"Who found who?" Blue teased, unable to resist.

George smiled that boyish grin that transported Blue back to his childhood and the bond of friendship these two men shared.

"I guess you found your people, huh? We've wondered where you'd gone."

Blue nodded. "And when I finally found some peace in my life, this happened."

George looked away.

"Did I fight with the Indians here today?" Blue answered George's unasked question.

George's eyes snapped up to Blue's. "Did you?"

Blue sighed. "I did. I had no choice. They gave me no choice. They attacked our peaceful village and had to be stopped."

George was about to protest, but snapped his mouth shut and nodded. "I guess we did, didn't we?

"Custer was supposed to wait for General Terry, but when this camp was discovered, he chose to attack. He was afraid the Indian's would run away before he could catch them," George snorted. He smiled sadly. "I think he miscalculated."

"By several thousand."

Shouts in the distance brought Blue back to the crisis at hand.

"We have to get you out of here," Blue said. "First we have to stop this bleeding. Do you have anything we can stuff inside your coat?"

"My kerchief, that's about all. Here." George jerked the scarf from around his neck and handed it to Blue. Blue shoved it inside the coat, grabbed George's hand and started to climb, pulling his friend behind him. By the time they reached the crest of the hill, George looked like a washed out sheet.

"Can you make it?" Blue noticed the makeshift bandage wasn't stopping the flow of blood; the scarf was already soaked.

"I'll make it. Just lead the way."

He tugged George over the rise toward his horse. "We've got to hurry."

With little urging George mounted. Blue headed the animal between hills and away from the battlefield while he tried to decide what to do next.

He had to get away from the Indian encampments. If he could get north of the Little Bighorn, well above where the Cheyenne were camped, maybe they could cross the river. With luck, he'd find a cave or somewhere to hide his friend. Then he'd ride back to camp, get Amy then go back for George.

It wouldn't be easy, but he knew it was the only hope any of them had of making it out of this valley.

He headed the horse west, careful to stay hidden between the sloping hills that made up the terrain of the Little Bighorn valley.

Blue began to relax as they worked their way from the river.

"How's your pa?" he asked. "Have you heard from Ben and Sarah since you've been gone? What's it like being a soldier?" Blue was suddenly overwhelmed by the need to know what was happening to his other family.

George remained silent.

"What's wrong?"

"Pa's been gone two years. Got a letter from Sarah that told me he'd passed on. Wound up with the consumption. He lingered, but she wrote it was peaceful in the end.

"She said he didn't talk about anything but me those last few days of his life. Remembered me as a kid, then when we were living out at White Oaks. Finally, as a soldier, even though he never got to see me in uniform. She said he died proud of me."

"I'm glad, George."

Blue suddenly felt uncertain of himself and all he'd accomplished. *Would either of his fathers, white or Indian, be proud of him for the things he's done the way George's father had been? Would his white father hate him because he fought as*

209

an Indian, or be proud because he fought with a people for what was right? And is Jumping Bear proud or ashamed?

"What about Sarah? And Ben," he asked to change the subject. "Are they well? Have you heard from them recently?"

"I heard from them about six months ago. They're doing fine. They're worried about you, though. If only you'd found some way to let them know you were all right."

"I know." Blue's throat grew tight.

"Where are we going?" George asked after they'd ridden in silence a few minutes.

"To find someplace to hide you, well away from the encampments. I'm going to take care of that wound, go back to Sitting Bull's camp, then come back and get you."

"What? Go back! Why?"

"For Amy. My wife." There was pride in Blue's voice.

George clapped Blue on the back. "Well, I'm damn sorry I missed your wedding," George joked, his voice sounding thin.

Praying he'd gone far enough to miss any stragglers, Indian or white, Blue turned his horse north.

The day wore on and George fell in and out of consciousness behind Blue.

George moaned.

"We'll stop soon," Blue said.

A half hour later they came to a tiny pool formed by a trickle of water cascading down the side of a cliff. Blue slid to the ground and helped his friend from the horse.

"Sit here." He pointed to a soft patch of grass. "I'll be right back."

George's eyes were ringed red, his forehead slick with sweat.

Blue searched the area for several minutes until he found a small cave in the wall of a nearby hill. The interior was only eight feet deep and five feet high, but there were no animal droppings so Blue felt it would be safe to use. The cave was nestled at the front of a rising bluff with a sheer drop to the rear and a twenty foot hill on both sides. Blue felt George would be safe inside for a few days. With a few leaf-covered branches dragged in front of the entrance, no one would even know it existed.

210

Blue made his way through the woods back to his friend. George was pale and Blue knew he had to do something soon, before the wound became infected.

His thoughts must have been obvious. When he sat down next to George, his friend immediately asked, "How bad is it?"

"Not as bad as you think, soldier boy." Blue tried to keep his voice light.

George sighed heavily. "Let's get on with it. Do whatever you have to."

Blue helped George to the cave and made him as comfortable as he could. He opened George's jacket and the stench almost made Blue gag. But he couldn't let George see his concern, so he continued his observance of the wound with a blank face, while his stomach churned and rolled. Crusted black blood was stuck to the linen kerchief and had probably kept George from bleeding to death. But it also kept the material glued to George's shoulder. Rather that, Blue supposed, than uncontrolled bleeding, he thought with a grimace.

Blue removed the jacket and George's shirt. He tore it into strips and went to the stream to soak them.

When he returned, Blue made George look at him. "We've got to get this wound cleaned so infection doesn't set in."

George drew in another heavy breath and closed his eyes. "I can take it. Just get me something to bite down on."

Blue gathered kindling and set a tiny fire just outside the entrance. When the wood glowed red, Blue put his knife on a rock so the blade rested in the flames. Then he knelt down beside George.

"We really shouldn't have a fire, Blue. Someone could spot the smoke."

"We've got no choice. There's no other way to sterilize and seal this wound."

Blue leaned over his friend and dribbled water onto the blood-encrusted linen to soften it so he could peel it away. The sour odor assaulted Blue again when he removed the last of the cloth after several minutes of carefully pulling the material away from George's skin.

George's breathing was ragged one minute, even the next. Blue knew he was slipping in and out of consciousness and he worked faster. He dribbled more water over the now open wound until he felt it was as clean as it could get.

He handed George a thick stick when he roused again.

"It's time. Bite down on this. I'll be as quick as I can."

George shoved the stick between his teeth and took a deep breath. He searched Blue's face, nodded and closed his eyes.

Blue grabbed his knife from the fire. Seconds later, the stench of burned flesh filled the cave. George passed out, but he didn't cry out, to Blue's surprise.

Drained and exhausted, Blue leaned back, swiped his forehead, then dabbed his friend's forehead with some wet strips of cloth. George moaned, smiled and opened his eyes, but quickly closed them again.

An hour passed. Blue shook his friend gently. "It's time for me to go back. I've been gone too long already."

He covered George with his cavalry jacket and hoped it would be enough to ward off the cold.

George nodded.

"I'll be back. I promise. Don't think for a minute I won't come back for you." Blue tucked the jacket under George's chin and a vision of the past they'd shared exploded into Blue's mind. Two boys, thrown together by fate. Boys who understood each other's pain and dreams.

Blue traced the faint white scar on his palm and swore again he'd be back.

Chapter Twenty-six

Blue rode hard back to camp. While he rode he tried to come up with a plausible story to cover where he'd been for the last six hours.

It was almost night before he reached the campsite where he'd left Amy. She was wrapping a warrior's injured calf when Blue came upon her.

His heart swelled with love as he watched her ministrations, chattering in both Lakota and English. An errant hair fell across her face and she brushed it aside with the back of her hand. As though she sensed his presence, she turned. And their eyes met.

Before Blue could breathe, she was in his arms, smothering him with warm, wonderful kisses.

She pulled away and checked him for wounds. She found the dried black blood on his leg and gave him a questioning glance.

"I'm fine. Just a flesh wound," he answered her silent question.

He pulled her into his arms and tried to kiss her, but she would have none of it. She shoved him away.

"Then where the hell have you been? I've been worried sick for hours."

He pulled her into an embrace, twined his hands through her hair to hold her still.

"Please, Amy. For once just stay quiet," he whispered into her ear. He met her lips, quieting any further questions.

When he looked into her eyes, he saw her concern. Her love. And her understanding.

Tipiziwin had been dressing the wounds of another brave. She saw Blue and stepped toward him.

"I'm glad you've returned safely, Blue Fox. Your wife was worried."

"I see her worry was without cause, my brother," Wild Wolf said when he came up behind them. "Why have you waited so long to return?"

213

Blue sensed antagonism in his question.

"I was upset after the battle," he said.

Wild Wolf's eyes clouded. "I remember. In a matter of minutes, I watched you transform from a strong, Lakota warrior to a white man with a woman's stomach." He spit and glared at Blue.

"And then you ran away, your heart too weak to look upon the dead."

"I needed some time to sort things out. Ask Jumping Bear."

"He told me," Wild Wolf said. "But you've been gone a long time. Where were you?"

He caressed Amy's cheek and smiled at her.

"I rode farther than I thought trying to get away from the sounds and smells of battle."

"You were upset the whites paid for their treachery?" Wild Wolf asked. "They killed our women and children!"

Blue looked at his brother.

"I know that. And they were wrong, but how can I make you understand what I'm feeling? They were men, just like us. You. Me. Jumping Bear, with families of their own."

"Who came to take what isn't theirs. Who killed our families and loved ones!"

"I know what they did was wrong. But was it any more wrong than our raiding the Crow village and taking their winter stores?"

Wild Wolf tried to interrupt, but Blue waved him silent.

"Both sides are wrong. And too many people are already dead. On both sides."

Wild Wolf stared at Blue, his lips tight with rage. Finally, he grabbed Tipiziwin's hand and stalked away, dragging her behind him.

Blue watched his friends disappear around the lodges and his heart felt heavy. He could only admire Wild Wolf, who was willing to fight and die for everything he believed in. For the land. For his people.

But hadn't he done the same?

Amy took Blue's arm.

214

"I'm sorry," she whispered. "Someday, he'll understand."

"Someday. If he's still alive." Blue looked at Amy's grimy face, dried streaks of tears evident through the dust on her cheeks. She had cried for him. The thought warmed him.

Amy pulled Blue to their lodge. The instant she was inside she whirled on him.

"Now tell me where the hell you've been."

In as few words as possible, Blue told Amy about George, her eyes wide when he finished.

"We've got to leave here. As soon as the sun comes up, we'll go to George and ride back to White Oaks."

Amy threw her arms around his neck, smothered him with kisses. In that moment he understood more about her than ever before. Amy had stayed with The People for him. Him alone. He held her tight, thankful that through all this madness, he hadn't lost her.

"Before we go, I have to talk with Sitting Bull and Crazy Horse."

"Why?" Amy's voice was laced with fear. "What if someone saw you with George. Accuses you? It's not safe. We should just leave."

Blue shook his head. A new kind of strength filled him.

"I have to try one last time to make them understand it's futile to keep fighting. I can't leave without trying at least once more."

Amy gave him a sad smile. "Before you go to the chiefs, Jumping Bear wants to see you. He's been waiting for you and asked me to send you to him as soon as you returned."

Blue kissed her cheek. "I'll talk to him, then go to the council."

"Jumping Bear." Blue called at his father's lodge flap. It slapped open and before Blue could blink, Jumping Bear had him in a crushing embrace.

"My son! You're not dead." Jumping Bear examined him up and down. "Come. Tell me what's happened to you since we spoke."

215

Blue stepped inside and sat down on a pallet across from his father. His shoulders slumped and he sighed. "You won't like the story I'm going to tell you."

"I'll be the judge," Jumping Bear responded. "Speak it."

Again, Blue related the story of George. Jumping Bear listened, intent on Blue's words. He never moved, never interrupted.

"So Amy and I must leave." Only then did the old warrior's body tighten.

Jumping Bear didn't say a word. He just stared. Finally, he broke the heavy silence.

"If this is what you must do, my son, so it must be. I don't fault you for your loyalty to your white brother. But I know no one here will have forgiveness in their hearts if they find out. Are you certain this is what you want?"

"Yes." Blue nodded. "But I won't leave until I talk again with the elders. Until I make them understand that next time, there'll be more soldiers. And more after that. Until every woman, child and brave is gone."

"I know your words come from your love of The People. We'll go to Sitting Bull and Crazy Horse and speak of it."

Jumping Bear stood stoic and strong as always. But there was sadness in the older man's eyes and a wave of guilt washed over Blue.

"Come with us, Jumping Bear," Blue pleaded. "I can't leave you here to die or be hunted down like an animal."

"But this is where I belong. With my people."

The words rang in Blue's ears. To belong. That was all he'd ever wanted.

A chill swept over Blue as he walked beside Jumping Bear.

"Thank you for understanding, Father."

"You are my son. The son of my heart and of my choosing. I made this so when I spoke it to The People. I know what you must do. But as your father, I grieve for your choice. I will miss you."

Blue smothered the sob in his chest and then he was in Jumping Bear's arms, holding his father in a farewell embrace he knew would have to last a lifetime.

"I will never forget you," he whispered. "For what you taught me when no other would. And for what you are to me."

Jumping Bear squeezed Blue one last time before he pushed away, but not before Blue saw the shimmer of tears in the older man's eyes.

"We must go. The elders meet in the council lodge. Tell them what is in your heart, Blue Fox. Make them understand."

At the flap of the council lodge, Blue sucked in a huge gulp of air to calm himself. Again his inner strength took hold.

He threw open the flap and entered, Jumping Bear behind him with unspoken support. The chiefs, elders and headmen stopped speaking as they came in.

"I must speak with Tatanka Yotanka."

Sitting Bull inclined his head. "You may speak."

"I come to speak to The People. To warn them again. Today a great victory was won. But the war is not over, it is only just beginning. Many more soldiers will come.

"Even if you fight to the last man, woman and child, *Paha Sapa* will still be gone. You must not fight or the white men will make this land your graves."

Shouting erupted, but Blue stood steady.

The great chief crossed his arms over his chest and waited for the room to quiet.

"You say more whites will come. If they do, we'll know. Already scouts have been sent across our land. When they return, we'll know what to do. When the sun rises we will speak again," he said, ending the conversation. He turned and addressed the council.

"Tonight we grieve for our fallen warriors. Along with those white men who died at our hands in battle. This night we shall mourn both as our own. Hetchetu aloh. It is so indeed."

Blue left the council lodge with Jumping Bear beside him and wondered where Wild Wolf was. He hadn't been inside.

Jumping Bear said goodnight and headed toward his lodge. Blue went to his own lodge where Amy waited.

"Is everything all right?"

"Jumping Bear is a good man. He understands our situation and will keep our secret. Of everything I'll leave behind, I'll miss him and Wild Wolf most."

217

"I know," she whispered. She guided Blue toward their pallet to rest before their journey. But for Blue, tomorrow would only bring unspoken goodbyes.

Blue couldn't sleep. His thoughts rolled and tumbled in his head. Guns exploded. Horses and men screamed. Warriors whooped and women wept. Before he realized, the sun was up.

Amy bustled about. She gathered only what was absolutely necessary for the trip: small amounts of dried meat, two knives, water, extra clothing.

"It's time for me to meet Sitting Bull for the last time."

Amy stepped forward and caressed his face. "Good luck."

He nodded, gave Amy a brief hug and left the lodge.

He entered the empty council chamber, allowing his eyes to roam the confines of the huge, airy room. Hides and furs covered the entire floor. A raised dais was at the front where the chiefs and elders sat in deference of their position in the tribe. A large fire pit was at the center, the ashes gray and cold. Pictures, drawn on the hide walls, stretched around the room.

Blue stepped up and traced his fingers around the pictures and faces that stared back at him. The history of The People. He was studying the pictorial history when Sitting Bull entered.

He stepped onto the platform, sat down and motioned for Blue to sit beside him.

"Tall Bear has returned with word that many Bluecoats march toward us," the chief began. "Many more than we met yesterday. The line of soldiers is nearly a mile long." He paused.

"As I have already spoken, I believe the whites who invaded our camps came as the fulfillment of my vision. I do not think the men who march today will be so easily delivered.

"Most of the ammunition for our guns and rifles is gone. I don't think we can defeat a great army of guns and rifles with bows and arrows, tomahawks and lances."

He stared across the room.

"I've already told the headmen we must leave this place. We will go north among our different tribes. I told Crazy Horse to take his people in one direction. I will take mine in another and so on for the other chiefs. This will make it difficult for the whites to track us.

"Many of the chiefs agree," he continued. "But others want to stay and fight."

"Because they will take the Black Hills from us if we run like scared women!" Wild Wolf shouted from where he stood in the entrance, his fists balled beside him. He took long strides into the room and stopped in front of Sitting Bull.

"If we don't fight they'll take our sacred lands and we'll never be able to return."

"You forget the Treaty of 1868," Sitting Bull reminded the angry warrior. "Only when three-fourths of our men make the mark of the pen on paper can the whites, by their own law, take the Black Hills from us. If they cannot find us, how can we sign a new treaty to give away our land?"

Wild Wolf opened his mouth to speak again, but was silenced by a wave of Sitting Bull's hand. He stood, leaned over and placed a hand on Wild Wolf's shoulder.

"Come. We have much work to do." The grizzled warrior straightened and stepped from the dais, Wild Wolf beside him, his anger burning beneath the surface like a flame.

Blue followed behind, a knowledge deep in his soul that if there was some way the government could get around that old treaty, they'd do it. The same knowledge told him Sitting Bull knew it, too.

Blue headed toward his lodge, but Wild Wolf stepped in front of him. Danger ripped up Blue's spine when he looked into his friend's face. Wild Wolf's black eyes were cold and hard, the killing fever still hot inside him.

"I suppose you're happy we will run away like sheep," Wild Wolf snapped.

"Damn it. What does it take to make you understand what you're up against?" Blue said. "Sitting Bull and the other chiefs are doing what they have to in order to save The People."

"Bah!" The warrior threw his hand out from his chest. "This is our land. And no one will take it from us without a fight!"

He shoved his way past Blue before he could utter another word.

219

Blue wanted to say something to Wild Wolf. He didn't want to leave with bad feelings between them. Didn't want their last words to be hard ones. *But what could he say? That he was going away never to return?*

He looked up and spotted Jumping Bear. Unable to leave his father without final words, he called to him.

"We'll be going soon," he said only loud enough for his father to hear.

"I know this, my son. Go safely. Know my heart goes with you."

Blue pushed down the anguish in his chest and took Jumping Bear's hand.

"I love you," he whispered. The strength of his emotion for this man shook him. Unable to remain without breaking down, Blue quickly strode to his lodge.

Amy waited inside, anxious to be on their way.

Within minutes, they were on their horses, riding from The People.

At the edge of camp, Tipiziwin stepped in front of them. "Would you leave without saying goodbye?" she asked.

Blue caught his breath. "We're not leaving."

"Don't lie to me." There was no trace of anger in her voice. "I know you leave us now. I know your heart is heavy because of what happened yesterday."

Blue dismounted and took Yellow Lodge Woman's hands in his.

"Please. Don't tell Wild Wolf. He's angry enough at me right now. If he finds out we're going, he might come after us."

Tipiziwin nodded. "My husband's heart is bad right now. He has unkind words for you. He says you weep over the dead like a woman. His words make me sad, Blue Fox. But don't worry. I'll keep your secret."

"Thank you."

Her eyes sparkled with tears.

"When I saw you weren't dead, my heart sang with joy. I thanked the Great Spirit for bringing you back alive. For a moment, I forgot you came back only for Amy." She looked at the white woman and gave her a slight smile. Amy smiled and nodded back.

220

"I'm sorry. So many things have happened. So many things have changed." He took her shoulders. "And so many more things are going to change."

The Indian woman looked away and nodded.

"I know it," she said softly. "I've felt it. I know we won't be free much longer. Our way of life will die with the buffalo. Many of our people are already on reservations. Red Cloud, Spotted Tail, both great warriors, both tired of war. Soon, we too, will be tired of running and tired of war and will go to the reservations."

She turned sad eyes back to Blue. "But you're half white. You can go among the whites and make them understand us. Tell them all we want is to be left alone on our land. Land that is sacred to us, to hunt and fish and grow old with our loved ones as we have done for all time remembered."

Her words were good and true. Maybe he was the one person *because* of who and what he was that could make the men in power understand. He realized he was nodding his head and Tipiziwin's smile brightened.

"Go, Blue Fox with Two Hearts. Take the wife of your heart and find your place among the whites. But in doing so, make a difference for The People."

She touched his hand one last time and tears spilled down her face. A moment later, she ran away as little clouds of dust floated up behind her in her haste.

Blue watched her go, his mind in a whirl. *Was she right? For once in his life did he have the power to do something good because of what he was? Could he make a difference for The People?*

Blue remounted. Amy touched his hand, her eyes filled with understanding.

"She loves you, you know."

Blue was stunned. He had no idea Amy knew.

"It's all right." A smile came to her face. "How could she not?"

They rode from camp in silence for many miles.

Stopping at a stream to water their horses, Amy finally broke the silence between them.

"I'm sorry," she said.

"Why?"

"Because I know how much you're hurting right now. And it makes me hurt, too."

He thought about leaving Jumping Bear and Wild Wolf behind. He wished he could have said goodbye to Wild Wolf. Wished he could have made him understand. But he knew it wasn't to be.

"In the last few months, I've seen too much," he said. "Too much has happened. I know now where I must go. Their world will never be the same."

He glanced over the rolling hills around them and bitter sadness welled up inside him.

"Where are we going?" Amy asked.

"Home."

Chapter Twenty-seven

Blue was concerned about George when they reached the cave by the river. The brush had been pushed away from the entrance.

"George?" he called softly before he looked inside.

Terror swallowed him like a living thing. The cave was empty. He shimmied his way back outside then scanned the area frantically.

"Don't panic like an old woman," came the familiar voice from not far away.

Blue whirled to see George walking toward him from the thickness of the trees.

"You're alive," Blue said. "When I looked inside and saw you weren't there..." He couldn't finish the sentence.

"I'm fine. Calm down." George shook his head. "I just went to the stream for water." He swayed on his feet.

Blue grabbed him and sat him down on a rock.

"You've still got a fever." He touched his friend's head and felt the heat.

"Had some crazy dreams last night," George said with a chuckle. "I'm far from better, but I'll live. I hope."

Amy stepped into George's view and he tried to stand, but Blue pushed him down.

"This, I presume, is Amy?"

"My wife." The pride was unmistakable in Blue's voice.

George gazed at her, an expression of appreciation on his face. "Beautiful. Pleased to meet you Mrs. Devlin."

"What?" she asked them both, her eyes full of surprise.

"Devlin. That's our last name. You are Mrs. Blue Devlin. But enough of this small talk. It's time to go," Blue answered, anxious to be away.

"Would you leave The People without saying goodbye to me?" Wild Wolf shouted the words as he stepped from a shadow of trees.

Blue's breath caught and his body went stiff. He looked into his Lakota brother's eyes. Eyes that burned like a funeral pyre, full of pure rage.

"Wild Wolf. You don't understand."

"What don't I understand, my brother?" The word dripped with sarcasm. "Why do you sneak away from The People like a slithering snake? Because you hide this white soldier!" he shouted. "A Bluecoat who rode with the others and killed my people. Our people!"

Wild Wolf stepped toward George, his hand on the hilt of his knife.

"Don't even think about using that," Blue shouted, his blood like ice.

"Why do you protect this white man?" The Indian took another step toward George. His fingers curled around the knife.

"I mean what I say," Blue said evenly. "Don't do it."

"Or what?" The veins in Wild Wolf's neck popped up, pulsed with rage. "What will you do to me, Brother? He is a white man and all whites must die!"

"Not this one."

The brave charged, but Blue knocked him sideways, away from George.

Wild Wolf came up with a bellow, his face twisted with hatred.

"No!" Blue raised his hands. "You can't kill this man. He's my Brother!"

Blue stood his ground in front of George, shielding him with his body. Wild Wolf, his chest heaving, glared past Blue at the white man who tried to stand.

"Get out of my way, Blue Fox. He will die. *I'm* your Brother."

Blue drew his back up like a lance. "He won't die. And you won't kill him."

The brave stared at Blue as though he were someone he'd never seen before.

"This man attacked our village. And you defend him?" the warrior shouted. "All whites must die!"

"But I'm part white," Blue said. "Will you kill me?"

"You are no longer white," Wild Wolf said. "You are my brother."

"One part of me is your brother, but another is this man's brother. Which part will you kill?"

Confusion clouded the Indian's face. Seconds ticked away.

"You must choose," Wild Wolf said.

"I can't choose," Blue shouted. "I love you both."

"That isn't possible. You must make a choice, or step away and I'll choose for you."

"No."

"Then you have chosen."

Wild Wolf stepped back and raised his right hand in front of him. He stared down at the gold ring on his finger, then jerked it off and threw it at Blue's feet.

"We are no longer brothers."

"Don't do this, Wild Wolf. Don't make me choose life or death for either of you. You're both my brothers!"

"The choice has been made. You are white. He is white and she is white. You will all die."

Blue couldn't believe what he was hearing. He glanced at Amy's stricken face. George swayed like a willow. He was the only thing between death and Wild Wolf for all three of them.

Wild Wolf threw himself at Blue and knocked him over, the warrior on top.

"I trusted you," Wild Wolf screamed. "You were my brother!"

"I'm *still* your brother!"

"You are dead, Blue Fox with Two Hearts. Dead!"

Blue shoved Wild Wolf off him and scrambled to his feet. His brother-friend was beyond reasoning.

"Don't do this, Wild Wolf. Don't make me fight you."

Wild Wolf charged, driving Blue backward. But Blue held his ground, angering the warrior more.

"I don't want to fight you!" Blue yelled.

Even as he shouted the words, Wild Wolf squared off in front of him. A high-pitched war cry exploded from the Indian's throat and he lunged again.

225

Blue dropped to the ground, rolled away then jumped back to his feet.

"Stop, Wild Wolf. I don't want to fight you!"

"You have no choice, white man!" The brave charged again and grabbed Blue around the belly. They hit the ground rolling.

Amy screamed. Blue fisted his hands and pounded Wild Wolf's arms. When he started to roll away, Blue hit him in the chest. All the pent up anger, fear, sadness and anger inside him exploded with wild fury. He hit Wild Wolf with every ounce of rage he possessed and drove him off him. Blue jumped to his feet.

A flash of silver. Blue froze. The brave rolled the knife in his hand.

"Damn it! Why won't you listen to reason?"

"Fight or die wasicun!" his Indian brother screamed.

Blue drew his own knife. Terror and fury coursed through him.

They squared off again, both soaked with sweat, Blue's heart pounding like the wings of a giant eagle. If this was going to be to the death, Blue couldn't let Wild Wolf win. He had too much to lose besides his own life. He could lose Amy and George.

He lunged forward and grabbed Wild Wolf's knife hand. The two staggered as each tried to gain control. Stones rolled and fell over the nearing precipice, bounced and clinked their way down the slope.

Locked in a dance of death, Blue jammed his knee into Wild Wolf's stomach. The brave doubled over and his knife clattered to the ground.

Gasping for breath, the brave dove toward the fallen knife. Blue snatched up the weapon before he could reach it and placed his foot on top of Wild Wolf's extended hand.

"I didn't want things to end this way." Blue leaned over the prone Indian, adjusted the blade in his hand and angled it toward Wild Wolf's neck.

The brave's eyes grew wide, but only for a second before his body relaxed.

"You have defeated me. Now you will take my life." He looked up at the trees. "Perhaps it is better this way. It is a good day to die!" Wild Wolf shouted.

Eyes hard and full of hatred, lowered back to Blue. "My only regret is I will not take more soldiers with me before I go...or you and these others!" he added with a gleam in his eyes.

He grabbed Blue's forearm with his free hand.

"If it's your intention to kill me, then do it," Wild Wolf challenged, pushing the knife closer to his throat.

Blue looked at the knife in his hand and a sickening dread enveloped him. Wild Wolf pushed the tip far enough into the softness of his neck to draw a pinprick of blood.

"Damn you!" Blue shouted. "I don't want to kill you. Whether you believe it or not, I'm still your brother. And as far as I'm concerned, I always will be."

He flung the knife away.

Wild Wolf sat up. "You have proven you are more white than Indian." A thin red trickle of blood oozed down his neck. He touched the spot and smiled.

"A true brother of the Lakota would have slit my throat and taken my scalp as a trophy."

In the next instant Wild Wolf was on him again, pushing Blue toward the cliff.

Suddenly Amy was draped over Wild Wolf's back, her fingers gouging at the warrior's eyes and cheeks. She screamed in his ears.

"Leave him alone, Wild Wolf!" Her finger nails raked across his face and left long red welts and blood on his skin.

The brave squared his shoulders and flung her toward the cliff like a gnat. Her feet landed at the edge, and she began to slip down the side. She screamed.

Blue scrambled toward her, but Wild Wolf blocked his path. "No my brother. You will watch her die."

Blue charged and knocked Wild Wolf aside in his haste to reach Amy. But Wild Wolf was intent on keeping his brother from his wife. He grabbed his arm as he ran past and swung him away from her.

"You will not stop her from falling, Blue Fox. I have chosen that she will be the first to die!"

"No!" Blue screamed as he rounded a fist on Wild Wolf. The blow caught the warrior on the jaw and knocked him backward.

Blue turned toward Amy, relieved to see George laying over the top of the cliff, pulling her up.

In the seconds he'd taken to see that Amy was all right, Wild Wolf was on him again. The warrior jerked him upright and flung him toward the edge of the bluff.

"Even as I send you to your death, you worry about your white wife and white brother!" Wild Wolf sneered. "Will you think of them as you fall?"

"I won't die. I'm not ready!" With a burst of strength born of fury and desperation, Blue surged forward and pushed the Indian aside.

The brave dropped his shoulder and charged again. But Blue had lived and fought with this man too long not to know his style of fighting. Wild Wolf ran straight in. Blue jumped to the side.

Wild Wolf staggered to a halt at the precipice—but his moccasins slipped. Blue heard before he saw.

Rocks broke away under Wild Wolf's feet and the earth slid away. In the blink of an eye, he was gone.

"Wild Wolf!" Blue scrambled to the ledge.

The Indian frantically pawed at the side of the cliff, trying to keep from falling.

"Grab my hand," Blue shouted. He slid over the edge as far as he could and reached for his brother.

The warrior looked up. His eyes reflected panic, yet the rage was still there, smoldering. He reached up and their hands locked. Wild Wolf's other hand clamped over Blue's wrist. Wild Wolf jerked.

Blue slid forward. Against his will, he inched closer and closer to the edge of the ledge.

"You will die with me, Wasicun!"

Amy and George grabbed Blue's feet and kept him from sliding further forward.

Wild Wolf began to struggle, kicked his feet.

"Damn you," Blue shouted. "I can save you. Hold on."

The warrior jerked again, but his hand slipped. Blue squeezed, but Wild Wolf's fingers eased from his grasp.

Blue watched his brother's face as surprise, rage and sadness swept over it as he fell.

Wild Wolf's body hit the side of the ravine twice and, finally, the bottom where his body lay contorted. Still. Amy tried to coax Blue away from the ledge. But he was frozen, unable to take his eyes away.

"There's nothing you can do." Her soft voice finally penetrated the haze in his mind.

He inched his way backward, away from the threat of the ledge, and sat up. Every part of him felt numb.

He staggered from the cliff, his mind and body frozen with sorrow and guilt that he couldn't save Wild Wolf from plunging to his death.

He looked down and something caught his eye. He reached over and picked up the small golden band half hidden in the dirt where Wild Wolf had thrown it.

All he had striven for, *all* he had possessed in the last years were gone.

The band lay dull and cold in his hand to match his heart—cold in his chest.

Chapter Twenty-eight

Anxiety grew like a seed in Blue's chest; he peered through the bright sunlight up the tree-lined entrance—up the lane he'd ridden so often in another lifetime.

Beside him, George and Amy sat in silence. Their horses snorted and swished their tails trying to dislodge the stubborn flies that seemed to have followed them all the way from the Black Hills. But Blue ignored the insistent buzzing of the insects, his eyes and mind focused only on what lay ahead of him. White Oaks. Ben and Sarah.

He clucked his horse forward, Amy and George behind him.

They emerged from the tree cover and Blue scanned the surrounding buildings. Things were as he remembered. To his right was the corral, its split-rail fence still sturdy. Behind it stood a newly built barn. To the rear of the barn were the bunkhouse and the well where Sarah had confided to him her capture by the Lakota. To his left, still proud against the deep azure sky, stood the main house. A spiral of gray smoke rose from the kitchen chimney at the rear.

A rush of time flashed through Blue like an opening of Heaven's gates. He saw the love he'd received from his foster parents. The joy he'd felt in this place. He saw George's smiling face as a young, awkward boy. The two skipping rocks over the pond in the south quarter.

He heard the bellow of cows off in the open pasture, and the memory of helping Ben with the branding and herds flooded his mind. Smells of hay and dust, horses and cattle, and the sweet aroma of Sarah's cooking, assaulted his senses.

He shielded his eyes with his hand and looked up at the fiery orange ball in the sky. From where it hung, Blue knew it was close to the supper hour. He turned and looked at George, who was already smiling. Blue couldn't help but laugh. He reached out his hand. Amy moved her horse forward and took it, a wary smile on her face.

230

"Do you think they'll like me?" There was an uncertainty in her voice he'd never heard before.

"Of course, they'll like you. Especially Sarah. You have a lot in common." He released her hand and ran his finger down her cheek. "Besides, what's not to like? I've loved you from the first moment I saw you."

Amy cocked her head and grinned. "Sure you did, every time you chased me down or protected yourself from my attacks or wondered *why* I was put off by your touch."

"Like I said, what's not to love? Come on, it's time for supper."

The three dismounted and tied off their horses. Blue took a deep breath, clapped George on the back and knocked on the door.

It creaked open and Sarah stood in the doorway. In a heartbeat, Blue was in her arms, Ben rushing to greet them.

With the speed of a lightning bolt, Blue understood all he had been searching for was here in this place. Gathered around him.

True acceptance is how you are loved and cared about despite who or what you are. Simply enough. Acceptance among strangers has to be earned, as Sarah once said. He had proven that. He'd been accepted among the Lakota. Accepted by Jumping Bear and Wild Wolf. Even by Sitting Bull and Crazy Horse. But it was only through his deeds that he'd found that acceptance. Ben and Sarah accepted and loved Blue for who he was, not what he could do or prove. Blue realized true acceptance was love. And with that realization, he understood one thing above all else.

He was home.

~The End~

"What treaty that the whites have kept has the red man broken? Not one. What treaty that the white man ever made with us have they ever kept? Not one.... What law have I broken? Is it wrong for me to love my own? Is it wicked for me because my skin is red? Because I am Lakota; because I was born where my father lived; because I would die for my people and my country."

-Tatanka Yotanka (Sitting Bull)
Hunkpapa Lakota

REFERENCES CONSULTED FOR ACCURACY:

Bury My Heart at Wounded Knee – Dee Brown
Lakota Belief & Rituals – James R. Walker
Native Americans – William C. Sturtvant
American West in the 19th Century – John Grafton
In the Spirit of Crazy Horse – Peter Matheson

About the Author...

Diane was born on "The Jersey Shore" and spent much of her youth on the beach, but for the past 20+ years she's lived in the Kansas City area. She currently resides south of Kansas City with her husband, horses, and a multitude of cats. She has two grown children and five grandchildren. She's always loved the old West and history of the Civil War period. Her favorite movie is Dances With Wolves, an inspiration for the first book in the White Oaks Series. Having parents from both the "North and the South" and a cousin whose parents were reversed, they called each other "Yebels" as children and, imagined themselves, as children will do, 150 years ago fighting on different sides of the war.

As a kid, Diane played "Cowboys and Indians" more than she did Barbie, and it comes through in her writing, as she relates stories of the struggle of common people and what made this country great.

When Diane isn't working on her next book in progress, one can find her curled up on the sofa engrossed in a good book or watching and old western movie. She currently is employed as a legal administrative assistant at a major law firm in Kansas City.

Diane would love to hear your comments on the books... e-mail her at dlrogers2@peoplepc.com.

Brothers by Blood
by D. L. Rogers

E-Book Published by Awe-Struck, Inc.
Copyright © 2008

33545123R00133

Made in the USA
Middletown, DE
17 July 2016